T0076368

To Err
is Cumin

To Err is Cumin

A SPICE SHOP MYSTERY

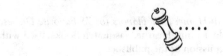

BY LESLIE BUDEWITZ

SEVENTH
STREET
BOOKS®

Published 2024 by Seventh Street Books®

To Err is Cumin. Copyright © 2024 by Leslie Ann Budewitz. All rights reserved. No part of this publication may be reproduced, stored in a retrieval system, or transmitted in any form or by any means, digital, electronic, mechanical, photocopying, recording, or otherwise, or conveyed via the Internet or a website without prior written permission of the publisher, except in the case of brief quotations embodied in critical articles and reviews.

This is a work of fiction. Characters, organizations, products, locales, and events portrayed in this novel either are products of the author's imagination or are used fictitiously. Any similarities to real persons, living or dead, is coincidental and not intended by the author.

Cover images © Shutterstock
Cover design by Jennifer Do
Cover design © Start Science Fiction

Quote from *World Spice at Home: New Flavors for 75 Favorite Dishes*, by Amanda Bevill and Julie Kramis Hearne, Sasquatch Books, used with permission of the publisher.

Inquiries should be addressed to
Start Science Fiction
221 River Street, 9th Floor
Hoboken, NJ 07030

Phone: (212)431–5455
www.seventhstreetbooks.com

10 9 8 7 6 5 4 3 2 1

ISBN: 978-1-64506-085-7 (paperback)
ISBN: 978-1-64506-095-6 (ebook)

Printed in the United States of America

*To the readers, who take my imaginary friends
into their hearts.*

A Menu for Murder

Aka the cast, serving you a tasty story!

AT SEATTLE SPICE

Pepper Reece—Mistress of Spice
Sandra Piniella—assistant manager and mix master
Cayenne Cooper—creative cook and problem-solver
Kristen Gardiner—Pepper's BFF
Vanessa Rivera—the new girl, wise beyond her fears
Arf—an Airedale, the King of Terriers

THE FLICK CHICKS

Pepper
Kristen
Laurel Halloran—widowed restaurateur and houseboat dweller
Seetha Sharma—engineer-turned-massage therapist
Aimee McGillvray—owner of Rainy Day Vintage

IN THE NEIGHBORHOOD

Talia Cook—new in town
Edgar Ramos—chef, Pepper's favorite customer
Jason Warwick—just another businessman
Cynthia Warwick—loves Pilates and the good life
Boz Bosworth—Edgar's onetime nemesis

THE LAW

Detective Michael Tracy—Major Crimes, fond of baked goods
Detective Cheryl Spencer—they've heard the jokes, and they aren't laughing
Officer Tag Buhner—Pepper's former husband, on the bike patrol
Sergeant Manny Reyes—keeping an eye on trouble

One

In 1991, a group of scientists gathered in a bar in Seattle's Fremont district declared that since no one could prove otherwise, the neighborhood was the Center of the Universe, and erected a guidepost establishing that fact. The King County Council has since made it official.

"YOU CAN'T CALL AN UBER FOR A WINGBACK," I TOLD LAUREL.

"Why not?" she said. The chair in question slumped on the sidewalk outside a three-story apartment building in Seattle's funky Fremont district, the autumn-floral upholstery tattered, one wooden leg askew. "Ask for a truck or a van."

"Guaranteed they'll send a Prius with a trunk that wouldn't hold a week's worth of groceries." I glanced at my own car, a black Saab with enough miles to have circumnavigated the planet a couple of dozen times and the dents to prove it. And a roomy trunk, but not that roomy.

I handed Laurel Arf's leash and dug for my phone. "No. I know who to call."

This was a moment made for a best friend who drives a rig big enough to haul two teenagers, their friends, schoolbooks, sports gear, and science projects with room left for a stray chair. At ten thirty on a Sunday morning, I could almost guarantee that Kristen's girls would be sound asleep, her husband would be out for a run, and she'd be delighted to help us rescue the wingback. Any luck, she'd let me stash it in her garage. No room to spare in my downtown loft, even without my honey around.

I found the phone and made the call. Not unusual to see old furniture put out for the taking, especially in Fremont, an area thick with apartments. A lot of coming and going. Pickings are best in university neighborhoods at the end of the semester, but never look a gift chair in the mouth. This one had good bones— just add stuffing and upholstery for a whole new look. And fix that wonky leg.

"She says twenty minutes, unless the bridge is up." I dropped my phone in my jute tote and stashed the bag in my car. "Wonder what else is here?"

Laurel sat in the chair, and the dog sat on the sidewalk beside her. A stack of cardboard boxes stood beside the big trash can, put out a day too soon. I popped the flaps on the first box and waved away a puff of dust that threatened to make me sneeze.

"Kinda lumpy," she said, her long, gray-brown curls bouncing as she squirmed. "Needs a new cushion. Do you even know how to reupholster furniture? You're not still on that 'I need a hobby' kick, are you?"

"No, and no. But it can't be hard. There's got to be a million YouTube videos. It will be perfect for my parents' house." As the owner of the Spice Shop in Seattle's Pike Place Market, I was much too busy for a new project. Tourist season loomed. We were training new employees and expanding our production and shipping operation. Plus I'd agreed to oversee the remodel of the house my parents had bought when they visited over Christmas. They were planning to return from Costa Rica on May 1, not three weeks away, and the to-do list was long.

But when you hook up with a commercial fisherman, as I had, there are a lot of lonely hours at night and on weekends. And until Nate safely returned to land, a hint of worry hovered in the back of my mind much of the day. A project might help.

The box held a set of melamine dishes that were popular fifty years ago, white with a green floral pattern around the rim. Much as I love vintage, they didn't qualify.

A cluster of people approached, the adults carrying shopping bags, no doubt coming from the Fremont Sunday Market. Laurel and I meet for brunch almost every Sunday morning, and today we'd braved the crowds to see what was new at the first outdoor market of the year. Happily, the day was dry, though the sun had not appeared, and we hadn't needed the rain jackets stuffed in our bags. Part craft fair, part garage sale, part costume party, punctuated by a few farm stands, the Sunday Market is a long tradition in this, one of Seattle's funkiest and most creative neighborhoods. We weren't far from the colorful signpost marking Fremont the center of the universe and helpfully pointing the way to local landmarks: the Troll, a twenty-foot-high concrete sculpture that lives under the Aurora Avenue Bridge, a red Volkswagen bug clenched in one meaty hand. The topiary dinosaurs who once roamed the Pacific Science Center. *Rapunzel*, a neon sculpture inside the window of a control tower on the Fremont drawbridge.

And for the seriously misplaced, or those who'd eaten too much and wanted to walk it off, Rio de Janeiro and the North Pole.

"Great chair," a woman said. "You taking it?"

"Yeah." I waved at the boxes. "But help yourself to the rest."

She and another woman began rummaging. A girl of about ten held a black Lab's leash. My Airedale and the Lab studied each other.

"This is Arf," I told the girl. "He's very friendly. What's your dog's name?"

"Swisher," she said, and the dog's tail swished back and forth. I smiled.

"Could your brother use these dishes?" the first woman asked her friend. "Now that he's on his own again?"

"What are you doing?" An angry male voice interrupted the conversation, and we all turned toward a scruffy white man in a tie-dye T-shirt and denim cargo shorts. His fury was aimed at Laurel and the chair. "What is that chair doing out here?"

"Yours?" If she was rattled, you couldn't tell.

"No, but what's it doing out here?"

"For the trash or the taking, obviously," I said. Where had I seen him before? That's the side effect of having lived in Seattle all my life and working retail in a busy place like Pike Place Market. I'd seen a lot of faces in my forty-three years.

"Where's Talia?" he barked. "Are all these boxes hers? Why are they out here?"

"Who's Talia?" I replied. He threw me an exasperated look and stomped up the sidewalk to the front of the building. A couple emerged and he grabbed the door, almost smacking into them in his rush to get inside.

The woman holding the box of dishes gave me a questioning look.

"Stuff's on the curb. Might as well take it," I said.

"We'll put them to good use. Cute hair, by the way."

Reflexively my hand went to my head, my fingers raking my short, spiky hair. I hoped she didn't see the gray creeping in at the dark roots. I hadn't decided what to do about that.

"Thanks," I said. A horn honked. Kristen had made great time. No open spaces, so she double-parked and hopped out.

"Great find," she said, eyeing the chair as she raised the back door of her white Suburban. Laurel stood, and we boosted the chair into the rig. A man from the group of market goers had stepped toward us, offering to help, but we didn't need it.

I was slapping the dust off my hands when the man in the tie-dye shirt burst out of the building and charged toward us.

"She's gone! Talia is gone!"

And a moment later, so were we.

GETTING THE CHAIR out of the Suburban had been a lot harder than getting it in. But we'd managed, and now the three of us stood in the century-old garage behind Kristen's house on Capitol Hill. Built for a Model A, back when family cars were a new thing. It was a storage and garden shed now, too small for most modern vehicles. Kristen's great-greats had built the house, and the garage was about the only thing she and Eric hadn't changed in their top-to-bottom remodel. She and I both grew up here, the center of the peace and justice community her parents and mine had founded in the 1970s, and I loved it as much now as I had back then.

I could not say the same of the wingback.

"What was I thinking? It's lumpy and the fabric is torn where it isn't worn-out. It needs a whole new leg. That one's too damaged to repair."

"No, no," Kristen said. She's blonde and pretty and often underestimated. "I mean, yes, all that's true, but it's a classic shape. With the right fabric, your mom will love it."

Her older daughter, on the verge of sixteen, had joined us. She flopped into it. "The seat's all lumpy and crunchy."

At a motion from her mother, Savannah stood. Kristen patted the cushion, then yanked it free and stood it on end. The zipper stuck and she waggled it back and forth, poking a finger into the tiny opening to loosen whatever was caught in the old metal teeth. After several tries, she worked the zipper free and peeled the cover off.

"What's this?" She drew out a fat manila envelope, bent at the corners, then a second. I took one. A metal prong broke off in my hand as I opened the flap.

"Holy marjoroly." I pulled out a stack of green bills, bundled with a thick rubber band. "Hundreds."

Laurel opened the other envelope. "Hundreds of hundreds."

We exchanged nervous glances. Definitely not your typical curbside find.

Inside, we piled the cash on the table in the breakfast nook and began counting. My hands trembled as I counted the bundles a second time. Laurel and Kristen watched me, holding their breath. Weak at the knees, I slid onto the bench and reached for the coffee Kristen had poured me. I cradled the cup and exhaled, my breath ragged.

"Thirty-five thousand," I said.

We sat in stunned silence. After a few moments, I took a closer look at the envelopes. No addresses or stamps, no notes about the contents.

"Is Eric home?" I asked Kristen.

"He and Mariah are helping clean up a park in Lake City. It's project day for her environmental club at school."

"Oh, right." I'd forgotten. Eric is a lawyer, my go-to whenever sticky stuff comes up in my business or personal life. "Obviously we have a legal obligation to return it, if we knew who the owner is—"

"Which you don't," Laurel said. "And the chair is yours, not ours. I'd have walked right past it."

"Or if I can find out," I continued. "At the very least, I've got a moral obligation. Someone hid this money to keep it safe."

"Finders, keepers," Savannah said.

"No," her mother said. "A quarter, yes. Or a dollar bill. But not someone's life savings."

"But they gave the chair away," the girl countered. "Ooh, what if it's evidence of a crime?"

I stared at the stacks of cash. Picked up the top few bills, their surfaces dry and slightly rough, and found the dates. Older, but not old, and not all the same. Ordinary paper could be fingerprinted, I knew, but the special textured paper used for currency? No doubt any money that had circulated would have been handled too much to give up usable prints.

Talia, the angry man had called the woman he'd been looking for. Or Dahlia. And he'd said she was gone. She'd left behind a broken-down old chair, a box of cheap dishes, and what else?

It gave me the willies. Something not right had happened here, I was sure.

"I'm guessing that Talia, whoever she is, owned the chair," I said slowly, piecing it out. "And she didn't know the money was hidden inside."

"You hear stories like that," Laurel said, "where someone stashed money and forgot it. Or died, and no one knew. And the landlord cleaned out her apartment and set out the things he considered trash."

"That's possible. But the man looking for her recognized that chair. Seeing it surprised him. He went inside, and when he came out, he said she was gone. He seemed—I don't know. Shocked. If you know someone well enough to recognize their furniture, aren't you likely to know if they died? Or moved?"

And clearly, he hadn't.

Who was he? I could almost see his face at the edges of my memory, but couldn't quite make it out. Or rather, I could see the face but couldn't remember where I'd seen it before.

But I knew what I had to do.

I had to call Tag.

Two

With all the herbs used in ancient burial rites—
cumin and lavender in mummification, cinnamon
and cassis in preparing the body and on funeral
pyres, even pepper up the nose for eternal life—the
path to the afterlife must have been a fragrant one.

"I CAN'T MAKE A CLAIM, NOT IN GOOD CONSCIENCE," I TOLD
my ex-husband over the phone. "It's not my money."

"At this point, it's as much yours as anyone else's. If they
don't find the owner, then you can say you don't want it. Give it to
charity—the meals program your parents started at the Cathedral,
or the Market Foundation."

Officer Tag Buhner of the Seattle Police Department rides the
bike patrol. It's been his beat for years, and he loves it. He knows
the department and its procedures inside out.

And he knows me. Sometimes too well.

"Anyone see the three of you take the chair?" he asked.

I paced back and forth across Kristen's stone patio as I told
him about the man who'd recognized the discarded wreck, seem-
ingly upset by the sight, and the families who had walked by, the
women drawn to the dishes.

"Listen, Pepper," Tag said in his cop voice. "Let the police do
their job. Don't go sticking your nose into this."

I refrained from telling him that what I did with my nose was my business, not his. We were divorced, after all. We'd been married thirteen years when I went out for drinks after work with friends from the law firm where I managed staff HR and nearly tripped over him and a meter maid (I should say "parking enforcement officer," but I can't) practically plugging each other at a table in the back corner. On an evening when he'd told me he was picking up a shift for a friend with a sick kid. I'd moved out and lucked into a downtown loft. Not long after, the law firm imploded in scandal, taking my job with it. What a way to turn forty.

But the past was behind me now. I'd bought the venerable Spice Shop in Pike Place Market, a place I'd loved since my mother had begun taking me along on her weekly shopping trips. Back then, I was barely tall enough to drop a quarter into Rachel, the bronze piggy bank near the Market entrance. Rachel is a kid magnet, collecting donations for the Foundation that provides social services. The Market is the heart and soul of Seattle—and its stomach. I like to think the Spice Shop gives it a flavor like no other city in the country.

And the Spice Shop had been my refuge and salvation. People think I get my nickname from the shop. Truth is, my grandfather named me Pepper when I was a little girl, sealing my fate. It just took me a few decades to figure out that selling herbs and spices was my calling.

Tag's beat includes downtown and the Market, leading to some uncomfortable encounters my first few months in the shop. We worked it out, uneasily at times, more smoothly at others. I can honestly say we're friends now, and for that I'm grateful.

"They'll find the rightful owner," he said. "Take the cash to the East Precinct station and get the process going. I'll call the desk sergeant, give him a heads-up."

I thanked him and punched off the phone. Despite Tag's assurances, I didn't share his confidence in his colleagues in blue. Not that they wouldn't care. But they have shootings and assaults and arson on their minds. Real crime.

And while thirty-five thousand was a fortune to anyone who didn't have it, to "the process," as Tag put it, it was just another piece of unclaimed property.

Back in the kitchen, I took pictures of the piles of cash. Then, using a dish towel to protect the envelopes and avoid further smudging any prints, I repacked the envelopes and slid them into a paper shopping bag. Kristen offered to take Laurel home, and Savannah begged to go along and practice driving. While they debated possession of the car keys, I downed the last of my coffee, kissed them all, and said goodbye, Arf trotting beside me.

I opened the car door for the dog, then stepped into the narrow, tree-lined street and climbed in the driver's side. Nearby, a bird chirped. In the distance, a lawn mower whirred. These houses had been built in the city's early decades, and some were on their third or fourth remodel. Grace House, as this one had been known for years, bore little resemblance to the hippie house of my childhood, when projects and protests were launched from the scarred surface of the kitchen table. It had always been a home, a sanctuary, but with time, effort, and a lot of money, Kristen and Eric had reclaimed its beauty. I loved this street. Always had, always would. The life it represented was not the life I'd been dealt, though, and that was okay. I'd created a life I loved.

But it was nice to visit this one from time to time.

I wound my way down to Twelfth, the homes smaller but sweet. The street became increasingly commercial near the trendy Pike/Pine corridor. A few blocks down stood Seattle University, the Jesuit college my brother and I attended, though only he had managed to graduate. The neighborhood had changed dramatically since then, with modern apartment buildings replacing run-down duplexes. A sushi joint occupied an old plumbing-supply business, and restaurants and cafés dotted the east side of the street across from SU.

Click. That's how I knew the man we'd seen in Fremont. I pulled over at Twelfth and Olive—parking was a breeze on a Sunday afternoon—and dug my phone out of the bottom of my tote. (Why it never stays in the inside pocket where I put it, who knows.) I thumbed a text to my buddy Tariq.

T, what's the name of the chef who ran the place where you worked in Madrona?

The chef who'd engineered the theft of a spice blend we'd created for another customer, hoping to spark up his crab cakes and other dishes. But he hadn't known the secret ingredient, exposing his charade. It's one thing to be influenced or inspired by work you admire, but outright theft is a whole other kettle of hot water and stinky fish. I'd attempted to lower the temperature by offering to create a blend for him, but instead, he'd fired Tariq for telling me what was going on. Then he himself had been fired, and the restaurant closed.

He'd given no indication that he recognized me in our brief sidewalk encounter. But maybe he was having the same conversation with himself right this minute, in reverse.

The phone in my hand rang.

"Hey, Pepper," Tariq said in a sleepy drawl. "All that chopping and cooking, I'm too tired to text. What's up?"

It was past noon, but restaurant staff work late on the weekends. I asked him about the chef.

"I can't remember his name. It isn't Bob."

"Ah, geez. Boz. Boz Bosworth." From Tariq's serious tone, I could almost picture him sitting up straight. "Careful. He's bad news."

Boz. That was it. But being a petty thief with a flying temper didn't mean he hadn't been legitimately concerned about the woman.

"Yeah, thanks. Hey, do you know a woman named Talia? Or Dahlia? Lives in Fremont." Or had, but I skipped over the nuance. So she'd moved in a hurry. So she hadn't told all her friends. If Boz was one of them, his hot head might have been the very reason she'd packed up and picked up. If that was the case, I didn't want to be the one who led him to her.

"No, sorry. Hey, I owe you big for smoothing things over with Edgar. Working with him rocks."

"Good to hear." Tariq had settled down nicely since I'd met him, when he and Edgar had both worked for a man I'd sort of been dating. The restaurant world has a rep for Spin the Wheel, staff moving around, but in every business, a stable team is key to success.

Once a personnel manager, always a meddler.

"He cooking somewhere?" I asked. "Boz, I mean."

"Not that I've heard. Too hot to handle, you know? I mean, the spice thing was so not cool. Firing me, I get. I deserved it. But then the whole staff quit, and word gets around, you know? I'm not saying he was blackballed, but . . ."

"But who would hire trouble on purpose."

"'Zactly. Hey, you gotta come 'round. You and Nate. We're cooking hot, man."

"Next time he's home. I promise."

The East Precinct station stood on the next corner, in a gray building that anyone who didn't know better would assume was a parking garage. It was back to normal now, the graffiti that had covered the bricks and the plywood that had covered the windows during the city's Black Lives Matter protests both long gone.

I opened the door, the glass front trimmed in royal blue, and walked in, greeted by the astringent smell of recent cleaning. Half a dozen people sat in the lobby. A thumb-sucking toddler stared up at me. A woman called her name, then swept her into her arms.

"Pepper Reece," the officer at the desk called. A glint from the overhead lights shone on his dark, bald scalp. "Sight for sore eyes."

"Manny Reyes," I said, matching the desk sergeant's grin. "Tag didn't tell me it would be you. Busy place, for a Sunday."

He rolled his eyes. "You would not believe."

After a brief catch-up on the wife and kids—they are always older than you think—Manny introduced an officer who escorted me into a small interview room. A second officer joined us, and I repeated the story of finding the chair and the cash. Then we went through the process Tag had outlined. The officers switched on their body cameras. Gloved up and counted the money twice. I clutched my elbows, reminding myself I had no reason to be nervous. One officer recorded the amount of cash and the break-down by denomination on the outside of a special envelope. At his direction, I signed both the envelope and another form, documenting the chain of custody. The officer slipped the stacks inside the evidence bag and sealed it.

"What this does," he told me, tapping the form with a finger, "is establish that on this date, at this time, in this place, you gave us thirty-five thousand dollars in US currency, and I have signed it to acknowledge receipt. Officer Edwards and I will walk this to the evidence unit and go through the same steps."

Then we repeated the exercise with the envelopes—they were evidence, too.

"Do you need my fingerprints?" I'd been printed before, for elimination, but didn't know if those prints stayed on file.

"Yes, ma'am." He gave me the receipt for the cash and a form spelling out the process to claim the money if the owner wasn't found in the next sixty days. On their way to the evidence room, they escorted me to a counter where my prints were taken. Quick and easy, inkless and painless.

Back out front, I waited for Manny to finish with a woman demanding to see her son. Manny clicked a few keys on a computer screen and told her the man was being held in the jail down in Kent. He took a printed information sheet from a cubby behind him, wrote in a name and case number, then handed it to her, pointing out visiting hours, bus routes, and other details.

"You could probably recite all that in your sleep," I said after she'd left.

"Sadly, yes. You get that claim filed?"

"Yep. What will you do to find the rightful owner?" Who might or might not be Talia of the unknown last name. Truth was, I had only Boz's word that the chair belonged to her and no idea who had put it out on the curb. Though I'd faithfully reported the details, who knew if they were accurate, let alone helpful?

"A property or patrol officer will contact the landlord and attempt to identify the owner of the chair. If they don't know, then we'll ask who's moved out recently. Make contact, ask questions."

"Tricky, dealing with cash." With art or jewelry, you could request a description, photos, a receipt for purchase. But cash all looks the same. And too many people would be eager to claim it, rightfully or not.

"Our people are pros." He flashed me another toothy grin, then turned serious. "And we'll run a check of our records. See if your report matches up with any reports of lost or stolen property."

In other words, found property was long odds and low priority, requiring a boatload of footwork at a time when the department was short-staffed and demand was high.

It might have been Sunday and the street sleepy, but officers came and went. Citizens came and went. Phones rang. Radios squawked.

"You've done your part, Pepper," Manny said. "We'll be in touch. You take care now."

I felt almost as reluctant to leave as I'd been to make the claim. I did not feel done with this.

Three

Scratch a dog and you'll find a permanent job.

—Franklin P. Jones

BACK AT THE CAR, I GLANCED AT THE SKY AND PUT ON MY jacket. Some errands are necessary, rain or shine. Arf and I headed for Cal Anderson Park, a hop and a skip away. It's one of the city's Olmsted Brothers parks, designed by the sons of the man who created Central Park in New York City. I'd recently discovered that its reservoir, now covered by grassy play fields and a small reflecting pool, was built to supply water for homes and firefighting after the Great Seattle Fire of 1889 destroyed the entire business district.

And it's ideal for a quick walk for dogs and humans alike.

"What do you think, Arf?" I asked my copilot after a quarter mile or so. "Will they find this mysterious Talia? Will they figure out who that money belongs to?"

The more I thought about it, the more convinced I was that Talia, or whoever had owned the chair before it was left for the taking, had not known about the cash. It had taken Kristen all of thirty seconds to unzip the cover and find the envelopes stuffed inside. So why hadn't Talia bothered to figure out what was making the cushion so lumpy?

Either she hadn't had the chair long, or she'd left in such a hurry, under such awful circumstances, that she hadn't had time to grab the money.

At the northwest corner of the park, an escalator leads to the light rail station deep underground. A woman emerged, beaded braids flying as she rushed by, phone to her ear, the wheels of the hard-sided silver suitcase she pulled clattering on the sidewalk. A woman on the move.

Like Talia?

"Come on, Arf," I said and picked up the pace. "We've got some investigating to do."

THE MARINERS WERE on the road today. The Saab's radio crackled, the play-by-play broken up by the brittle wires and ancient innards that a wise mechanic—my boyfriend, Nate—had told me could not be fixed. He'd followed that with a shrug I interpreted to mean, "You don't need a new radio. You need a new car."

Ahead of me, a short line of traffic waited for the University Bridge, one of four drawbridges that cross the Ship Canal. One giant span jutted into the air. I braked, then fiddled with the radio dial. Maybe it wasn't the wires. Maybe the bridge's electronics were interfering with the signal.

I had not actually agreed when Tag told me to turn in the money and walk away. No man controls my decision-making, and Tag knows better than to think he can order me around. He was still skeptical of my investigative abilities, though no doubt he'd claim he was only concerned for my safety. But I try not to make promises I don't intend to keep.

Then there was Nate. While my safety mattered deeply to him, he would never hint at any doubt or lack of trust. I'd already solved three murders when we met, and he knew my drive for justice was as much a part of me as my spiky hair, my love of coffee, and my passion for herbs and spices.

Nate had been away since mid-January, plying the waters off the coast of Alaska, save for a week home earlier in the month. The catch had been good and the crew needed a break. So did he and Bron, his brother and co-captain. A chance to spend more than a few hours on land. To hug the people they loved and sleep in their own beds. Eat food they hadn't cooked themselves and see other faces. Bron was four months into a long-distance relationship with a pizza restaurateur named Daria, and needless to say, we hadn't seen much of them that week. We'd been otherwise occupied. Retail shop owners don't get vacation time, but I'd managed a few days off. One day we drove up to the Skagit Valley for the Tulip Festival. Another day, we only left the loft to walk the dog. The ten months since we'd met were the sweetest not-quite-a-year of my life.

But he's a practical man. I could almost hear him ask, "So, what are you hoping to accomplish?"

I was hoping to find someone at Talia's building who could tell me about her or the chair.

The play-by-play returned long enough for me to figure out that it was the bottom of the third and the Mariners led by two.

I knew for sure that both Nate and I were committed to a future together. What it would look like, I didn't know. Over the winter he'd dropped hints about selling the boat or finding other work, but he hadn't mentioned either option since then. I'd taken to heart the advice Laurel and my dad had given me: let him be. I process my thoughts out loud, but he needs to work things out himself before talking about them. My nephew, Charlie, had spent a Saturday with him tinkering on the smaller vessel he keeps at Fishermen's Terminal, under Arf's supervision, and all had seemed well. Not that I would expect Nate to unburden himself to an eleven-year-old. And if he'd talked to the dog, I hadn't heard about it. Arf is the soul of discretion.

The bridge decks lowered. Lights flashed, crossarms rose, and cars crept forward. The metal grating rumbled under my wheels, competing with the broadcaster barking out the stats from the first third of the game.

I skirted the University District, dropping down to the semi-industrial area along the lakeshore, and in a few minutes, we were back in the People's Republic of Fremont. Crowds had not yet thinned, and I circled Talia's block twice before lucking out. A van pulled out, and I pulled in.

The dog aimed his soulful eyes at me, the message unmistakable: "Take me, take me!"

"Okay," I said. "As long as you work your magic and wheedle out some useful information."

Assuming we met someone who had useful information.

We crossed the street to the pale-yellow building, its exterior brick on the first floor and wood siding above. Outside the front door, I studied the directory. No luck—last names only, and I didn't know hers. No on-site manager listed.

A red-and-white FOR RENT sign taped inside the front door advertised a furnished one-bedroom. No rent listed; it would probably give me a heart attack. I tried the handle. Locked. I cupped my hands around my eyes and peered in. A small, basic lobby, although the wood floors gleamed. A lot of older buildings in this part of the city had been razed and replaced with bigger, better, newer. Without obvious charm, how had this building survived? Though as the owner of a shop in a building closing in on its first century, I was keenly aware that reliable plumbing and electricity have their own charms.

No signs of life.

"Looks like we're out of luck, Arf." Back on the sidewalk, several boxes remained. I opened one. Books.

A direct route to my heart. I stuck my wrist through the loop in Arf's leash, grabbed the box, and crossed the street. Opened the trunk and set the box inside. Returned to the stack and opened another box. Knickknacks and other things I wanted to sort through, vaguely protected by a swath of pink-and-white gingham.

"Hey, you. What are you doing?"

Not the angry ex-chef this time, but a fiftyish Asian man in a turquoise polo and olive-green cargo pants tight around the belly and loose in the hips. Splotches of white paint covered one knee.

I spread my hands. "Trolling for treasure in the trash. That's the point of leaving boxes on the curb when it isn't trash day, right?"

"You're not going to find any treasure in this cr—" He stopped himself, mindful of my tender female sensitivities, though I had no trouble with the word he hadn't said. "Tenants come and go. They leave stuff behind and expect me to deal with it." He started to walk away, but I couldn't let him.

"You're the manager? Did Talia move out?"

"Why you asking? You a friend of hers?"

I sidestepped the question. "I was surprised she left the old chair."

He glowered at the space where it had been. "Somebody nabbed it. I guess the legs might make decent firewood."

"Were the rest of these boxes hers, too?"

"I wouldn't know. She claimed to be apartment-sitting for a friend, but I'd bet a bundle that her 'friend'"—he made air quotes—"is working out of town and it's an illegal sublet. Some kind of analyst or engineer for one of the tech companies. They've all got bright, shiny offices down by the canal. I don't know what they do, but they move around a lot."

"Talia's an engineer?" His rant had me confused. And I was pretty sure subletting was legal, though the lease might prohibit it.

He blew out a dismissive breath. "I couldn't tell you what Talia does. Comes and goes during the day. No regular hours, and now she's gone. I offered to rent her a unit upstairs, but she said no. My guess, no cash. This sublet farce continues, I may have to cancel that lease."

So Talia was subletting in a building with a vacancy. Maybe she didn't want the commitment of her own place. Maybe the manager was right and she couldn't pull together the money.

But she'd had a chair, and I was increasingly certain she hadn't known about the cash in the cushion.

I wanted inside her apartment. Lacking that, I wanted inside the building.

"Can I see the apartment for rent?" *Think fast.* "I've got an employee who needs a place. With the bus stop close by, it's easy to get downtown. Could be just right."

He scanned me tip to toe, his gaze not entirely comfortable. If my imaginary employee were young and female, I would not send her here. But I matched him for height, at five seven or so, and given his appearance, I figured I could knee him and sprint away if I had to.

Besides, I had Arf. Airedales aren't guard dogs, but he is a terrier. Those teeth are bred for gnashing.

"I get first and last month's rent and a damage deposit. But no dogs." The manager marched toward the building entrance. I decided he didn't mean no dog right this minute, and followed.

"I'm Pepper Reece. I didn't catch your name." He hadn't given it.

"Vernon Phan. What kind of business you run?"

For half a second, I considered lying, but that's not really in my DNA. Except in emergencies. "I own the Spice Shop in Pike Place Market."

His grunt might have been approval, but probably not.

As I'd thought from outside, the lobby was utilitarian, not a place to linger and visit with your neighbors. An artificial ficus tree stood between a built-in bank of locked mailboxes and a stairway going down.

"Laundry and storage downstairs," Phan said. "Sign says keep this door closed, but nobody pays any attention." He closed the stairway door with a clang, then continued walking. At the end of the hall, he pulled a heavy key ring out of the lower pocket of his cargo pants.

Show me a man with a lot of keys, my grandfather used to say, *and I'll show you a man with too much on his mind.*

Phan found a key and stuck it in the lock, cocking his head toward the door across the way.

"Same size as your friend's place, not that you'd know it—all that junk crammed into it."

"Sit," I told Arf, who sat in the open doorway. "Stay."

Wherever the paint on Vernon Phan's knee had come from, it wasn't here. The walls needed a fresh coat and the greige carpet a good shampooing. In truth, the carpet needed to go. Not a big project—the whole unit couldn't have been more than five hundred square feet.

Bed and bath were small and plain. The queen-size mattress was bare but clean, the black metal bed frame cheap but decent. The windows looked out on a narrow passage between this building and the larger, newer one next door.

"Fridge is new." Phan waved a hand at the galley kitchen.

"Nice," I said. Black appliances, speckled black Formica counters, and plenty of cupboards. It would do, if you cooked alone. Anyone standing at the stove would have to back out to let someone else get to the refrigerator.

The dark-brown couch was not as old as I'd expected, flanked by two tan-slipcovered chairs. Next to the wall stood a small wooden desk with a single lap drawer, the kind sometimes called a sofa table, and a single chair.

To my eyes, the apartment hovered somewhere between decent and a dump. An optimist would call it a blank slate.

"Your employee single?" Phan asked. "Bit tight for a couple, but plenty of room for one, if they don't hang on to everything they ever owned, like your friend's friend."

I gave him a knowing smile, totally fake. "She is a collector, isn't she? Do you have a card? I was hoping to drop in on Talia. When did you last see her?"

"Couldn't say for sure." He fished in a pocket, then handed me a grubby business card. "Monday or Tuesday? A while."

I patted my leg, releasing Arf from his stay. We followed Phan out of the apartment, and as he locked the door behind us, I sent mental vibes to Talia's unit.

Vernon Phan couldn't help me find Talia. Or if he could, he wouldn't. He wanted nothing to do with her, except to keep on collecting the rent from his rule-breaking tenant.

Maybe Talia, whoever or wherever she was, had no better claim to the money in the chair than I did. But if I didn't do my best to find her, I would feel like a thief.

And now that I'd seen where she'd been living, finding her seemed even more important. But how?

How?

Four

Waiting for the Interurban, a *cluster of cast-aluminum statues of six people and a dog*, sits near the Fremont Bridge commemorating the rail line that ran between Seattle and Everett for forty years, doomed by the 1939 completion of Highway 99.

AFTER PHAN LOCKED THE DOOR BEHIND ME, I GRABBED THE box of knickknacks. At the car, I stashed the box and settled Arf into the back seat, leaving the windows open several inches. Then I strode down Fremont Avenue toward the Ship Canal. Some retail shops were closed, others open, counting on foot traffic from the Sunday Market.

And where there's foot traffic, a bakery is always a good bet. Breakfast had long worn off. I hadn't spent much time around here in years but would lay odds there was still a bakery on the corner.

When it comes to food, my memory is rarely wrong.

A row of gold "Best of Fremont" stickers lined the bottom of the bakery's glass door, one for each of the last umpteen years. Inside, the scents of sugar, yeast, and coffee mingled, and the walls screamed with color, as if to make up for Seattle's too-frequent gray skies. Customers filled about half the tables. A few more perched on stools at the counter inside the front windows, nursing cups of coffee and tea, little but crumbs left on their plates.

"Hey, doll," a fortyish man with blue streaks in his platinum hair and a white apron called from behind the counter. "We're a bit low right now, with the after-market rush, but I'm sure we can find a treat to hit your sweet spot."

"When it comes to treats, I'm easy to please." I studied the trays of cupcakes, cookies, and éclairs in the display case. Despite the gaps, I knew my mouth and I would be happy. This level of baking and decorating is an art form. And while I'm no artist, I excel at art appreciation.

"How about an Americano and a German chocolate cupcake for here," I told the counterman. "And three of those cherry-cheese-cakey things to go."

"You got it." He touched a screen, ringing up the sale.

"You've created quite the neighborhood hangout," I said.

"From morning coffee to after-school cookies and cupcakes, and cakes for special occasions, we feed Fremont. Fewer familiar faces on Market Sundays, but we serve you once, we know you'll come back." Sounded like he was reading from his own ads.

I found a table that offered a view of the room, admittedly small, and the passersby. The day had been filled with emotion and activity, and the moment I sat, the combo hit me hard, followed immediately by a flood of questions and doubts. Had I done everything I could to reunite the cash from the chair cushion with its owner? Both Tag and Sergeant Reyes thought so. In their eyes, I was nothing but a claimant, a signature on a form, my duty done.

Was it?

Blue Hair delivered a plate crowned with a divine cupcake, drew a napkin from his apron pocket, then presented a tall, clear glass mug of liquid nectar.

"Wow. That is one seriously gorgeous cup of coffee." I held out a hand to keep him for a minute. "Long shot, but do you know a woman named Talia? Young. Lives close by."

"Oh, sure. Dark hair, cute smile. About this tall." He leveled a hand near his shoulder, indicating five three or four. I nodded, as if his description wasn't news to me. "Come to think of it, I haven't seen her in a few days."

I frowned to show my worry, and he called to the ponytailed blonde wiping the table next to mine. "Hey, Stelle. You seen Talia this week?"

"No. Not like her to miss a Tuesday or Friday." She straightened. "Lemon cream scones. And Sundays, when the outdoor Market is on."

"On Fridays, she buys a bag for the weekend," Blue Hair said. "Using tip money, my guess—mostly singles. Don't tell the boss, but I put a few aside for her, pretending they're day-old."

Stelle snorted. "He is the boss."

"Talia is obviously a woman of good taste, and you are a man of good heart." I sipped the coffee, a lively dark roast. "And a fabulous barista."

"Thanks, doll," he said, clearly the kind of man for whom endearments come easily, without insult or innuendo. "But you know, you're the second person who's asked about her recently."

"Oh, that must have been Boz. White guy, late thirties, always in a tie-dye T-shirt?"

"No. No. White, taller than average, salt-and-pepper hair. Kinda twitchy, like he thought the Troll might get him. Musta been Wednesday." He looked at his employee for confirmation, but she shook her head. "That's right. He ordered a nonfat latte and a blueberry scone. I mark the days of the week by our baking schedule."

The description ruled out Vernon Phan from Talia's building, my other guess.

Two women entered, and my blue-haired friend reclaimed his place behind the counter. I took a bite of the most amazing chocolate cupcake I had ever eaten. I was going to have to take Arf for an extra-long walk this evening to work off the calories.

But now I had a vague idea what Talia looked like. And reason to think she'd been gone most of a week. Who had been searching for her, and why? Did it have anything to do with the cash, or her decision to abandon the sublet?

I'd learned something else, too. Stelle and Blue Hair hadn't recognized Boz from my description. If he lived in the neighborhood, surely he'd be a regular here. I didn't know what kind of work he did now or what hours he kept. Tariq had been certain he was out of the restaurant biz. But he still had to eat, and what food lover wouldn't love this place?

I finished my cupcake and sat back to relish the last of the coffee.

The owner whisked my plate away and replaced it with a pink

cardboard box. "Your cheesecakes. We're closed Mondays, so I tossed in a couple of freebies. To bring you back."

"Count on it," I said.

When I reached the car, I tucked the pink box safely under the front seat and let Arf out to stretch his legs and water the fire hydrant. I glanced at Talia's building just as a woman in a red raincoat emerged and came toward us. More likely, to the bus stop on the corner. All these raincoats today and not a drop.

"Oh, an Airedale!" she exclaimed.

"The King of Terriers."

"We had one when I was a kid. A holy terror."

Arf stood motionless, as if he understood the conversation and knew it was his responsibility to redeem the reputation of his breed. My little ambassador.

"I wanted to catch Talia," I said, pointing toward the building, "but the manager thinks she moved out. Do you know her?"

"Oh, the retro-hippie chick with the goth eyes, subletting on the first floor? Yeah, I haven't seen her since Sunday night. Okay to pet him?" At my nod, she stroked Arf's ear. He sighed happily and leaned into her hand. "We were both doing laundry, up and down the stairs. At least both dryers were working then. Building looks okay, but you complain and it gets worse. Guy in the apartment across from Talia moved out last week. Got sick of waiting for the fridge to be fixed. I'd leave, too, if I could afford it."

"Hmm. Could she have gone back home, to her parents' place?"

"Not likely. She doesn't talk to her mom much. Her father was never in the picture. We talked while we loaded the washers or waited for the dryers."

"Her boyfriend?" A shot in the dark. "I thought I saw him here earlier."

"The guy in the tie-dye T-shirt who was asking about her? No. She's taking a break. The story she told me . . . well, you probably know it." Her fingers continued to work Arf's fur.

"Right. The last guy, in—I forget where."

"In San Diego. Begs her to move in with him, some high-end apartment with an ocean view. Then he waltzes in one day and says he took a job in, I don't know, Las Vegas or somewhere, and off he goes. Sticks her with rent she can't afford, no car, no job. Nothing."

"That's crazy," I said in my best *oh wow, girlfriend* voice.

"Yeah, well. Men. You know." Her fingers moved to Arf's other ear. "Joke was on him. Before he could come back for the rest of his stuff, she sold it and moved up here. Sublet was perfect for her—she didn't own a stick of furniture. Not that the tenant made room in the place for much more than a toothbrush."

So I'd heard. "Smart move."

"Seems like half of Seattle moved here to get away from somewhere else. Make a fresh start. She knew the city a little, from summers with relatives as a kid."

That would be like me moving to St. Louis, where my dad grew up. I'd visited three times in my entire life. Of course, I had twenty years on Talia, which would make a major transition both harder and easier.

"Do you know where I might find her? At work, maybe?"

"Doubt it. She cleans houses and I don't know what else. Patching together jobs here and there. But she usually had Sundays free. Gotta go." The bus was approaching. She gave Arf's ear a gentle tug. The bus stopped, and the door opened with a hydraulic swoosh. "Give the little guy an extra treat, for me."

The doors closed, and the bus pulled away. Arf gazed up at me.

"Yeah, yeah. It's only fair. I had my treat. You'll get yours."

SOME SUNDAYS, I swing by the shop, but I'd been on the go all day on what was supposed to be my day off. Today's crew was a mix of new hires and veterans. Good to let them work together without me or Sandra, the longtime assistant manager. Besides, if an emergency cropped up, I was only a text away.

The ball game had ended while I'd been poking around in Fremont, the Mariners victorious on a late-inning two-run homer. I was sorry to have missed that, but I'd picked up decent intel, along with dessert. Not that I was investigating anything. Or assisting the police with their inquiries, the phrase my pal Detective Michael Tracy uses when describing me. Although coming out of his mouth, it could have been truth or sarcasm.

The door to the garage beneath my building opened on the first press of the magic button—more cause for celebration—and I parked the Saab in my usual space. The last few summers, I'd taken custody of my dad's classic '67 Mustang ragtop. The downside to my parents' return was that my dad was going to want to drive his car himself.

I grabbed one of the boxes I'd salvaged, set my pink bakery box on top, and headed for the elevator, Arf trotting beside me. My loft is one of a pair on the third floor. The top floor. My brother calls it the penthouse, though it's no bigger than any of the others in the converted warehouse. My neighbors had gone for the sleek, modern look, in contrast to my vintage-industrial style. They'd bought the unit below theirs and spent the last six months combining the two spaces. The remodel was finished enough for them to move back in, but unfinished enough that every conversation seemed to revolve around light fixtures or refrigerator styles. I'd thought it all kind of fun, since the problems were theirs, not mine, until I had to deal with some of the same nitpicky details at my parents' house.

I managed to unlock my door without dumping dessert on the floor. I set the larger box on the boot bench and carried the precious baked goods to the butcher-block counter that divides the kitchen from the dining area. Hung up Arf's leash and my coat, then sat to pull off my wellies. Those things are great for puddles but not meant for all day. I'd dressed for rain without needing to, a sort of insurance policy I was happy to pay for, though my feet were squealing at the moment. I flexed my toes and sighed in relief.

"You were a good boy today, Arf," I said as I set fresh food and water on his mat. "Waiting in the car, letting strangers pet you."

I got out the extra treats I'd promised him, then changed my clothes, poured myself a glass of pinot grigio, and sank onto the couch to check my texts. One from my mother, Lena, reminding me I was supposed to meet the designer at the house Tuesday afternoon. *I'll be there!* I replied. We'd FaceTime her so she could see the new kitchen cabinets, scheduled to be installed this week. Another from Tag, asking how things went at the precinct.

Good, I thumbed back. *Nice to see Manny.*

See? he answered. *Told you they'd take care of everything.*

I didn't tell him I wasn't persuaded. He didn't need to know.

I scrolled through my photos. Never had I seen such a pile of cash. With that kind of cushion—pun intended—Talia could pay for a decent apartment and furnish it. She wouldn't need day-old scones. She'd be free of that old boyfriend, free to do what she wanted.

The boyfriend. I sipped my wine. Had the cash been his? Only if the chair had been his, and that didn't make much sense. A woman without a car, who'd sold what her boyfriend had left behind, would not have hauled a ratty old wingback twelve hundred miles or more.

Besides, the neighbor had said she didn't have any furniture. That would have made a sublet attractive, legal or not. The wingback meant she was making plans. Without any idea that she'd been literally sitting on a pile of money.

Truth be told, I kinda liked her for selling off the creephole boyfriend's stuff, sneaky as it was. No sneakier than the stunt he'd pulled.

Ohhh. Was he the man who'd been asking about her, tracking her down to get his revenge? The bakery owner had said the man was older, and she was young. So maybe, maybe not.

If the cops didn't trace the cash to its rightful owner, it would come to me. The thought made me squirmy. Not that I couldn't use it. We were expanding production capacity at the shop, and that took capital. I'd never felt much urge to travel until I met Nate, and now we had lists of places we wanted to see together. I could use a cushion of my own, although I was set for furniture.

And I did need a new car.

But the money felt tainted. Even if the law said I could keep it, did I want to? Bonuses for my employees, or what Tag had called my causes.

No need to stress over any of that now.

The next photo was the chair. I debated sending it to my mom, then decided to keep it a surprise. A housewarming gift with history, for a house with history.

Instead, I sent it to the designer. *Nabbed this today. Living room or study? Red, with a pattern or texture? Bring swatches!*

I stood, ready for dinner and a refill. The sun was setting over Elliott Bay and the Olympic Mountains. When I bought the loft, it had been little more than an open space and a set of plans. The old double-decker elevated highway known as the Viaduct had hunkered less than thirty feet away while visions for replacing it with a tunnel danced in city planners' heads. The Viaduct, and a decent divorce settlement, were the only reasons I'd been able to afford this place. Now traffic moved underground and I give thanks daily for the twelve-foot-high multipaned windows that line my western wall, though why a brick warehouse built early in the last century for the cannery business had windows at all remained a mystery.

Purple, pink, and orange streaks tinted the clouds layered above the horizon. I watched the lights of the waterfront and Alki begin to come on, deeply content. Deeply grateful.

In the kitchen, I cut roasted, peeled beets into chunks. Sliced green onions and crumbled feta. Popped a tangy chunk into my mouth. I'd discovered the salad on our excursion to the Tulip Festival, but lacking a recipe, I'd had to recreate it myself. My new favorite, the feta's sharpness balancing the earthiness of the beets and toasted cumin seeds.

Before I tossed the salad, I opened the box of treats. Next to the three cherry cheesecakes were two lemon cream scones—not wrapped as day-old—and two chocolate crinkle cookies. If they were half as good as the cupcake, I'd be back in Fremont before I knew it. That had been Blue Hair's intent.

I nestled two cheesecake squares on a red Fiestaware plate and carried them across the hall. Glenn answered my knock. It was immediately obvious that this was not a good time.

"I brought dessert, from a scrumptious bakery in Fremont." I held out the plate.

"Oh, gosh, thanks." He took the plate. "I'd invite you in, but we're having a discussion." His tone underlined the last word. The remodel had been tense at times, leading to a few such discussions between Glenn, a city councilman, and his husband, fondly known on my side of the landing as Other Nate, to distinguish him from My Nate.

"One bite of these and you'll forget all about it," I said. "I promise."

"You're a good friend, Pepperoni."

"That I am."

As I closed the door to my own place, I spotted the box I'd brought up. The box in my trunk could wait. I cut a hunk of bread and served up salad. Refreshed my wine and set the glass on the old packing crate that serves as my coffee table, next to a first edition of one of my favorite Brother Cadfael mysteries, a gift from an old friend. A thank-you gift after I'd identified the man who'd assaulted her, put her in the hospital, and come back to finish the job. She knows I consider the mystery-solving medieval monk and herbalist my spirit guide. I cued up my latest binge watch, *Father Brown,* featuring a village priest in postwar England who saves souls and solves crime. But as I watched and ate, my mind kept wandering to a missing woman and found money.

Then it was time to catch up with the love of my life. It had bothered me, briefly, to realize I'd once given another man that title. When I was young and foolish, before my heart and trust had been broken. Before I'd made my own share of mistakes.

Despite all that, I had never felt the need to hold myself back with Nate. Just the sight of his name as my phone began to ring got my blood moving.

"Hey, little darlin'. What's cooking?" Even from twenty-five hundred miles away, his voice melted me. I asked about his day, he asked about mine. I squeezed my account of the morning with Laurel into a couple of sentences, then told him about the chair and the money.

"Wow. And you don't think this woman—Talia, you said— had any idea it was there?"

"Couldn't have, or she'd have taken it with her. My guess, she knew the chair was lumpy—you couldn't not know—but hadn't had time to rip into it yet. I asked around, but no one seems to know where she might be."

"What if something happened?"

"You mean, like she's sick and in the hospital? Then I guess she's safe, and I'll find her eventually. Or the police will track her down. Hard to fathom stashing that much money in a chair cushion."

"Do you suppose it might be stolen? Drug money that someone hid?"

"Or simple safekeeping. But I don't want to talk about that. I want to talk about you. And you and me."

And we said sweet things to each other, and though Nate was far away on a boat in the middle of the North Pacific and I was here in our cozy nest, I felt his love wrap itself around me like the night embracing the stars.

Five

*A self-guided tour in Amsterdam, complete with a
Rub 'n Sniff map, allows visitors to explore the city's
past and present through stories connected to its
canals, perfumers, colonial history, and natural
setting—and its role in the spice trade.*

IT IS IMPOSSIBLE TO SAY WHAT I LOVE MOST ABOUT PIKE PLACE
Market. The sights, the sounds, the smells. The familiar faces,
friendly or distracted. The architectural styles that should clash
but don't. The cobblestones that rattle wheels and bones.

Monday mornings in the Market are a particular stripe of
chaos. Fridays buzz. Saturdays rock and roll. Sundays hum, the
pitch varying with the season and the weather. On Mondays, we
regroup. We restock. We take deep breaths.

And we greet each other. From the moment Arf and I emerged
from the elevator we'd ridden from Western, our street, up through
the bowels of the Market, our progress was slowed by hugs and
kisses for me and scratches behind the ears for him. We returned
the greetings in ways specific to our species, happy to be among our
people. The baristas and bakers. The flower sellers, many of them
Hmong. The Orchard Girls, two sweet young sisters who sell jams
and jellies made from fruit grown in their family's Central Washington orchard. The high stallers peddling produce from around
the region and beyond. And the fishmongers in their orange rubber

aprons and knee-high boots, filling their display cases with fresh ice and fresh fish, warming up their voices for the songs and jokes they'd trade as they tossed salmon and flung halibut, entertaining the crowd they fed.

A morning chill cooled the spring air, and I appreciated the warmth of my go-cup, the scent of hot coffee invigorating. I often stop at one of the Market bakeries. But I never look a gift scone in the mouth, and today, I had a lemon scone from Fremont in my tote bag.

During the winter and early spring, some vendors and merchants close on Mondays. I'd debated it, but a slow day is a good catch-up day, and there's never a shortage of work in retail. Many of the restaurants we supply place their herb and spice orders early in the week, and a quick turnaround is essential.

Travel mug and leash in one hand, I dug in my bag with the other for my keys. A moment later, we were enveloped by the scent of paradise.

Almost every first-time visitor to the Spice Shop stops a few feet inside the front door. It is a veritable feast for the senses, and not just taste and smell, so intertwined. There is much for the eyes to drink in: Row upon row of clear jars filled with every shade of green, gold, and red you can imagine. Stacks of tins holding blends. Jars of salt and pepper. Gift sets curated for the backyard grillers, the bakers, the cooks aspiring to recreate the regional flavors of their travels. Teas and accessories. Spice grinders. Aprons. Shelves of books, from spice guides and cookbooks to chef memoirs and foodie fiction.

And then there are the memories. Not strictly a sense but intimately connected to smell. Everyone has a story of a scent that transports them, often before they're aware of that hint of lavender or cinnamon.

I unhooked Arf's leash and gave him a chew toy. Dogs are technically against Market rules but tolerated in retail shops as long as they don't cause trouble. Arf spends most of his time on a comfy bed behind the front counter or in my office, napping or chewing. Or dreaming of chasing cats.

Ha. Arf is far too well-mannered to chase a cat. No thanks to me—he came into my life a year and a half ago when his former owner, an occasionally homeless man named Sam, decided to return to his family in Memphis. We'd all agreed that Arf belonged in the Market, his home ground. Heck, the dog had more friends here than I did.

I stashed my coat and tote in the tiny back office. Switched on a few lights, then readied the till. Some days we take in a lot of cash; others, not so much. When I first bought the place, I'd been boggled by the amount we spent on credit card fees, but I got over it. Cash and checks have their costs, too, mostly in time and error.

Cash. Yesterday's find and the missing woman hovered at the edges of my mind. I took my coffee and scone to the nook, the built-in table and benches in the corner of the shop. Arf brought his chew bone over and sat at my feet. The nook is where we gather for staff meetings, where we test new blends, where we take breaks or quiet moments. A customer will sit there occasionally, nursing a sample cup of our signature tea. We never mind. A well-rested customer is more likely to find something they simply must have than a tired, grumpy one.

I picked up the scone. It was lemon love at first bite. Bits of zest dotted the glaze—not too many, just enough to counter the sweetness. Good crumb, with more lemon flavor and a hint of vanilla. I'd been right: Talia's love of these scones showed her good taste. And everything I'd tried from the Fremont bakery proved it deserved those gold medallions for excellence.

I'd be making up excuses to get back there soon.

Then my staff arrived. Vanessa helped me roll out the big metal racks of herb seedlings we carry for a few weeks in the spring. Then she and I filled the electric samovar that brews gallons of spice tea every day. A tea purist would cringe at us calling an electric model a samovar, but that's what the kitchenware and appliance dealers say, so we follow their lead. She wasn't as perky as usual, despite the space buns on top of her head. I chalked it up to working all weekend while taking college courses.

Cayenne made sure the front of the shop was ready for business. Customers laugh at our names and ask if Rosemary and Ginger work here, too. I say if you know one on the job hunt, send her in.

Good flavor tastes even better served with good humor.

At five minutes to ten, the door flew open and Kristen swept in. She'd offered to help out part-time when I bought the place, largely to give me moral support in my first venture into retail. Temporary had turned into years, and I wouldn't want to try to run the shop without her.

"So what happened at the police station?" Kristen said as she emerged from the back room, fiddling with her apron strings. "What are they going to do about the cash?"

At the mention of cops and cash, Cayenne and Vanessa froze. My staff are used to visits from the major crimes detectives, and Tag stops by regularly. But familiarity does not dampen curiosity.

I told them about the find. "They say they'll do everything they can to track down the owner of the chair. But who knows?"

"Wow," Cayenne said. "I read a story like that, about a woman who bought a bunch of furniture on craigslist and found cash stuffed in every crevice. Some guy's mother had died and he'd never known she'd been hiding all this money in the furniture. The woman called him and gave it all back."

"Every penny?" Vanessa sounded skeptical.

"Every penny," Cayenne echoed. "He sent her flowers every month for a year."

"Well, I'd give it all back if I knew who it belonged to," I said. "No flowers necessary."

"Flowers are always necessary," Kristen said.

Time to do business. We unlocked the front door. I retreated to my office to review the weekend sales and do the books. Readied the bank deposit. Then I brought up our website. Most restaurant customers submit their orders electronically, but I scan them before giving Hayden, our warehouse and production manager, the green light. He'd been on the job since January, and so far, so good.

Back out front, I answered a customer's questions about the different types of paprika and gave her samples to taste and sniff. She chose two, smoked and sweet Hungarian. Small businesses got a boost during the pandemic when customers realized how essential, how responsive, and how endangered we were. But we were still battling the online sellers and big box stores. The best defense is good product and the personal touch—real people answering questions, not a chat bot regurgitating answers from a guidebook compiled by another bot.

I was in the back room swapping my apron for my jacket and the dog's leash when Vanessa stuck her head in.

"Boss," she said, a nickname the staff had picked up from Sandra. "There's a man here asking for you. Says no one can help him but you. He's kind of—sweaty."

That was odd. I thanked her and followed her to the shop floor.

Boz Bosworth. I hadn't known his name when I'd seen him yesterday, outside Talia's building. And he did look sweaty—from nerves, I suspected, not exercise. He blinked rapidly, vibrating with suppressed urgency.

I held out my hand. "Pepper Reece. I admit, I'm surprised to see you."

He ran his hand down the leg of his denim shorts before taking mine. Damp, despite the effort.

"What can I do for you?" I asked.

"Is there somewhere we can talk, in private?"

I often meet with customers—and cops—in the nook, but it's not exactly private. My office was too small, and I was too cautious. His poor judgment and lack of self-control had destroyed a business and cost an entire restaurant staff their jobs.

Yesterday, he'd been seething with fury over Talia's disappearance. He'd remembered who I was and tracked me down.

No. We were meeting out in the open.

I held up the leash. "Dog walk. You're welcome to join us."

At the magic word, my dog emerged from behind the front counter and sat next to me, waiting. I snapped the lead onto his collar and he stood. I glanced at my scowling visitor, then gestured to the front door, leaving the man no choice.

We strode up Pike Place, the Market's cobbled main street. As we passed the original Starbucks—no outside line at the moment—I broke the silence.

"What can I do for you?" I asked again.

He cleared his throat. "Help me find Talia."

"Why me? I sell spice. I don't even know her."

"Pepper," he said, his voice low. "Everybody knows you solve crimes."

"What makes you think a crime's been committed?" Though the crowds were thin today, I dropped my voice, too. Arf tugged gently on the leash, reminding me of our necessary errand, and I picked up the pace. Was the cash the proceeds of a crime, as Nate and I had speculated? And how was it connected to Boz—if it was?

"I don't, not for sure." He exhaled heavily. "But Talia is—gone."

"She wasn't home when you came by. Why do you say she's gone?"

"Nobody in the building has seen her in a week. She left—stuff. The manager—" His eyes were wild, the cords in his neck taut. "I may have gotten her in trouble. No, not like that. I mean—I didn't mean to cause trouble for her, and I need to help her. To make it right."

"Have you been to the police?" I asked.

"This morning. But they said she was an adult and I had no reason to think she was actually missing or in danger."

Did that mean they hadn't talked with Vernon Phan? From his perspective, Talia had no right to live in the building anyway. More likely it meant they hadn't connected Boz's request with my found-property claim. While I'd linked the cash to Talia's address, I knew only her first name.

Did Boz honestly think she was in danger, or was he searching her out for another reason? Just because I thought he was a jerk didn't mean his concern wasn't sincere.

We reached the corner and crossed to the little park with the big views, the grass bright, the scent fresh and earthy after the overnight rain.

"How do you know her?" I asked. "Why do you care so much about her?"

He stared past me, as if deciding how much to say. I found a small bag in my coat pocket and scooped up after Arf, then the dog and I headed for the railing overlooking Elliott Bay. Boz had sought me out, then clammed up. Maybe the brisk air would clear up this confusing nonconversation.

"You know I lost the restaurant." Boz stood beside me at the rail. "No one wanted to hire me. Seemed like time to do something else. I've been driving for Uber."

An easy gig, if you owned a decent car.

"I gave her a ride home last week. Her and that chair. Helped her haul it in. That's why I knew where she lived. When I saw it on the curb yesterday, I knew she was in trouble."

Ha. Laurel had been right—you *could* call an Uber for a wing-back. And I'd been right to think Talia hadn't had the chair long. Not long enough to find the stash.

"So yesterday, why were you coming to see her?"

"I—I wanted to check on her."

"Because she's young and cute?" He had a good dozen years on her. Maybe she liked older men. Maybe he was a predatory sleaze. "Are you trying to help her ex find her? I hear he holds a grudge."

"What?" He squinted, not understanding. "No. Nothing like that."

"What, then? Why are you trying to find her?"

"Because—" he squirmed, that nervousness on display. "Listen, Pepper, I know people are upset with me. I don't blame them—not after how I behaved. But there's stuff going on. And if that sweet kid gets hurt because of it, I—I couldn't live with myself."

That all sounded very well and good, but I still didn't like or trust him. You can't just flip the switch.

I gazed at the ferries and the freighters and tugs cutting through the diamond-blue waves, the paths in the water closing as quickly as they'd opened.

What would Brother Cadfael do? The old monk felt duty-bound to help people in trouble, especially the sick or injured, out of devotion to God, but also as penance for the harm he'd done as a soldier. I had no ties to Talia. No obligations to her, or to Boz. I'd turned in the money, told the police what I knew. I owed neither of them anything more.

I had enough on my plate. I just wanted to live my life for a while without being involved in other people's problems.

"Pepper, you have to help me." He reached out a hand. Beside me, the dog tensed.

I stood my ground, half expecting him to fling a name I'd been called a time or two before, a name often aimed at women who won't do what men want.

It was flattering to be asked, to think that someone needed my help, that I had a reputation. But I would not be bullied.

"There is nothing I can do."

"At least take my number." He pulled his phone out of his pocket. It was one of the bigger models, the back a vivid tie-dye pattern like the shirt visible beneath his open jacket.

I agreed and put his number into my phone. Then, deflated, he stumbled off, head down, hands in his pockets, not caring who he elbowed or brushed aside as he crossed the park and stepped into the street. A horn blared and a car jerked to a stop. Boz kept going through the intersection and up the hill.

"Goodbye to you, too," I muttered. *And good riddance.*

Six

*There is a special place in hell for women who
don't help other women.*

—Madeleine Albright

"A-OKAY, SPICE QUEEN?"

The nickname jarred me out of my mental whirl. It was one of several the media had given me. Others included the Mistress of Spice and the Spice Sleuth, referring as much, I hoped, to my skill in tracking down the freshest and finest ingredients as to my experience rooting out killers.

"Hey, Vinny. What's up?"

"I been up the street, checking in with a customer. The white Bordeaux he loves is outta stock, so I took him a few other options." Like me, Vinny believes retail thrives on individual relationships. He jerked a thumb over his shoulder. "Saw Bosworth jawing at you and figured you might need a hand. Shoulda known you could handle him."

"You know Boz?" In his late fifties, balding and a little paunchy, Vinny Delgado, aka the Wine Merchant, was an unlikely white knight, but I appreciated the thought. At least the vestiges of a Brooklyn accent made him sound tough.

We left the park, Arf between us, and walked down Pike Place. "Was he a wine customer of yours, when he had his own restaurant?"

"Nah. He asked, but word gets around and I'd heard enough to say no. Matt told me about your run-in with him last fall."

Ah, yes. My former employee Matt, a retail whiz, now Vinny's business partner. A good move for them both, despite the tragedy that had precipitated it.

"So what's the buzz on Boz?" I asked, hoping to sift a little fact from the gossip.

"Not a team player. Thinks he's the only one who knows the game." Vinny loves baseball even more than I do. "You put a guy who wants to call all the pitches in charge, you're asking for trouble. In any business, but especially a restaurant."

I thought of Talia, young and on her own. "Sexual harassment?"

We stopped in front of the Soames/Dunn Building, one of my favorites for the peaked glass roof visible from inside. A metal staircase in back leads to Upper Post Alley, home of Vinny's shop.

"Not that I've heard, but I wouldn't put it past him."

"Thanks," I said. "When Sandra and I had lunch at his place, we guessed he wouldn't last six months, and we were right. 'Course, he might have succeeded if he'd used our spices."

"Fat chance. I gotta get a move on. Chiller for the whites and sparklers is on the fritz. At least we've got a reliable tech. You don't want to get hooked up with some of these sales and service outfits. Louses and scumbags."

"Every business has 'em. Scumbags, scams, and schemes."

"Why can't they use that energy for the good, instead of bilking people?" He scratched his bald head over the question that baffles every honest business owner. "You take care now, Pepper."

"That I will." I waved, and Arf and I continued on our way.

So why was a *don't tell me what to do* guy like Boz Bosworth begging me for help?

All was well in spice land. I finalized the bank deposit, then slipped out the side door and ducked into the fragrant warren known as the Post Alley shops. Not to be confused with Upper or Lower Post Alley, though it inevitably is. I stopped at the chowder joint and placed an order for staff lunch. Used to be, I bought lunch on Saturdays, when the Market was too busy for my staff to fight the crowds. Then the pandemic hit and many restaurants switched to takeout. Our mail-order and curbside pickup businesses boomed. I decided buying lunch for the crew every day would be good for them and our neighbors, and the benefit paid off so well that I'd made it permanent.

Then I strolled past other shops and stalls, seeing what was new. Now that Vanessa had gained some experience, she'd taken over most of the deliveries in the Market, and we'd hired a bike service for the rest of downtown. The gain in efficiency cost me some of the critical personal contact with customers, so I tried to make up for it in other ways. See and be seen.

And everywhere, I saw the signs of spring. Tulips and late daffodils. Early-season produce—asparagus, rhubarb, fresh herbs, tender young leeks. I chatted with the produce sellers. Laughed when the old lady perched on the stool outside the Asian grocery teased my ankles with a paper snake on a string—as if she doesn't do it every time I see her. Swayed my hips to the rhythm of the bucket bass an elderly busker played near Pike Place Fish. Waved at the bookseller inside Left Bank Books, another business that sprung up fifty years ago, back when activist energy helped revitalize a Market that had become shabby and ripe for change. Overripe.

At the corner of First and Pike, I waited for the light. Why was Boz so hot to find Talia? He knew she'd loved that chair. If he'd known about the cash, he never would have let me take the chair yesterday afternoon.

But even if he'd known about the money, that didn't prove he was the rightful owner.

The light changed, and pedestrians flooded into the street. The cherry blossoms on Pike were in full bloom. There had been a kerfuffle when the city proposed replacing the decades-old trees with elms. Even without fruit, cherries were messy. All those pink petals! The trees were old, past their pride and prime. Elms would grow quickly to provide leaf cover and shade.

But Seattle's cherry trees are as symbolic as their better-known cousins in the Other Washington. Before World War II, a majority of the Market's farmers and vendors were of Japanese ancestry. The original trees had been planted to honor that heritage and frame the entrance to the Market. And they're beautiful. After the outcry, the city agreed to plant new cherries, expanding the number of trees in the downtown plan.

Don't ever think public opinion doesn't matter. It's the whole reason the Market still exists.

At the bank, I headed for the drop slot, then changed course. Went inside and made my deposit with a real, live person. See and be seen.

"I need to swing by," the teller said. "Now that she's tasted your Cinnamon Toast blend, my daughter won't eat toast any other way. And she's four, so there's no changing her mind until she's ready to change it."

"She's a creature of good habits," I said.

Then it was back to the Market. No meandering this time. I picked up the lunch order, a container of seafood bisque bursting with Northwest flavors, and a bag of sourdough rolls. Made it back to the shop just in time to prevent a hunger mutiny.

Kristen had left for the day. I poured myself a cup of our signature blend tea from the blue enamel samovar and stood behind the counter while Cayenne and Vanessa sat in the nook to eat. They were a contrast, the tall Black woman in her early thirties, the small Hispanic woman ten years younger, and worked together well. Our new production manager, Hayden, had fit in beautifully, and Sandra hovered over us all like a mother hen. With summer coming, we needed one more employee in the shop and could easily add one or two to the production crew.

I took a sip. Our tea was a scent and taste from my childhood, always comforting. My mother had been friends with Jane, the woman who opened the Spice Shop shortly after the voters saved the Market from urban removal in 1971, and there had always been a bag of Jane's special tea in our house. I could picture my mother and Kristen's mom, who died years ago, sitting in well-worn chairs in the Grace House living room, the black tea spiced with cardamom, allspice, and orange peel perfuming the air. And I could picture my mother sipping it again in the newly re-covered wingback, in the new house. The instant I saw that chair, I'd wanted to recreate those moments for her.

The chair. I stopped myself from calling Sergeant Reyes at the East Precinct. He'd replay what he'd said before: when he had news, he would call me. Even if I didn't quite believe that, it was too soon to call him. The squeaky wheel doesn't always get the grease; sometimes, to mix my metaphors, it gets the brush-off.

Yesterday, I'd had no qualms asking questions about Talia. Thinking I could find her. Thinking I *should* find her. I'd been in her neighborhood, and the shock of the discovery—first the cash, then her seeming disappearance—had been fresh.

Was I letting my distrust of Boz get in the way? It's hardly mature, let alone ethical, to refuse to do something you want to do simply because it might also help someone you dislike.

My phone buzzed with a text. A chef who'd worked for a loyal customer of mine was taking over a French bistro in Belltown. His former employer had told him not to work with any supplier but me. Could we meet later this week and talk spice?

We could. I replied, and we made a date.

The shop was quiet for the moment, and I picked up a business magazine that lay on the back counter, open to a piece on market trends in retail. Some were out of the question. I wasn't going to automate a system of price-matching the competition. Price isn't the only value; our staff's knowledge of food and flavor and our commitment to personal service were key to our success. Customer engagement, the trend talkers call it. Good business sense, in the words of my Market mentors.

Flash sales had been moderately successful for us, and I was intrigued by an account of a retailer who held special sales every Wednesday afternoon. Customers came in to see what the "deal of the day" was, making both planned and unplanned purchases. It would take time and tech help to pull that off.

In other ways, we were ahead of the curve. "Branded merchandising," for example. We'd long created custom blends for our restaurant and producer customers and were now taking the next step, providing specially labeled jars of the blends for on-site resale. First up was a butcher's special salt and pepper combo, and we were about to roll out Speziato Speciale, the blend we'd created for our buddy Edgar.

And while that particular blend had triggered the whole Boz fiasco, the idea was still a good one. Our goal was to create more such connections—with less drama and no crime.

But "experiential retail" was a trend we could build on. More spice tastings and demos in the shop. And I had another idea, if we could pull it off.

The chimes on the front door sounded and I laid the magazine aside, a pleasant retail expression on my face.

"Good morning, ladies," I said to the new arrivals, a pair of fortyish women with eagerness on their faces. "How can we spice up your day?"

The woman with dark, collar-length curls and red glasses answered. "A friend is going through a hideous divorce—"

"To put it mildly," her companion said.

"And she's throwing herself into cooking. She's always been a decent cook, but now—wow. It's like Julia Child on steroids. All we have to do is bring the wine." She adjusted her glasses. "Of course, we have to listen to her whine, but that was a given. At least this way, we get a great meal out of it."

"So you're hoping to find a few spices she may not have tried yet? Cookbooks? Tea?"

"All of it," the other woman said. She wore a shiny black trench I'd seen in Nordstrom's window. Trendy. "The paperwork should be final this week, so we thought a gift basket would be a good way to celebrate. Commiserate. Or whatever."

"I understand." I came out from behind the counter to pour them samples of tea. "We've got gift sets for every palate." I beckoned to a table stacked with small boxes, each holding three jars of spice blends. Potted tulips brightened the display. The woman with the red glasses picked up a box.

"Dukkah," she read.

"It's a traditional blend from Egypt. The herbs and spices mixed with sea salt combine the Mediterranean and Middle Eastern flavors, including cumin. Sesame seeds and ground hazelnuts give it a little crunch. Our hazelnuts are grown in Oregon, for a Northwest flavor."

"I've never heard of it."

"We love introducing cooks to blends from around the world that they may not know. Dip flatbread into olive oil, then the dukkah. Sprinkle it on carrots or cantaloupe. Use it anywhere you want a crust, like lamb or fried goat cheese."

We talked about what their friend liked to cook, where she'd traveled, and, most importantly, what food and flavors they hoped she'd add to her repertoire. I grabbed a shopping basket, and in no time, it was full.

My staffers had finished lunch and returned to the shop floor. I put a hand on my stomach to quiet its growling. Hungry as I was,

I wanted to finish this sale first. The friends chose a pair of my favorite spice reference books, then added a trio of gift sets, a jar of French fleur de sel, and a natural sea salt from a producer on San Juan Island.

"And this is for me," the woman in the black trench said, putting a bottle of blueberry-lavender Joy Juice on the counter. Not to be outdone, her friend took a bottle of the lemon-sage.

"You'll love those," I said, as I handed back the credit card. "Super local, super good. Great in cocktails and mocktails and on desserts. Check out the recipes on Joy's website. The address is on the label." I added a flyer for our spice club to their very full shopping bag and sent them to Vinny for champagne.

Curious cooks and loyal friends. Now that's a business trend that will never go out of style.

Seven

There are few, very few,
that will own themselves in a mistake.

—Jonathan Swift, satirist and political essayist

I DIDN'T NEED A BUSINESS MAGAZINE TO HIGHLIGHT THE importance of keeping on top of our social media. Both the women shopping for their about-to-be-divorced friend had used their phones to sign up for our blog on the spot, earning an instant discount code. That was as far down the trend tunnel of text-message marketing as I was willing to go.

On our afternoon break, Arf and I were interrupted only by pleasant interactions, including a fresh-baked dog cookie for him and a raspberry macaron for me. Fuel that let us work late, he supervising while I added new recipes to the queue, linking them to our spice blends and other products, and caught up on a few projects. Happy campers, we were.

The cobbles were quiet when we stepped outside. "Quiet" here is a relative term. The Market is home to more than seventy-five farmers, two hundred shops and restaurants, two hundred craftspeople known as daystallers, a score or more of buskers ranging from musical trios to balloon artists, and nearly five hundred residents, all on nine acres. But it was Monday evening, and most of our ten million visitors a year were home now, though I imagined a few upscale tourists were clinking glasses as they watched the sun set from the Inn, the Market's sole hotel.

I waved to the security guard patrolling the North Arcade and started down the Hillclimb, the wide steps that connect Pike Place to Western, then continue to the waterfront below.

Seeing the evening watchman reminded me that there's a difference between keeping an eye open, as Vinny had done, and searching someone out, as Boz and the older man Blue Hair had mentioned had been doing.

Why were they looking for Talia? Who was the other man? Were he and Boz connected?

In the loft, I fed the dog, then flipped through the mail. I was getting a lesson in the downside of marketing, from the recipient's perspective. Every plumbing and lighting fixture website I'd visited for my parents' remodel now had me in its sights, sending email reminders ("New exhaust fans blowing your way!") and actual paper catalogs. I slid a couple directly into the recycling bin but kept one advertising blinds and shades ("Treatments for every window!") and for my dad, a flyer from a landscaping-supply company.

Coatless and shoeless, I poured a glass of viognier and put the leftover bisque in a saucepan to reheat. Happily, there were extra rolls, too. I carried my dinner to my weathered round picnic table. My former mother-in-law had spotted it in her neighborhood and immediately thought of me. Sidewalk pickings are a noble tradition. It's perfect for my dining space—not quite a room, in a loft intentionally short on walls.

No ball game on Monday nights, so I turned on the radio. Seattle has a terrific jazz station, and I was practically raised listening to it. I was just in time to catch the weather report.

"Record winds and waves were reported off the coast of Alaska," the announcer said. "The storm could be sending dark skies and wet days to Puget Sound."

My guy was off the coast of Alaska. *Keep him safe,* I told the Universe. Keep him safe.

Then I sat. After leaning over the computer for hours, my back craved an actual chair. Besides, it's hard to eat soup on your lap on the couch. And the bisque, a creamy, tomatoey combo of shrimp, cod, and salmon accented with a hint of basil, deserved all my attention.

It didn't surprise me that Boz had said the police weren't worried about Talia. The neighbor Arf and I had met at the bus stop claimed Talia hadn't been around all week, but that wasn't proof that she'd gone missing. Particularly in light of potential trouble over the questionable sublet. I took a sip of wine, creamy and heavenly scented. Did the money in the chair change the situation? Not necessarily.

What about the fact that two men were looking for her? Was that even evidence?

In a court of law, no. In my mind, maybe. Enough to keep asking questions. I couldn't refuse to help a woman in trouble.

I spooned up a bite of soup. Boz had insisted on giving me his number. Did he think I might change my mind?

Might be better not to let him know he'd been right. If he believed I was out of the picture, he wouldn't try to pressure me. Would he do that? Yes. He was a cheat and a hothead who'd taken the consequences of his own mistakes out on his employees.

And who knew how many sins he'd committed against shrimp and tomatoes.

Could he be a threat to Talia? If he was, I had to find her.

Before he did.

ARF ENJOYS a sunset stroll along the waterfront, relishing the pungent sting of salt water and diesel-tinged decay. He may be a gentleman in many ways, but his nose is all dog.

At Pier 57, we stopped to watch the Great Wheel turn. Only the outer ring was lit up; on weekends, holidays, and days the Seahawks play at home, colored lights glow on every beam and strut. The views are spectacular, if you don't mind heights and going in circles above water.

We continued south, strolling along the water's edge. I had my wellies on, so the puddles from a brief afternoon shower didn't bother me, but keeping Arf out of them was not so easy.

After the Viaduct came down, the city created an expansive waterfront park. That and a surge in the number of downtown residents had increased the sense of neighborhood, despite the number of businesses catering to tourists. In my mind, a change is successful if it feels like it's always been this way. If the new doesn't crowd out the old. We passed the pier that serves as home port for local cruises—boat tours of the harbor, the locks on the Ship Canal, and other sightseeing routes. Then came the waterfront fire station and its fireboats, and beyond that, the ferry terminals.

Bright lights, big city. Where in all the hustle and bustle might Talia be? Without knowing more about her, I couldn't begin to imagine. The neighbor had said Talia hadn't been here long but that she'd visited the city as a kid.

Had she taken refuge with an aunt or a cousin? Had she gone back to San Diego or moved on, searching for home somewhere else? I'd left Seattle once for a few months, twenty years ago, though I'd quickly discovered my mistake. But not everyone is lucky enough to be born in the place that most suits them.

Arf and I looped back to the loft along Western and entered by the main door. Shucked off coat (me) and leash (him). I toweled his feet dry, made sure his water bowl was full and his chew bone wasn't stuck under the couch or some other hard-to-reach spot, then slipped into my comfies and called my guy.

"As storms go," Nate said, his voice clear despite the distance between us, "this one's not so big. Yeah, we got wet, but we get wet in good weather. Comes with the job."

True enough, but as reassurances go, it didn't do much. We talked about everything from the catch of the day to the shop to my meeting with the designer (in person) and my mother (by Face-Time) tomorrow.

And then we talked sweet mush, blew each other cyberkisses, and said good-night.

"Fisherman fish," I muttered as I set the phone on the packing crate. It's what Nate often says when people question his here-again, gone-again schedule. Our mantra since we met that sunny Sunday afternoon at Fishermen's Terminal ten months ago.

I poured a second glass of wine—a short one—and settled on the couch. I had a new-to-me book on the Age of Exploration and the spice trade, a fascinating subject but far too heavy for bedtime reading.

I'd finished all the Brother Cadfael books and the Dame Frevisse mysteries. I dip in and out of other historical series and love the foodie fiction we carry at the shop. A couple of boxes of new titles had arrived today, but Kristen hadn't opened them yet. Nothing in my to-be-read pile grabbed my attention.

What about the books I'd salvaged on the sidewalk? I didn't know if they belonged to Talia or some other tenant. Some possibly-not-illegally-subletting tenant.

I untucked the box flaps. Oops. Not the books, but the knick-knacks. I'd mostly been interested in the fabric used to cushion them. Carefully, I unwrapped a ceramic robin and a child-made clay turtle and shook out the fabric they were wrapped in. An old gingham apron. The woman who makes the aprons we sell in the shop would love it.

The books were still in the trunk of my car. Not that I'd necessarily find anything I wanted in a young woman's collection. Or her cast-offs. If they were hers. But it was worth a look.

Arf was snoring in his bed by the big windows. Quietly, I shoved my feet into shoes and grabbed my keys. They slipped out of my hand and hit the plank floor with a clatter. In an instant, my dog was awake.

"No," I said as he began to scrabble to his feet. "You've had your walk. Go back to sleep."

He tilted his head, watching me. As if he couldn't imagine me going anywhere without him. Then the tug of doggy dreams grew too strong to resist, and he sank into the bliss of his bed.

The box wasn't as heavy as I'd remembered, and I was back upstairs in minutes. I set it on the picnic table and opened it.

A Wrinkle in Time. A couple of old Mary Stewarts, from her Arthurian series, the spines of the fat paperbacks creased, the covers faded. Two Circle of Magic books by Tamora Pierce. Talia liked the classics, with a dusting of magic and fantasy, of myth and legend. And all, I realized, focused on strong girls and women who discovered deep within them the talents they needed to conquer their fears and work their way out of trouble.

I dug a little deeper. "The Hill We Climb," the poem Amanda Gorman had read a few years ago at the presidential inauguration. I began flipping through the slim book when a snippet of handwriting snagged my eye. I turned back to the title page.

For Talia.
There is no hill you cannot climb.
Love,
G.

So the books were Talia's. Who was G? Grandma? The hand-writing had the confidence of an older woman. Or it might be an initial, for a name I could never guess.

I reached for *Wrinkle* and opened it carefully. Inside the flyleaf, in a loopy scrawl, was the name Talia Ruth Cook.

A pang shot through me. Now I knew. Whoever Talia was, these books mattered to her. She had not left them behind on purpose.

What were the alternatives? I would have no better luck than Boz convincing the police that she was in danger, that she had gone on the run, or worse, been taken. Guesswork, they would say. The cash in the cushion didn't prove anything, not if she didn't know about it. And the police were not going to let themselves be used in a personal search not connected to a crime.

Boz claimed he'd picked her and the chair up in an Uber. Had he overheard us tossing around the idea of calling one? Unlikely. If I remembered right, he'd burst upon us after I'd called Kristen. Where had he picked Talia up? He hadn't said, and I hadn't asked. Stupid. Instead of probing for what he knew, I'd questioned his motives, letting my distrust get in the way.

I hadn't taken a lot when I left Tag, spending a few weeks in Kristen's guest room during the loft build-out, and I'd only moved a few miles. But I had kept the books I loved, including childhood favorites: *Calico Bush* by Rachel Field, *The Secret Garden*, and my own copy of *A Wrinkle in Time*.

My eyes sought them out on the low bookshelves I'd had built beneath the tall windows, drawing comfort from the memories and their presence. Right next to my Cadfael collection.

It was like a sign, the old monk telling me I was on the right track.

Eight

Seattle is home to roughly 125 bridges, including the four drawbridges that cross the Lake Washington Ship Canal, aka "the cut," connecting the saltwater Puget Sound to the fresh waters of Lake Union and Lake Washington.

I'VE NEVER MET ANYONE WHO DOESN'T LIKE TULIPS, AND I'M pretty sure I wouldn't trust them if I did.

But it was nice to see a few irises and painted daisies in the buckets clustered on the green wooden tables of the Main Arcade. I buy flowers for the shop on Tuesdays and again on Friday or Saturday, working my way down the line, then back to the beginning. Today's flower lady didn't speak a lot of English, but that didn't stop us: point, pick, point, pick.

"Pepper!"

Arf recognized Jamie Alexander's distinctive contralto as quickly as I did. Her wardrobe, like her artwork, is as colorful as the spring bouquets. Today she wore a bright-yellow slicker, reminiscent of the Morton Salt Girl and a little yellow number Arf sometimes wears, a purple-and-orange woven scarf around her neck. Coffee in one hand, her portfolio of new work in the other. We touched cheeks, then she leaned down to smooch the air near Arf's nose.

"I hear we might actually need these raincoats today," she

said. "Pray for dry skies until after closing. Oh, it was you who got the last caramel roll. You lucky dog." She nodded at the white paper bag in my hand, sticky goo outlining the shape inside.

"Take it," I said. "Don't say no. I know how hard it is to get away from your table." The daystallers watch each other's spots during bathroom breaks and lunch runs, but other than that, selling your work at the Market stalls is an all-day affair. Fortunately, the rules only require artists and craftspeople to staff their own tables a couple of days during the week to get a coveted Saturday spot, though some hire sales agents to increase their presence. Jamie had come to the Market last fall and fit right in. I was sure her playful acrylics would be a huge hit with tourists.

"Thanks, Pepper. Hey, have you heard the new busker? He sings and plays banjo. He's great."

An old joke popped into my mind. "Did you hear about the banjo player who didn't lock his car? Came back and found two banjos."

"That's terrible!"

We exchanged more air kisses, and the dog and I crossed the street to our happy place.

After my morning chores, I decided to call the police, now that I had Talia's full name. They might have already gotten it from the building manager. Or not. I assumed he knew it, even if her name wasn't on the lease, but had they talked to him? A quick scan of the morning paper confirmed the impression I'd gotten at the station that it had been a busy weekend in cop world—an armed robbery outside a nightclub, a carjacking, and several arrests in an ongoing drug investigation. And the discovery, pursuant to a tip, of a bronze statue commemorating fraternity members killed in World War I that had disappeared from a U Dub frat house during a remodel a few years back. Why, I wondered, would anyone steal that—until I read that it was valued at over fifty thousand dollars. No suspect had been identified, and the frat boys, bless them, were not interested in pursuing criminal charges. They were just happy to have the statue, portraying two wounded soldiers in the distinctive combat helmets of the era, back where it belonged.

All that was more than enough to keep the officers too busy to track down the owner of a ratty old chair, even if someone had used it as a safe-deposit box.

"Reyes," the sergeant barked into the phone.

"Reece," I barked back. "Pepper Reece."

"Pepper, I told you we'd be in touch when we had something to report." I heard beeps and buzzes and chatter in the background and hoped that, not me, was the source of his impatience.

"That's why I'm calling you, Sergeant. I have something to report."

I'd shocked him into silence.

"I told you that the woman who owned the chair was named Talia or Dahlia. Now I know, from some books I found at the same time, that her full name is Talia Ruth Cook. With a T." I heard the sergeant clicking keys. "I also discovered that she moved here recently from San Diego but that she found the chair in Seattle. Where, I don't know, but I know who to ask."

"And who might that be?"

I told him. "I'm sure he'll tell you where he picked her up. That would give you a place to start, to figure out where she got the chair."

"You're doing great so far," he said. "Forget I said that. Your ex would have my hide if anything happened and he found out I encouraged you."

And then Tag would aim that fury at me.

"Why didn't you tell us about this Boz character on Sunday?" Reyes continued.

"Didn't seem important. At that point, I had no idea how he knew Talia or why he got upset when he saw the chair." I still didn't know, not exactly. There was some reason he wanted to find her that he hadn't let on.

The good sergeant thanked me for the call, repeated his assurance that they'd be in touch, and added a caution to let them handle it.

As if.

We hung up. Truth be told, I was surprised not to have heard from Boz again, continuing his pleas. I hadn't given him my cell, but there were no messages from him on the shop line.

By ten thirty, it was clear that this was going to be a slow Tuesday. The threat of rain or the unpredictability of retail? Didn't matter. The staff had the shop well in hand, giving me time to run up to Fremont and see what I could dig up. Though I'd heard nothing but raves about the downtown doggy day care, I hadn't had time to check it out. To be honest, I was procrastinating, because I like having my boy around during the day. My staff loves him and happily watch and walk him when I'm out, but was it fair to him? I'd save that conundrum for another day. Before the weather warmed up.

The midmorning sprinkles had dried to a gloomy gray when the dog and I stepped out onto Pike Place. At my building, I retrieved the Saab and drove north on Westlake, then waited with the other cars and buses at the Fremont Bridge. It's said to be the most frequently opened drawbridge in the country—at barely thirty feet above the water, it's too low for commercial vessels and all but the smallest sailboats to clear.

I was a few cars back, my line of sight partially blocked, but I didn't see the bridge deck up. Good. If the bridge was already closing, I wouldn't have to sit here long.

But both wait and line grew. The bridge didn't go up and it didn't go down. People were milling around, pointing. What was going on?

Then, on some magic signal, people jumped back into their cars. Engines came to life and traffic began to move. I caught a glimpse of flashing lights west of the bridge, near the Burke-Gilman Trail on the north side of the canal. Curious.

The wait had given me time to make a plan—sort of. My plan amounted to finding a parking place close to Talia's building, but not too close. If someone other than Boz was watching for her, I did not want to blip onto their radar screen. Before anything else, I did what a local would do and headed for the bakery. My stomach was rumbling, but I didn't regret giving Jamie my caramel roll. It was Tuesday, and the staff here knew Talia. If she'd been in, lured by the promise of lemon cream scones, they would tell me. And I wanted to get a sense of the neighborhood, see if I could find someone else who knew her.

The bakery was steamy and sweet, about half the tables full, mostly with women alone or in pairs. I fit right in.

Blue Hair stood behind the counter. "Hey, doll. I knew you'd be back, but I didn't think it would be so soon. You new in the neighborhood?"

How could I explain my presence? Talking spice was always a

good excuse, but not this soon after meeting him. I didn't want to appear pushy and squash any hope of getting his future business.

"I'm a sucker for a good Americano, and those scones were divine."

His eyes sparkled at the compliment. "Coming right up," he said, sidestepping to the espresso machine. I laid a twenty on the counter—using a card would give away my name. He might make the connection between me and the shop and feel played.

Of course, I was playing him a bit. Not for business, but for talk.

Stelle emerged from the back, wiping her hands on her white apron. "I still can't believe it," she said to Blue Hair, quietly but not so quiet that I couldn't hear. "In the canal."

"Too weird." He matched her somber tone. "I mean, there's lots of foot traffic on both sides, but in all the years I've been here, nothing like this. A jumper?"

"I don't know. Musta gone in overnight, or early this morning." She clutched her elbows. "Can you imagine the poor guy who found it? Biking to work and you find a body in the water? I mean, I'm a wreck and I was just passing by."

The heck with my coffee and scone. And my change. I threw my bag over my shoulder and ran.

Ran out the door and toward the canal. Toward the police cars, the reason for the traffic stoppage on the bridge. It was three blocks and I am so not a runner, but I had to know.

It could be nothing. It could be unrelated. It might not be a body, despite what Stelle had said.

Or it could be Talia.

A few tech companies have offices in Fremont, part of a decentralization trend that eases traffic congestion, keeps employees happy by keeping them closer to home, and generally spreads the wealth around. Vernon Phan at Talia's building had said the woman who leased her apartment worked in one of them. A cluster of those employees now stood outside a brick-and-glass building, faces somber, as they watched the police officers prowl the banks of the canal. Up the street is a small grassy park, more a greenbelt than anything else, but in this section, the paved trail is separated from the water only by a short, steep slope of rough-hewn rocks. The trail was cordoned off and I saw a runner surge into view, then stop, forced to stay and watch or redirect his steps to surface streets. He stayed.

We almost can't help it, can we? It's as if we're programmed to stare when tragedy strikes. Morbid curiosity, sure, but also caution. We want to know what happened so we can avoid a similar fate. As if we believe that disaster striking someone else increases our own odds of staying safe one more day.

But drowning—flailing in the water, unable to breathe or to know which way was up. I could almost feel the panic swell in my chest and shut off my senses. And I was perfectly safe, on dry, solid ground.

What had looked from the bridge like a police car or an ambulance turned out to be a cluster of half a dozen police and fire vehicles. The flashing lights had been turned off. A pair of fire department divers in wet suits stood beside a red SFD Rescue rig, talking to a woman in uniform. Marine odors, a mix of diesel, mud, and rotting algae, swirled around us.

And there in the midst of it all were my pals.

I first met Detective Michael Tracy when I was married to Tag and they worked in the same unit. I'd known they didn't care for each other, but it wasn't until a year or so ago that the truth came out during a murder investigation. My investigation. Only then did they realize their mutual resentment was based on a misunderstanding, and tensions eased. That had changed Tracy's attitude toward me, too.

Fifteen feet away, Tracy stood with his hands in the pockets of his camel hair jacket. I'd often wondered if he had a closet full of them or if he always wore the same one. He's short, Black, and a bit rounded, in contrast to his tall, blonde partner, Detective Cheryl Spencer, who stood next to him. She's nicer than he is, as well as a better dresser, and an equally good cop. They'd heard the jokes their names inevitably brought, but the humor had long worn off. They were assigned to Major Crimes, aka Homicide, and I'd provided intel in several of their cases, even solving a few. I'd earned a grudging respect, and an honorary badge. I keep it pinned to my shop apron.

But that didn't make them happy to see me.

They were talking to a man in tight black cycling pants and a yellow jacket. A bike lay on the grass nearby. Spencer shook the cyclist's hand, then he leaned down to pick up the bike.

As if they sensed me watching, the detectives turned in my direction.

I ignored their disbelieving faces. Stepped forward before Tracy could spear me with a smart remark.

"Tell me it's not a young woman named Talia Cook," I said.

Tracy's eyebrows rose. "And you tell us why you're asking, but no. White male, aged thirty-seven. Found shortly after sunrise, but how long he was in the water, ME couldn't say yet. Lucky for us, he still had his wallet and ID."

"Who is he?" I asked.

"Keep this between us," Tracy said, and read from his phone. "Name of William Anthony Bosworth."

Now I knew why I hadn't heard from Boz.

He was dead.

Nine

*I don't care if the glass is half-full or half-empty. I
just want to know if there's coffee in it.*

—Overheard in a Seattle coffee shop

"YOU FIRST," TRACY SAID AFTER WE'D SETTLED AT A CORNER
table. Blue Hair had promised me a fresh coffee and taken my
companions' orders. By the way he eyed them, I guessed that he'd
made them for cops the moment we walked in and was no longer
so sure about me.

Even when you want to be helpful, when you have nothing
to hide, the presence of the police makes most of us stand a little
straighter and watch our words. Not that we seriously believe a slip
of the tongue could get us thrown in the slammer. But when they
show up, we know we are dealing with serious shiitake. When life
and death are on the line, we all want to mind our peas and cukes.

I told the detectives how I'd first met Boz last fall, when my
longtime friend and customer, Edgar at Speziato, accused me of
selling the spice blend we'd created for him to another chef. Talk
about a no-no. Worse, the rival chef was, in Edgar's not-so-humble
opinion, second-rate.

In a quest to save our reputation and our customer relationship,
Sandra and I had gone on a spice spy mission, ultimately discov-
ering that Boz had been romantically involved with a bartender at
Speziato, who stole a jar of the stuff for him. When it ran out, he

attempted to recreate it, but his taste buds weren't up to the task and he'd missed a key ingredient.

"We decided it wasn't a matter for the police," I said, wrapping up the story.

"And this chef," Spencer said, "was William Bosworth."

"Yes." I rubbed a spot on my temple that was starting to throb. "Fair to say, he had a temper. When he found out that his sous had given me inside info, he fired him. The rest of the kitchen staff quit, and the owner canned Boz and shut down the whole operation."

"Sounds like he made a lot of people unhappy," Tracy said. "We'll need names."

"Edgar Ramos. Tariq Rose. They would know the girlfriend's name, and Tariq can tell you the other employees. I didn't see Boz again until Sunday, around noon." I described the brief encounter on the sidewalk and our conversation Monday in the Market.

"Two Americanos and a vanilla latte." Blue Hair called out the coffee order before he reached our table. "And fresh lemon scones."

Tracy plucked a scone from the plate and bit off the end, then reached for his latte. Spencer and I sipped our coffee. I appreciated the pause in the conversation almost as much as the hot brew. I hadn't done anything wrong and I knew it, but that didn't stop me from feeling shaky.

"So who's this girl he was after? Young woman, I should say," Tracy said around a bite of scone. "And you're asking questions and poking around because of a chair?"

"That's where it gets weird." I told them about the hidden cash and the report I'd filed.

"I'm on it," Spencer said. Phone in hand, she left the bakery.

"Tell me more about this Talia Ruth Cook," Tracy said. "Who is she? Why was Bosworth looking for her?"

"That, he didn't say. I assumed he was trying to hustle her. Though I think she's quite a bit younger than he is. Or was." Despite everything he'd done, I was sorry he was dead. He'd made mistakes, but you're never too old to correct course. And he might have held a clue or two about where Talia had gone and why she was on the run. If she was. "She was semiregular here. Her neighbor said she worked part-time, cleaning houses. Maybe other jobs, too. The building manager might know more—she claimed to be apartment-sitting, but he calls it an illegal sublet. You can check Boz's story about giving her an Uber ride, right? Do you need a warrant? Will you take over her case?" If there was a case. Odd as it was to haul home a big, unwieldy chair, then split and leave it behind, there was no reason to think a crime had occurred, just because people who barely knew her didn't know where she'd gone. Although the cash stash put a different angle on it.

Tracy grunted. "We may or may not have a missing person. We definitely have a dead body. Is there a connection?" He brushed scone crumbs off his lapel.

"You mean—" I paused, my throat going dry. "You mean Talia might be a suspect in Boz's death?"

"Man goes after a woman, won't take no. She takes the opportunity." He opened his hands. "Wouldn't be the first time."

No. It wouldn't. Or the last.

"But why would she have been down by the canal at sunrise?" I asked. "She hasn't been seen in Fremont for a week."

"She hasn't been seen at the apartment that may or may not be hers for a week," Tracy said, correcting me. "Doesn't mean she isn't close by."

True enough. Crashing somewhere else, changing her routine. Skipping her favorite bakery. "Check Boz's phone. He would have her number and address." I stopped when I saw Tracy shaking his head. "Oh. It's soaked. Can your tech people get the data off it, to track his calls and movements? Besides the Uber stuff."

"No phone," Tracy said.

"Hey!" A woman's cry pierced the chatter in the room. She stood at the counter, pointing to the door. "That guy took my coffee. I came back from the restroom and it was gone."

Instinctively, I glanced at the door. No sign of anyone. The sprinkles had become light rain. Tracy shrugged. Bigger trouble on his mind.

"It happens sometimes, with go orders," Blue Hair told the wailing woman. "Usually by accident. I'll make you another, no charge."

"You don't have his phone," I said. "The divers. That's why they went back in, and why you've been sneaking peeks at your phone every two minutes. See?" I said at Tracy's surprise. "I'm an observant witness."

"When you saw him Sunday, did you notice what he drove?"

"No," I admitted. "The Fremont Sunday Market was on. He could have parked blocks away, like we did. Must be a van or SUV, to fit that chair. But you can find out easy, right?"

Tracy grunted again. He would commit to nothing.

"Okay," I said. "Your turn. How did he get into the canal? Did he drown or was he already dead?" I remembered Stelle's speculation, then leaned closer, my voice breaking as I spoke. "He didn't jump, did he?"

"We're waiting on the ME for all that. Though jumpers— and thank God we don't have many—usually choose Aurora, not Fremont."

That made sense. The Aurora Avenue Bridge, carrying U.S. 99 a few blocks east of here, was much higher than the drawbridges, especially this one.

I cast my eyes down, biting my lip.

"I'm sorry, Pepper. Honestly, I am," Tracy said. "If I knew, I would tell you."

His kindness hit a tender spot. "So we need to find his phone and his vehicle," I said. "And Talia. And figure out when he died."

"Not 'we,'" Tracy said. "That badge is honorary, remember?"

I hid my smile behind my coffee cup.

Spencer returned, rain dripping from her black coat. "Time to go. Got a lead on the rig. Nothing on the door-to-door yet." I wasn't invited. Okay by me.

"You see, hear, learn, think anything," Tracy said, pointing at me, "you call."

I cradled my cup as I watched them leave. Phones know us. They track who we talk to, who we text, where we go. Boz's phone was critical evidence. If they found it and could salvage it, they might be able to confirm his story about Talia. More importantly, they could trace where he'd been before he died, who he'd texted or talked to, and when he went dark. Without it, they'd be relying on Uber and the phone company, which might not be the easiest thing in the world.

I needed to let Edgar and Tariq know. No love lost between them and Boz, but I couldn't see either of them as viable suspects. Edgar had been angry at the time, but the incident was hardly grounds to shove a man into the Ship Canal. And Tariq—well, blowups and firings are common in restaurant work, and he'd found a better job. Besides, as he'd said himself, he understood why Boz canned him. In exposing Boz's wrongdoing, Tariq had broken an unwritten code.

The rest of the staff? They'd quit in solidarity, though no doubt some had their own grievances with Boz. Up to Spencer and Tracy to suss that out.

Talia Ruth Cook, who are you? Where are you? Innocent or not, involved or not, she had me worried. I'd found something valuable that might or might not belong to her, and if she was driven by fear, as I suspected, that cash might be her way out.

Or it might be what had gotten her into trouble. A big help or a big complication.

I finished my coffee, got a bag for the remaining scones, and ventured out into the rain.

WHERE TO NEXT? I had to decide in a hurry, before I drowned. Then I remembered Boz and chided myself for the careless phrase.

I ducked into a recessed doorway and called Edgar. No answer. Voice mail was marginally better than texting for delivering bad news. I left a message and asked him to tell Tariq and anyone else who would want to know.

What next? I glanced up the block. Inspiration struck and I dashed through the rain twenty feet to a beckoning sign above a welcoming door.

With each step down to the lower level, past a mural of superheroes, icons, and sports stars, my vintage-loving heart grew a little happier. I am a modern woman, despite my hippie roots and my mythic first name (the one on my driver's license), and despite living in a warehouse more than a century old. But my style is eclectic, in the best sense of that ambiguous word. My furniture is a mix of Asian and mid-century modern, with wacky additions like the picnic table, and my kitchen is crammed with vintage dishes and utensils. I hadn't been in this place in at least two years. My bad.

At the bottom of the stairs hung an old metal traffic light. A musky mix of age and orange oil clung to the air.

Might be a good place to find a small table or desk for my parents' house. Not on my shopping list, but I'd been thinking about one ever since seeing the desk in the vacant apartment. A sweet companion for the wingback.

Along one wall, glass display cases held jewelry, souvenir spoons, and other shiny objects. Behind them stood a woman in a vintage black tuxedo jacket, the lapels studded with red sequins. A pair of black-and-red lacquered chopsticks pierced the pile of dark hair on top of her head, like knitting needles in a ball of yarn. Brow furrowed, lips pursed, she studied her phone. She did not greet me.

"Pardon me," I said.

She raised her eyes slowly and dragged her gaze in my direction. *Sweetheart,* I told her in my mind, *I am a customer, not an interruption.*

"A friend found this great old wingback chair, and I'd like to find a small desk or table to go with it." I held out my phone, showing her a photo of the chair before we'd ripped into it.

"Not my piece. She didn't get it here."

Not my question. "Right. I'm looking for a small desk—"

Ms. Chopstick's red nails flashed as she shoved her phone in her jacket pocket and stomped off, leaving me staring open-mouthed at the flapping tails of her tux. With that attitude, the chopsticks ought to be considered concealed weapons.

"Sorry about that," a man said. I hadn't noticed him earlier. Tallish and thin, north of sixty, his short hair once red but now fading. He pushed up the sleeves of his vintage tweed jacket as he approached. "Welcome to the Vintage Mall. Our merchandise is a mix of items my partner and I find, consignment pieces, and vendor-owned items. Some vendors work a few hours a month to cut their space rent, and they aren't always with the program. What can I help you find?"

I explained my quest.

"Good bones," he said, pointing at the photo. "With a wingback, even a smaller one like that, you'll want a desk with a narrow profile and interesting legs. We've got some good prospects I'm sure your mother will love." He gestured and I followed him through the aisles, past displays of Franciscan dishware, early Nancy Drews, and old records. Past a shelf full of blue canning jars with zinc tops and a stack of vintage suitcases. I stopped.

There is something about the smooth leather, the brass hardware and straps of a two-sider, the practical romance of a train case, that is almost irresistible. Old luggage speaks quietly but firmly of a bygone era, one with more flaws than you could shake a walking stick at but with an undeniable flair. I reached for a small caramel-colored piece with tan stitching and a leather-wrapped handle.

"This one has a lap drawer and tapered legs," the shop owner was saying.

But I wasn't looking at the desk. I was reading the business card tucked in the leather bag tag. "Cook's Upholstery. Robert R. Cook. Furniture restoration and upholstery," it said, above an address in Burien, a small city near Sea-Tac airport.

"Classic pieces." The shopkeeper had noticed my distraction. "Great way to add a little history to a room."

"Where did it come from?"

"Don't know. My partner bought that. There's a lot of coming and going in the neighborhood, and we pick up a piece here and there when someone wants to lighten the load."

Behind him stood a rack of vintage clothing. A red leather blazer caught my eye, and I ran my fingers down the sleeve. Too big and heavy for me. Behind it hung a black cardigan embroidered with colorful flowers, and I lifted the wooden hanger off the rack.

"Cashmere," he said. "I'd date it about 1960. Excellent condition. Not a moth hole in it."

"Perfect for my poodle skirt," I joked. Too small for me, but so cute. "My best friend's teenage daughter is totally into vintage. I'll take it, too."

"Wonderful. Now, shall we look at that desk?"

He showed me three options, all small but leggy, and I took pictures and measurements. One, without a drawer, bore several coats of chipped paint. The next option had a lap drawer, but it stuck, and when I peered underneath, I suspected it needed new bracing. Project pieces, both of them. The third desk, the one with the tapered legs, was stunning.

"Cherry," the shop owner said. "Always in good taste."

And a bit too much money for a spur-of-the-moment splurge.

"Oh my gosh. I've got to get going. I'm meeting the designer at the house. I'll let you know what she thinks." I snapped photos while he rang up my purchases, wrapping the sweater in tissue paper.

"Give me your number, in case I come across something else that might work." He laid the sweater inside the valise, as he called it, then slipped it into a giant black trash bag, wrapping the plastic around the handle so I could carry it easily.

At the foot of the stairs, the traffic light stopped me.

"You can see it's been rewired," he said. "If you have time—"

"Right this moment, I don't. But I'll be back. Promise."

"My pleasure. Apologies again for the attitude you encountered when you walked in. I'll speak to her. We are all about helping people find the treasures they had no idea they were looking for."

I'd found more than treasures. I'd found evidence. Of what, I didn't know. Not yet. But I was going to find out.

Ten

Truth is, with 149 days of measurable rain in a typical year, Seattle is not the rainiest big city in the United States. At 167 days, Rochester and Buffalo, New York, tie for the honor, edging out Portland, Oregon. But don't tell anyone.

OUTSIDE, THE RAIN HAD STOPPED, BUT I APPRECIATED THE dealer's care with the vintage valise. So different from Vernon Phan, dumping the chair, books, and other boxes on the sidewalk.

Not that the dealers at the Vintage Mall weren't trying to make a profit, but they loved what they sold. Although I had my doubts about Ms. Chopstick. What was her problem?

At the corner, I could not stop myself from looking toward the canal. A police car and CSU van remained at the scene. No sign of the Fire Rescue truck. The sidewalk was still blocked, but traffic flowed freely on the street and bridge. A few feet away, a woman stared in the same direction, huddled in her puffy purple coat. Stelle, from the bakery.

I approached cautiously, not wanting to startle her.

"Wonder if they found anything else?" I said.

She nodded, wordless.

"It must have been terrible," I continued.

"I was on my way to work. I stopped, but the man on the

bicycle had already dragged him out of the water and called 911. He tried to cover him up with his jacket, but I'll never forget that one bare foot—"

She covered her mouth with her hands. It was an image I'd never forget, either, and I hadn't seen it.

"I'm so sorry," I said.

"There was nothing I could do. Those were cops with you, weren't they?"

"Detectives. Friends of mine. They'll figure out what happened."

"You were asking about Talia when you came in on Sunday. It wasn't her, was it? I mean, I thought it was a man from the foot, but I couldn't be sure."

"No." I wished I could tell her I'd been in her position, that I knew how being close to unnatural death felt, but that was too much of a burden. Better not to say I'd known the dead man or that he'd known Talia. Let her go home—working early hours, she might be done for the day—and take a nap, then greet her children after school with cookies and milk, untroubled by fear. I could not take away the shock and grief, but I didn't need to add to it.

"Funny," she said, "how you can feel connected to someone you see regularly, even if you never exchange more than a few words. But I knew what Talia liked, and I liked making sure she got it."

"You have a generous spirit. And flour in your hair."

She ran her fingers through it, the flour and mist already forming a soft paste. "I wish I could tell you more about her and the man who was looking for her. But I'm back and forth from the counter to the tables to the kitchen. I miss a lot."

"What about your boss? Seems the observant type."

"And the honest type. If he says he didn't see the man you described, he didn't see him." She glanced toward the bridge and the official vehicles one more time, then back at me. "When you find her—Talia—tell her I've got a scone with her name on it."

BY THE TIME I got to the car, it was raining again. I didn't have time to track down the detectives and ask if the divers or CSU had found Boz's phone. The Saab's engine complained a bit, then took hold. What was wrong, I didn't know—probably couldn't afford to know—though I couldn't put off taking it to a real mechanic much longer.

I zipped across the Montlake Bridge and up Twenty-Third, then drove down familiar streets. I wasn't sure who'd been more astonished last winter, my brother or me, when our parents bought back the house they'd sold years ago before moving to Costa Rica. They planned to keep their condo near the beach as an escape from Seattle's dark, damp winters, but this would be their new home base. New-old. Too weird.

As I pulled into the driveway, I couldn't help but notice how overgrown the shrubs and perennials looked in comparison to the tidy yard next door. My dad would trim them into shape with glee. This was a 1920s house, but the garage was plenty big for his baby, the '67 Mustang he bought new. It was currently in storage but would soon be coming home to the house we'd lived in for so long.

This had been our family's first house on our own, where we moved after we left Grace House when I was twelve, after the tragedy I hadn't fully understood until last summer. It had been a healing place for my parents as well as their home for twenty-five years. Happy years. No wonder it beckoned.

I poked my head into the garage, relieved to see that the new cabinets had been delivered. The interim owners hadn't done much work so there wasn't much to undo, but my mother wanted an all-new kitchen. I snapped a photo for her, then crossed the brick walkway and climbed the steps into the mudroom–slash–laundry room. Slipped off my boots and laid my wet coat over the new front-loading washer. Snazzy.

Though the kitchen had been gutted, Mom had insisted on keeping the house's traditional details—the arched entries and coved ceilings—but with bigger windows for more light. I approved.

In the living room, I unlocked the front door for the designer. A "mood board" she and Mom had created stood propped against a wall. Would the desk and chair—assuming I could pull it off—fit the mood? I hoped so.

The smell of new paint drew me to my old bedroom. The walls were now a soft sage green, redolent of spring. My parents had designated it the future guest room.

My mother's goal for the redo was simple: She wanted to feel at home here, but she and Dad were different now. We all were. The house, she said, needed a refresh to help them live their "now" lives.

I'm always in the mood for that.

"Hell-oooo!" a woman called, and I rushed to meet the designer, Gabby Monroe. Where my mother had found her, I didn't know. My parents had been activists and teachers, far from the "hire-a-designer" crowd. I'd suggested my pal Aimee, owner of Rainy Day Vintage, but Mom had wanted someone a little older, who understood "what we want a house to do at this stage in our lives."

"I brought swatches." Gabby balanced a fat binder on the pony wall between the entry and living room. "For that darling wingback."

I told her my idea about the small desk and showed her my photos.

"Perfect. I can picture them right here." She marched to a corner between the fireplace and the front window, chopping the air with her hands. "The desk will function almost like a sofa table. The chair can stand on its own—I can see your mother here with her book and her afternoon tea. Or she can turn the chair to sit at the desk. Do you have someone to re-cover it or do you need names?"

"I was sort of thinking—"

"No, Pepper," Gabby said. "Your mother will be delighted with the find. You don't need to earn extra points by reupholstering it yourself."

Busted.

We picked out several fabrics that would fit the overall color scheme. The mood. "Best to have options," Gabby chirped. "You never know."

An excellent philosophy, not just in decorating.

Then we were on to FaceTime for a progress update. Gabby's presence saved me from telling my mother I was investigating the disappearance, if that's what it was, of a woman I didn't know, which could be linked to the death of a man I didn't like. Not to mention the discovery of a small fortune stuffed inside a chunk of foam.

That chair better clean up good. It had some answering to do.

"All good at the shop?" my mother asked when talk of recessed ceiling fixtures and matte versus gloss finishes for the countertops had wrapped up. "And with Nate?"

"All good." I told her I loved her and asked her to give Dad a hug for me, and we promised to talk next week.

"This is going to be sweet," Gabby said, surveying the kitchen one last time. "I don't know when I last enjoyed a project so much."

"Bet you say that every time."

"Bet you wouldn't lie to your mother if she were standing right here," Gabby said.

She wasn't talking about the desk and chair that neither of us had mentioned, and we both knew it. What she'd seen in my body language that gave me away, I couldn't guess, but I was busted again.

BACK AT THE MARKET, I parked in the merchant lot and headed for the shop, stopping along the way to pick up a couple of piroshky for a late lunch. Beef and cheese, and mushroom and potato, if you want to know. (And I know you do.)

Walking along Pike Place, where I'd walked with Boz yesterday, I was shaken by his death. Who would grieve the man? No one I knew. They'd be shocked, but nothing more. And that was about as sad a comment as I could fathom.

Two minutes later, I was behind the counter of the Spice Shop hugging my dog, the piroshky safely out of reach. Even a gentleman has his limits.

"Hey, Vanessa," I said as I washed my hands in the big sink. "How did the deliveries go this morning?"

"Um, okay." Eyes downcast, she straightened a stack of paper bags. What was up?

I had to tell the staff about Boz. Sandra had been my coconspirator on the spice mission to his restaurant. Neither of us had been impressed by his food, and she'd taken to calling him a "self-appointed chef" and a "glorified pancake flipper."

"No easy way to say this. Boz Bosworth, the chef who orchestrated the theft of Edgar's spice blend, is dead."

"What?" Sandra's hands flew to her mouth, fingers catching in the beaded chain that held her reading glasses as they went.

"Found floating in the Ship Canal this morning, near the Fremont Bridge. It could have been an accident, but I doubt it."

You could slip or trip easily, but fall down that slope into the water and not be able to crawl back up? Unlikely. "And I don't think Spencer and Tracy think so, either. They want to talk with Edgar and Tariq—"

Sandra gasped.

"They did have beefs with him," I continued, "and the cops—well, you know how our friends operate. But I'm sure they'll be cleared quickly."

"I am so sorry. I take back every mean thing I said."

I let out a deep breath. Took my second-in-command by the shoulders. "It's natural to regret harsh words now that he's dead. But you never said or did anything bad to him. You expressed your honest, valid opinion about his food and behavior. There is nothing wrong with that."

Her chin wobbled, but she nodded.

Was it murder? I didn't know. If it was—well, there's no justification. But what had Boz done to persuade someone otherwise?

Kristen hadn't known Boz, but she knew all about our encounters. And she knew me. "You're diving in, aren't you?"

"No. Well, I need to find Talia."

"Uh-huh." She was not convinced.

I retreated to my office and closed the door. The messages had piled up. I returned Tariq's call first.

"Listen to me, Tariq. There's no reason to worry," I repeated a few minutes later, for about the tenth time. "They just want to talk with you, see what you know."

"I don't know anything. I haven't seen the man since he canned my ass."

"Then tell them that."

Silence. "He did me a favor, is what he did. It's hard to quit a job you know isn't right for you, even when you know you got to move on."

That is the truth.

My conversation with Edgar took a similar tone. Pepper Reece, Reassurer in Chief. But I had no trouble with the role. I was honestly truly sure neither man had anything to do with the death of William Anthony "Boz" Bosworth.

Though to prove it, I might have to prove who did.

Back on the shop floor, I was straightening a display when two women arrived. One made straight for me.

"I went to a wedding in New Orleans a few weeks ago. Loved the food. I bought some Cajun and Creole spice blends—sorry, I should have waited and bought them here."

"No worries. You were in Cajun and Creole country."

"But now I don't know what to do with them. Do you have any suggestions?"

I plucked a business card from my apron pocked and handed it over. "Check out the recipe section on our website. One of our staffers has family roots down there, and she's created several recipes for us with a Louisiana flair. And take a look at Red Stick Spice Company, online. Technically they're competition, but their recipes are divine."

"Red Stick?"

"Baton Rouge."

"Oh my gosh. Am I a dunce or what? Never occurred to me what that name meant."

We found a cookbook focused on Louisiana flavors—Cajun, Creole, and more. "Do you like foodie mysteries? My book buyer and I devour them, and we have a couple set in New Orleans. Guaranteed to make you laugh and make you hungry."

"Right up my alley," the wedding guest's friend said when I showed them Ellen Byron's Vintage Cookbook series and *A Streetcar Named Murder* by T. G. Herren.

"One more question," the first woman said. "All the farm stands are showing off fresh asparagus and people rave about it, but what I remember is my mother cooking the heck out of it, all limp and mushy, then making soup."

"It makes your pee smell funny," her friend interjected.

'Twas the season. I was prepared. "That sulfury smell comes from the breakdown of the acids when your digestive juices hit them. It dissipates quickly, and yes, it can be annoying, but it's no reason not to eat asparagus. Just thank your kidneys for working right." I went on to describe my favorite cooking methods. "Remember, you want to keep that bright-green color and that tender-crisp texture. I think you'll like our asparagus soup. We love it with a bit of cumin, raw or toasted."

"Sounds like dinner to me," one said.

"That's what I like to hear," I said, then told them where to get the best baguettes to go with the soup.

After closing, Arf and I were on our way to the car when I heard my name and the whiz of bicycle wheels.

"My favorite ex-wife," Tag called, rolling his bike up beside me. Almost too late, I noticed the puddle within leash distance and led Arf away from temptation.

"Your only ex-wife," I said, as usual.

"So far," he replied, as usual. He'd dated plenty since our divorce—even, sadly, before our divorce—but while many had aimed to put a ring on Thomas Allen "Tag" Buhner's left hand, no one had succeeded. If and when some woman did, I would wish her well and honestly mean it.

"Vanessa talk to you?" he asked.

"What? No. About what?"

"Oh, sorry. Didn't mean to spill the beans." He straddled the bike between his long, shapely legs. "I saw her this morning down by the park, with a guy. Young, white, dresses like a surfer dude. I've seen him around—sales agent for a couple of vendors. Anyway, the tension was clear."

I knew the kid Tag meant, though not his name. I'd seen Vanessa walking with him a couple of times, and last week, he'd brought her flowers.

"He reached for her," Tag continued, "and she shook him off. He raised his arm and took a step forward, and I was about to intervene when he said something else, then stalked off. I gave her a few minutes, but when she still hadn't moved, I approached. Asked if there was a problem."

"What did she say?"

"Yes, no, maybe. I suggested she talk to you, and she looked horrified."

"What? We get along great." I pride myself on being approachable without interfering in my employees' personal lives. "Or I thought we did."

"Pep. She idolizes you. She doesn't want to tell you she can't handle her own problems."

"Ohhh. Well, that explains why she was so subdued this morning. The jerk. Thanks."

I was about to ask him how the police got data from the rideshare companies when his radio barked. He held out a hand to stop me. Listened. Keyed the mic. "On my way." Slipped one foot in the bike stirrup and shoved off with the other.

"Talk to her," he called over his shoulder. "Let me know if I can help."

And off he went, rolling through the puddle and sending splashes of rainwater all over my dog and me.

Eleven

*Spring seasons in Seattle: Still Raining. Fake
Spring. Rain, with Flowers. Real Spring. What's
That Yellow Thing in the Sky? Juneuary.*

"IT FITS ME BETTER," MARIAH TOLD HER OLDER SISTER. "YOUR
boobs stick out too much."

"The two of you can share it," Kristen said before Savannah
could reply. "You're not going to button it anyway, and you don't
go to the same school, so no one will know."

Having lost the argument that she should get the sweater
because she was older, Savannah sank to the kitchen floor and
buried her face in Arf's fur.

"Sorry," I mouthed to Kristen. I didn't have sisters or daugh-
ters. I hadn't expected them both to be drawn to it. Arf stood,
shaking himself, and Savannah took him outside. Mariah had
disappeared with the sweater.

I'd gone home just long enough to change my clothes and not
long enough to give in to the urge to stay there with Arf, the baseball game, and a good book. Movie night is a hallowed tradition.
Kristen, Laurel, and I had expanded the Flick Chicks to include
Seetha, an engineer–turned–massage therapist, and Aimee, who
owns the vintage shop on the ground floor of Seetha's building,
down the block from Edgar's restaurant. The girls had started
joining us when we met at Kristen's.

And besides, I'd known an evening with my girlfriends would perk me up.

"It's weird," I said. "First you move back into your old house, which was kind of ours, too. And now my parents are moving back into our other old house." I waggled my finger in one direction, then the other.

"Right?" Kristen laid slender spears of asparagus across the puff pastry, scored around the edges and layered with mustard and grated Gruyère. "I love the continuity, knowing this house has been in the family for generations. But I don't want the girls to feel like it's a lifelong responsibility one of them has to take over."

When Kristen's mother died a few years ago, her father had stayed put for a while, then bought a condo. Kristen's two younger sisters had quickly agreed she and Eric should take the house if they wanted it. It remained Family Central, and I felt at home here, too. Of course, it had been my home until I was twelve, but back then, it hadn't been anything like the showpiece it was now.

"Do you ever forget that you're forty-three, not thirteen, when you wake up in the middle of the night?" I asked.

"No. But there's a reason why we never slept in my parents' old room and created a new primary suite when we remodeled." She slid the tart into the oven. The fancy-schmancy oven, one of a pair, that matched the fancy-schmancy fridge and dishwasher and other appliances. This house had been highlighted in the *Seattle Times*' "At Home" section and regional lifestyle magazines, but it was still a place where you could kick off your shoes and where your dog was as comfy as you were.

Then the other Flick Chicks arrived, bearing food and drink. Kristen handed around glasses of Kir Royale—champagne mixed with cassis, aka black currant liqueur—and we clinked flutes, the tiny bubbles tickling our noses as we sipped. A few minutes later, we carried our glasses and plates to the basement theater.

Mariah queued up the DVD. The vintage sweater suited her, the perfect gift for the girl who chose the original *Mrs. 'Arris Goes to Paris* for movie night.

Talia couldn't be much older than Mariah and Savannah. She hadn't grown up in Seattle, but she'd had family here, and a routine. Where had she worked? Who were her friends?

I put the thoughts away and went to Paris with my own friends and the incomparable Angela Lansbury.

Intermission. Aimee and Seetha followed me out to the garage to see the chair.

"Good bones," Aimee said, echoing both the man at the Vintage Mall and Gabby the designer. "But a serious project. It needs all new stuffing. That broken leg can be repaired, but all four need to be refinished. You won't know what shape the webbing and other innards are in until you get it apart."

"Ooh," Seetha said. "Wonder if you'll find anything else hidden inside?"

"I said 'you,'" Aimee said, "but don't you dare think about doing it yourself."

I hate being predictable. "That reminds me. Do you know Cook's Upholstery? In Burien." Aimee had worked in a high-end antiques firm before opening her own shop, and she knew a lot of people in all aspects of the business.

"Name doesn't ring a bell." She was already searching on her phone. "Hmm. No. There's a listing on Yelp, but it says 'permanently closed.'"

I read over her shoulder. Same address as on the card in the luggage tag. Pooh.

We headed back inside, me showing Aimee and Seetha the desk photos on the way.

"That's your best option," Aimee said, pointing. "I've got a piece that might work, but it's more like an end table. Give me your specs and I'll check. But I'd go with that one."

Naturally, she pointed at the pricey cherry piece with the tapered legs.

Downstairs, I refreshed my champagne and took a dish of the Moroccan chocolate mousse, gently spiced with cumin, that Mariah and Savannah had made. The girls were parading back and forth, pretending to be Dior models. Kristen quizzed Seetha about Oliver Wu, her new sweetheart, then turned her attention to Laurel's love life.

"I keep telling you," Laurel said. "We are not dating. It would be super awkward if it didn't work out and he lives two boats away." Widowed with a son in college, Laurel loved the Lake Union houseboat community as much for the privacy as for the water and waves.

But it was a real community, with work parties and potlucks and even a shared cat, at home in half a dozen floating homes.

"How many times do you have to go to a concert or out to dinner with him before it's dating?" Kristen said.

Laurel rolled her eyes and sipped her drink.

"It's no more awkward than seeing your ex-husband the beat cop ride by your shop every day." The girls out of earshot, I told my friends what Tag had witnessed. "I'll talk to Vanessa tomorrow, after the staff meeting," I said to Kristen. "But we need to keep our eyes and ears open."

She made a disgusted grunt, reminding me of Detective Tracy. Then it was back to haute couture and dizzying displays of Dior floating across the screen.

AFTER OUR WALK, Arf and I collected the mail and let ourselves into the loft. Long day, but I knew I wouldn't be able to fall asleep yet.

A damp chill had rolled in from the Sound. I made myself a cup of lemongrass tea, letting it steep while I crawled into a long-sleeved tunic and fleece pajama bottoms. I'd missed a text from Nate and curled up on the couch to reply. Arf conked out on the rug. It can be exhausting, going for walks and getting pets and sitting for dog treats.

Nate and I exchanged texts about our days. Nothing earth-shattering, just the simple catch-up couples do, yet it made me warm and happy. I signed off with a string of emojis. At times, the midlife gift of this relationship turned me into a lovesick teenage girl—the kind of girl I'd never been.

I rinsed out my tea mug and saw Talia's books stacked on my picnic table. I'd never read the Circle of Magic series. I picked up the first, *Sandry's Book*, and took it to bed. How old had Talia been when she discovered them? A teenager, I supposed. I could give them to the girls. If I didn't find her.

Intriguing as the story of the young weaver Sandry was, brought to Winding Circle to learn how to use her powers, the sandman's power overcame me in a few pages. I woke with a start, the dull gray light of morning filtering into the bedroom, Arf softly snoring in the living room. I swung my legs over the side of the bed and ran my hands through my spiky hair. I was due, maybe overdue, for a cut.

I lowered my feet and hit something. Recoiled, then realized it was the book, sprawled open, spine up. I sent it a quick apology, my father's words to us as children echoing in my sleep-addled brain: "*Books are our friends.*" Just beyond it lay a piece of paper, maybe eight and a half by three or four. My morning-dry fingertips scratched at the wood floor but finally got hold of it. I turned it over and squinted.

"Queen Anne Cleaning—for Home or Business," it read, a preprinted number in one corner and "March services" followed by a dollar amount.

I worked HR for a long time before I bought my own business. Rare as they were now that most employers use direct deposit, I recognized a payroll check stub when I saw one.

Was this a lead, an honest-to-goodness lead in tracking Talia Cook?

The padding of paws on the wood floor told me I'd have to figure that out later.

THE SPICE SHOP gets rolling early on Wednesdays, for the weekly staff meeting. The rest of the crew had arrived, including the warehouse and production team, but no sign of Cayenne. I was about to text her when she burst in, breathless and red-cheeked, a covered tray in hand.

"Sorry I'm late." She set her tray on the nook table and shucked off her coat. Out of the corner of my eye, I saw Kristen and Sandra exchanging a glance. What was up with that?

"Jam roll," Cayenne said, uncovering the tray. "Blackberry, from my grandpa's vines. We froze gallons last summer. I added lemon zest and a dash of cardamom for balance."

It was brilliant, and we were happy guinea pigs.

Hayden, the warehouse manager I'd hired last winter, gave a quick update. "The Szechuan pepper is back-ordered again, Pepper. You said you might have another supplier you could call?"

I made a note. "What do you bet, soon as I place the order, the back-ordered shipment will show up and we'll be swimming in little red berries?"

"Sandra and I can brainstorm a new blend or two," Cayenne said. "Since it's not Five Spice season."

"Five Spice is always in season," Reed piped up. "At least in my family. When you're Chinese, it's not just for the Lunar New Year."

"If you're up to it," Sandra told Cayenne.

"Oh, I'm always up for spicery," she said.

"So, let me plant an idea, see what you think," I said. "For ages, I've wanted to do hands-on cooking classes focused on herbs and spices. Obviously, we don't have the room."

"Use the warehouse," Hayden said. "Plenty of tenants have full commercial kitchens you could use."

"Would our customers drive down to SoDo?" Kristen asked. "It's kind of out of the way."

The facility managers host regular tasting nights for producers, where tenants introduce each other to their newest and tastiest. But the thought of the organizational details and internal wrangling required to expand that to the public gave me the willies, and I love organizing and wrangling. "Great idea for the future. For now, let's narrow the focus."

"We talk about spices. They cook, then eat," Sandra said. "And they leave with the confidence that they can recreate the food at home. I love it."

"Experiential retail," Cayenne added. "It's all the rage. What about a theme night? Learn to make Indian food, with all the spices. Or Mexican."

"Instead of a full meal, it could be cocktails and appetizers," Sandra said. "Or using herbs and spices in desserts, and a wine pairing."

"But where?" Kristen brought us back to earth.

"What about Speziato?" Hayden asked. "The kitchen is big enough for three or four groups to work at the same time. Edgar would love it. It would be perfect for our first effort."

"Great idea. Plus, he's got a loyal clientele to draw from," I said. Edgar had transformed a run-down Italian joint into a true neighborhood restaurant.

Italian night was a no-brainer, but what else? The ideas flew. A sushi workshop. A paella party. Summertime picnic inspiration. Gluten-free baking.

"Not your average Taco Tuesday," Vanessa suggested.

"Date Night," Kristen said. "In February."

So many choices for sharing our love of spices. Some of my

staff are trained professional cooks while others, like me, are mainly professional eaters. They had different personal and work experiences, too, making for a rich stew.

We wrapped up the meeting, and the warehouse crew left. The shop staff dove into the morning checklist.

"Vanessa, can I have a word?" I said. The young woman's dark eyes widened and her skin paled, leaving two bright spots of color on her cheekbones. She'd swapped the space buns for a French braid.

In my office, I gestured for her to take the rolling stool while I perched on the edge of my desk.

"Tag told me about your conversation the other morning. You okay?"

"Yeah," she said, drawing the word out in a way that suggested otherwise. "I mean, I like him, but I have to work to go to school, and I have to go to school. I don't have time."

She was a first-generation college student, passionate about getting a degree that would help her help the farm and orchard community back home in Central Washington. Why she was in Seattle rather than at one of the smaller schools, I didn't know, but I loved having her here.

"So are you actually going out?"

"We grabbed a bite after work a couple of times. Walked along the waterfront. He slid into my DMs. That's okay, I guess, but now he wants to 'define the relationship'"—she used air quotes—"but I'm not sure I want a relationship. I'm not ready for that."

"Tell him."

"I know. Ask for what you want. Set your boundaries. That's what my mom would say, if I told her." She rolled back and forth on the stool, the tiny office too small to go far. "But it's hard some-times, you know?"

"Hate to tell you, it doesn't get easier. Who is he? Who does he work for?"

"His name is Logan Bradshaw. He's the sales agent for the beekeeper, and he subs for Herb the Herb Man. That's how I met him—they all get prime spots on the Main Arcade, right next to Angie and Sylvie." Her roommates, aka the Orchard Girls. They'd sent Vanessa to me when I was hiring. Farm vendors get priority in daystall selection, ahead of the arts and crafts vendors, who tend to move around. Now that I knew for sure who the guy was, I wasn't entirely sure I should stay out of it.

"Isn't he—? Never mind." I brushed away a wisp of gossip.

"This morning, I was so anxious that I'd run into him and wouldn't know what to do that I dragged the cart through the street. Turned out it's his day off."

"Hey, you have every right to go anywhere you want in the Market. Don't let him stop you." I couldn't take her off the delivery route. Sandra and Cayenne were too valuable on the shop floor, and Kristen worked part-time. We had to solve this.

No, Pepper, I told myself. *She* has to solve this. You can help, but that's all you can do.

I stood up. So did she.

"Thanks, Pepper. I feel better already."

I gave her a quick hug and watched her return to work.

That's retail for you. Something new every day.

Twelve

In the Middle Ages, superstitious brides and grooms carried cumin, dill, and salt in their pockets to ensure faithfulness.

BEFORE I HEADED OUT, I MADE A PHONE CALL.

Voice mail. Claire DaSilva of Queen Anne Cleaning was unable to take my call at the moment, but would I please leave my name and number and a brief message? I would and did. If she expected me to be a potential customer, good—no one in their right mind would call me back if I told the truth.

Then Arf and I took a stroll.

As long as I've been coming to the Market, it never gets old. The city of Seattle owns the property, but since 1971, when the voters passed a bond issue to save the place, it's been a city within the city, governed by the Preservation and Development Authority. The PDA is the official leaseholder and property manager. It's got all the problems of any other city, from parking challenges to aging utilities and maintenance issues, all managed quite well, in my experience.

Then there are the people. Any time you put this many individuals, each with their own flaws and goals and moods, in a tight space, there's bound to be trouble. Was Logan Bradshaw nothing more than a serial flirt? Was he a clueless kid or a harasser in the making? I kept thinking of that raised arm and worrying about his self-control.

As Vanessa had talked, I'd remembered stories I'd heard, stories that could have been about him. Now I wanted details. Not to interfere or intervene. To be able to watch out for my young employee. Young'uns have to learn by doing, and sometimes by failing. But it's the responsibility of the elders—though at forty-three, I didn't love the term—to guide them, when they ask. Which Vanessa hadn't, not in so many words, but I wanted to be ready.

I didn't know the beekeeper well, so Herb the Herb Man was first on my list. A tall, gangly man, he's sold fresh herbs and seedlings here for years and knows almost everyone. A whiff of sage and thyme greeted me.

"Hey, Herb," I called. Like me, Cayenne, and Vinny, he's got an aptronym—a name that suits his job. Unlike us, it wasn't his real name. (I do consider Pepper my real name, since it's what everyone calls me, except in doctors' offices.) But it suits him. "How's your garden growing?"

"Not bad, considering how little sunshine we've had. Soon as that yellow ball of fire lights up the sky for more than twenty minutes a day, I'll be rolling in the parsley. Got your email about restocking your seedling racks for the weekend. I'm on it."

"Thanks. Hey, can I ask you—the young man who works as your sales agent, Logan? He okay? He's sweet on Vanessa, and I'm curious about him."

"That who it is now? That's youth for you, always eyeing a different pretty girl." His long, narrow face turned serious. "He making a pest of himself?"

"Not sure yet."

"Can't say much. Met him through the beekeeper. Son of a friend, or a friend of her son—can't remember which. But he works hard, sells the stuff, and seems to be honest."

"That's all a good sign," I said.

"Someone's standing in for you, you want 'em to behave decently." Herb crossed his arms. "Flirt, okay, but show a lady some respect. Do I need to give him a piece of my mind?"

"Not yet," I said. "Let's see what happens."

A customer arrived in search of fresh basil.

"Thanks, Herb. I hear anything else, I'll let you know."

He acknowledged that with a bounce of his head and named

two varieties of basil on hand now, a third soaking up the heat in his greenhouse but available in a few days.

I walked slowly up the Arcade to the beekeeper's stall, thinking about what I wanted to know and how best to ask.

Business was buzzing, and I hung back until the woman was free. I kept my tone light, reminding her first of my name and shop, although my apron advertised that for me.

"Seems like your Logan has his eyes on one of my employees. Even brought her flowers."

"Oh, so Chloe works for you?" she said. "I didn't know. She's cute as a bug."

"Chloe?" I didn't hide my surprise. "No. Vanessa. Not sure we're talking about the same person. Though she is cute. And very smart."

A couple approached, and the beekeeper began handing out samples. "Kids," she said to me with a wave of her hand, then launched into her customer spiel. "We're a small, family-owned business. Our bees are free-range"—that got the intended laugh— "buzzing merrily from flower to flower in the shadow of Mount Rainier. Our honey is raw and unfiltered—"

I'd begun to drift away when I heard my name.

"I couldn't help hearing your conversation," the jeweler told me, her hair the same copper as the earrings and bracelets in her display. "Logan is her best friend's son, and she thinks his flirtation is harmless."

"But you don't?"

"My daughter fills in for me some days. At first, she thought it was fun to joke and tease with the cute guy in the next stall. Then she realized that he always waited until after she chose her location, despite the beekeeper getting farm priority, and took the spot next to her. He wouldn't leave her alone, talking to her even when she was trying to catch shoppers' attention. He stood too close and kept asking her out, no matter how many times she told him she has a boyfriend. He kept that up for weeks until she got the idea to request a table in the Market Front, knowing his bosses would insist he stay on the Main Arcade. That did the trick. He doesn't pay a lick of attention to me, so I can take a table up here when it's my day to run the show."

This was what I was remembering. My painter pal Jamie

had mentioned it but hadn't named names. "I don't suppose your daughter is Chloe?"

She shook her head. That made three young women Logan had targeted, in the Market alone.

"You could talk to the PDA," I said. "They take harassment claims pretty seriously."

"I wanted to, but she said no. Absolutely not."

"Thanks," I said. "Anything changes, give me a holler. I think we need to keep an eye on him."

It's one thing to joke around with your neighbor vendor, another to pressure her to go out, and yet another to raise a hand in anger. I reminded myself that I'd gone snooping simply to be prepared.

So now I was prepared. Not the end of the story, but the end of the chapter.

In the shop, Sandra was explaining the difference between toasted and raw spices to a young couple. She opened jars and handed out tasting spoons.

"This is cumin. First, the raw seeds." They each touched the tips of their tongues to their spoons.

"Mmm," the woman said. "Kind of—this may sound silly, but I'm not sure how else to describe it. Grassy. On the edge of pungent."

"A hint of citrus? Woodsy?" Her husband sounded tentative. "If that's not contradictory."

"It's perfectly fine to use words like that," Sandra said. "We often describe what we taste and smell by comparing it to other things. Now try the toasted seeds."

New spoons, new seeds, the tips of the tongues less tentative this time.

"Oh, now that's pungent," he said. "Pleasant, but sharper."

"Is it salted?" the woman asked. "I taste salt."

"That's the toasting. Any seed or berry will undergo a subtle flavor change. Raw cumin seed, as you noticed, can be a little bitter. Toasting softens the flavor and brings out the earthiness as well as the salt. Now let me grind them both and give you a taste." Sandra dropped a few seeds in two mortars, handing one bowl and a pestle to the man and grinding the other herself. Experiential retail in action.

A few other customers had stopped to listen. "I've always bought cumin in powdered form," one said.

I grabbed a basket of tasting spoons and handed them out. "No worries. But I think you'll notice the difference with freshly ground seeds."

She did. "That's almost not the same thing. I always thought cumin was hot, but it's not."

That led to a conversation about heat versus flavor and to questions about how to use cumin. I passed out copies of our carrot soup recipe, a staff favorite. "You toast the pecans in a skillet, then toast a few spices together, including cumin or coriander and some black peppercorns, and grind them. The lighter-colored spices help you know when the mixture is done. Of course, your nose is always your best guide."

"Oh, this sounds good," the young man told his wife as he scanned the recipe. "And it uses coconut milk, so it's plant-based. We can get the spices here and carrots at one of the farm stands."

She agreed, and Sandra helped them choose spices while I worked with the other customers. A few minutes later, we were alone behind the front counter.

"Plant-based." She snorted. "Why is it that every generation thinks they discovered eating their vegetables?"

"Don't laugh," I said. "Food trends are good for business. And we need to know what customers want from us."

That brought me back to the special events trend. Cooking classes were hardly a new idea, but they were new to us, with our space constraints.

Experiential? Heck, yeah. We'd make it an experience worth remembering.

Hayden was right—Speziato would be ideal. How to convince Edgar?

I felt rotten about spilling the proverbial beans to the cops about Edgar's argument with Boz, but it couldn't be helped. They were going to find out at some point, and if they discovered I'd known and hadn't told them, my credibility—and my ability to wheedle the inside scoop from them—would be toast.

I checked the pending orders. Nothing for Edgar, so I couldn't use a delivery as an excuse to drop in.

Be bold, Pep. It was closing in on one o'clock. If I knew

Edgar, he would already be in the restaurant, planning his menus, checking his stock, getting ready for prep.

"Up for an adventure?" I asked Cayenne, the best cook on my staff and a born planner.

She was. I texted Edgar and said we'd be stopping by.

The immediate plan, about as fully cooked as a three-minute egg, called for me to dash home and get my car, then swing through the Market for Cayenne. I was sorry to leave Arf. He and Edgar adore each other, even if the dog's loyalties are bought by the bones Edgar saves for him.

I zipped down the cobbled Pike Place, planning our pitch in my mind.

"Pepper!" the new owner of the yarn shop called, a bag from Three Girls Bakery in hand. "I've been meaning to swing by and say thanks."

"Uh-oh. What did I do?"

"Sent me to Fabiola. She created a brilliant graphics and advertising campaign and stuck to my budget."

"She's a trip, but she does good work."

"And so do you." She waved and dashed off in the direction of her shop.

"Oh, little Saab," I murmured to my car a few minutes later, as the check-oil light stayed on a hair too long. "Don't give up on me now." The light went off, and I breathed a sigh of relief. I pulled onto Western, wound my way up to Pine, and parked on the steep slope. First-time visitors often express surprise at the shop exterior. The Market is a collection of more than a dozen historic buildings, most built in the early decades of the last century, each with its own identity. And its own color scheme. The Garden Center Building, where my shop is, dates to the 1930s, when the salmon-pink stucco walls and forest-green trim were the height of Art Deco sophistication. Or so the story goes. Me, I simply adore it.

Cayenne popped out the side door, a teal raincoat over her shop clothes. We wear black and white, along with black aprons sporting the shop logo, a shaker sprinkling salt into the waves of Puget Sound. The lighted sign in our window echoes the design.

In the twenty minutes I'd been gone, my staff had identified more than a dozen Italian dishes that students could make featuring our herbs, spices, or blends. Cayenne read from the list while I navigated our way out of downtown and up to Eastlake.

"Eggplant appetizers and baked paprika cheese. They look harder to make than they are."

"Plus the baked cheese is Edgar's own creation, and it's such an elegant way to show off smoked paprika." I stopped at Denny Way, the Saab lurching slightly as I braked. I sent it a tiny prayer to hang on; I didn't want to have to call for a ride to get us back to the shop. "They'll love knowing they've got the inside view."

"He'll have ideas of his own. This will work best if it's a true collaboration."

Point. Edgar's opinions were as strong as an after-dinner espresso. I loved seeing Cayenne take charge of this project.

Then she read out the staff's list of open questions: demo only or hands-on, full meal or an alternative, how to promote, how to charge, and most importantly, our role. We tossed ideas back and forth like the fishmongers at Pike Place Fish toss crab and halibut for awestruck onlookers. Before I knew it, we'd reached Speziato.

"Pepper! Cayenne!" Grace Ramos, Edgar's wife, said as she opened the door, then locked it behind us. "I'm sorry. I shouldn't laugh at your names, but I always do."

"It's okay," I said as we exchanged a quick hug. The muted strains of Dean Martin singing "That's Amoré" wafted out of the ceiling speakers. "They make us laugh, too."

Edgar stood from the two-top where they'd been finishing lunch. Fettuccine Alfredo, judging from the nearly empty plates. My tummy growled.

"Bienvenida, bienvenida!" He pulled out a chair at the table next to theirs. "Sit, sit. What can I get you? A glass of pinot grigio? Campari and soda? Yes?" A garnet-red drink in a short, squat rocks glass sat by his plate.

"How about an Italian soda?" Cayenne asked.

"Perfecta," he said, then gave me a questioning look. The Campari was tempting. But Edgar's Italian sodas are bubbly and effervescent, and our conversation might go more easily if I didn't have any alcohol on board.

"I'll have what she's having."

We chatted with Grace while Edgar made the drinks. Now

that their daughter was in school all day, she was spending more time in the restaurant, handling the books and other details.

"Gracias," I said when he set the tall, frothy sodas, each topped with a splash of cream, on the table. "Or grazie, since this is an Italian drink in an Italian restaurant. Tariq and the prep cooks aren't in yet?"

"Soon, soon." Edgar checked his watch. "You know that one has trouble telling the time."

I took a sip, the sweetness of the vanilla syrup contrasting with the spark of the seltzer, all of it mellowed by the cream. Then I got serious. "So. About Boz. I don't know what happened, but clearly the police think it's suspicious. I hope you understand—I had to tell them about the hard feelings between you."

"Bah, no." Edgar waved a big hand, his drink in the other. "You tell them, Evie tell them. At least you tell me you tell them. So they know Boz unhappy with all of us—Tariq and me. And you." He tipped his glass toward me, then took a long drink.

Unhappy, yes. And yet Boz had come to me for help.

"Plenty of people had a lot more reason to be angry with Boz than you did," Grace said to her husband. "Besides, he blamed you for costing him his restaurant, but why would you go after him? After all this time, for something that's water under the bridge?"

An innocent metaphor, but it made me cringe.

"So the police interviewed Evie?" I asked. "I thought they broke up."

"They broke up every other week," Grace said.

"Then, when you discover the truth," Edgar said, eyes blazing at the memory of his bartender sleeping with a rival and giving away his kitchen secrets, "Boz burst in, furious with her, and they yell and scream right here." He pointed vehemently downward.

"In the restaurant?" Cayenne said, as surprised as I was. I hadn't heard this part of the story.

"Every table full. First time ever I fire an employee middle of their shift."

"Wow." Sounded like Evie might be nursing a grudge of her own against Edgar. As for Boz's death, if it was murder, she rose to the top of my suspect list. Admittedly, the list was short. "Where is she now?"

"Working in the deli at the co-op," Grace said. "I saw her last time I stopped in."

"Graciella, por favor," Edgar said. "Find her address for Pepper. In the person files." Grace nodded, collected their plates, and left the dining room.

"I tell you what I told la policía," Edgar said, leaning across the gap between our tables. "You know, in my home country—" He drew a finger across his throat, indicating both the violence that had gripped El Salvador for so long and his attitude toward the authorities. But he'd met Spencer and Tracy before, when he and Tariq worked for Alex Howard, my old flame. When Alex's longtime pal went too far to protect an old secret—I slammed the door on that memory.

"What did you tell them, Edgar? Do you have any idea who might have killed Boz?"

"I told them I am sorry when any man is dead, but I am glad he is no more trouble." He sat back, glancing at the kitchen door as he did. This was what he had not wanted his sweet wife to hear.

He sipped the Campari and continued. "They ask me where I was Tuesday morning, early. Home in bed, like any good chef. Yes, yes, we are dark on Mondays, but too many years in this business—I have my habits. Who else, they ask, might—" He paused, searching for the word, leaning forward when he found it. "Might benefit from his death. No one benefits from death. But plenty of people are mad at him. The employees, the restaurant owner, the building owner."

"Here you go, Pepper." Grace returned with a slip of paper.

"Thanks." I put it in my bag. "Oh, so his restaurant and the building had two different owners? Do you know who?"

He did not.

"Part of what we like about this place," Grace said, "is that the same family owns everything. It's such a difficult business—dealing with just one owner makes it so much easier. And less expensive."

"I am loyal," Edgar said. "Not like that Boz, always moving around. Never saying he was sorry, saying everyone done him wrong." He turned to his wife. "That is the phrase, yes, not just my English?"

She gave him an indulgent smile.

"Okay, so no one liked him," Cayenne said. "But none of that is reason to kill him."

"Oh, Cayenne, I love you," I said, squeezing her hand. "So refreshingly normal. But to the mind twisted by anger, greed, or revenge. . . . " My words trailed off as I pondered motives. I'd seen too many, heard too many stories. A victim might be an obstacle to what the killer wanted, or in the wrong place at the wrong time.

And sometimes they died to protect someone else.

That made me think of Talia.

Cayenne squirmed in her seat, despite the cushioned chair.

"I'm sure the police will figure it out," I said. "I don't want to keep you two from work. The real reason we're here is to make you a proposal."

We told them our idea for a collaborative event. They would provide the space and equipment, and we would organize and advertise. They exchanged excited glances, interjecting with suggestions on the menu, the wine, and more.

"It's the personal connection that people are hungry for," Cayenne said.

"I love it," Grace said, clapping her hands. "And Speziato does mean *spicy* in Italian."

"Perfecto," Edgar added. "Or should I say perfetto?"

Perfect, in any language.

Thirteen

One theory says French bistros got their name in early-nineteenth-century Paris, during the Russian occupation after the Napoleonic Wars. Russian soldiers shouted "bystro," demanding waiters serve them quickly, and the word came to mean a casual, cozy café serving traditional French dishes with a rustic but elegant touch—and wine.

"WE DID IT! THEY'LL DO IT!" ON THE SIDEWALK OUTSIDE Speziato, Cayenne bounced like a five-year-old waiting for an ice cream cone. We'd agreed to aim for our first class in a few weeks, before summer slammed both their business and ours.

"You did it," I said. "You convinced them, with your ideas and your focus on collaboration. As long as we're here, let's pop into Rainy Day Vintage. Aimee has a piece that might work for my parents' new house. Old house. Whatever it is."

"Sure," Cayenne said, and we started up the block toward Aimee's shop. "She's got all those great vintage quilts. I wonder if she has—hey, is that Tariq?"

A slim Black man in his early thirties, wearing a white T-shirt and black cotton pants, hopped down from the number 70 bus.

"Tariq!" I called.

"The real deal Spice Girls," he said and gave us each a quick hug, slinging his backpack out of the way. "I can't talk long—I'm late."

"Blame me," I said. "We just came from a meeting at the restaurant. So, the job is good?"

"Couldn't be better. I don't know what I was thinking, wanting to run my own place. I'd much rather let a real chef take the glory and the headaches." A chain of thoughts seemed to race behind his dark eyes. "Wait. Is that why you're here? Because that idiot Boz went and got himself killed?"

"Partly. We also had a business proposition—Edgar and Grace can fill you in," I said. "I hear the detectives quizzed you about your conflict with Boz."

"Sheesh." He ran a hand over his close-cropped hair, freshly trimmed. "Like they think I'd kill him because he fired me. Thank God Edgar understood."

I knew what he meant. By a certain age, nearly everyone has lost or left a job under unpleasant circumstances. When it happens to us, we feel like we're walking around under a black cloud—and we don't talk about it. Losing the sous chef job at Alex Howard's First Avenue Café hadn't been Tariq's fault. He'd applied for a head chef opening across town. Didn't get it, but in a classic case of insult added to injury, Alex had punished his ambition by firing him. Then Boz came along, and more chaos followed. Meanwhile, Edgar had left Alex's employ and taken on his own kitchen. Tariq knew he had a good thing going now, and he didn't want to mess it up.

"I was pissed off, I admit. But Boz did me a favor," Tariq continued. "Edgar knows what I can do in the kitchen, and he didn't hold the Boz sh—stuff against me."

"I hear Edgar got pretty hot."

Tariq's shoulders stiffened and he looked like he didn't know what to say, afraid it would be the wrong thing.

"With Boz and Evie screaming at each other on the doorstep," I finished.

"Oh, yeah. That." He let out a breath, visibly relaxed. "I heard. I wasn't working here yet."

"Funny," Cayenne said. "You took the job Hayden left when he came to work at the Spice Shop, running the warehouse."

"Lucky for me, man. It isn't all pasta, you know. We make a mean osso bucco, and once you eat our crab cakes, you'll be ruined."

"Listen, one more thing, then I'll let you get to work." I put a hand on Tariq's arm. "Since you left Boz's place, had you seen or heard from him? Was he involved in anything shady?"

"You mean that would have gotten him killed? Not far as I know."

"What about drugs?" asked Cayenne, who'd worked in restaurants and knew some of the risks.

"Yeah. No. He was clean, at least while I worked with him." Tariq shifted his pack to the other shoulder and drifted toward the restaurant's front door. "He mighta had one shot of tequila too many now and then, after hours, but nothing serious."

What about after losing the job? Had the chef forced out of his kitchen spiraled down into trouble?

And why, for the second time in half an hour, did I get the clear impression that a man I trusted wasn't telling me everything?

BACK IN THE SHOP, Cayenne filled the others in on our conversation at Speziato. Ideas flew like fly balls in batting practice as they talked over our first-ever Spice Shop cooking school dinner, between tending to customers.

It's a thrill, I tell you, to have a staff that plays so well together.

Had I been alone when we left the restaurant, I might have followed up on my conversation with Edgar. The grocery store Grace mentioned, a local chain, had locations all over the city, including one not far from them. But I wasn't going to waste Cayenne's time—for which I was paying—by dragging her around on my personal boondoggle.

Boz's death was not my business. Unless it had some connection to Talia and the cash.

Or to me. Edgar had pointed out that if his dispute with Boz made him a suspect, it made me one, too. My spice-girl spy mission had put me spank in the middle. Not that creating similar blends is necessarily a problem—great minds come up with similar formulations all the time. And imitation is said to be the sincerest form of flattery.

But had it led to Boz's death? I'd understood his rage. I'd offered to create a custom blend for him, in what I'd thought was a brilliant solution. (To be fair, it was Cayenne's idea.) Then he'd discovered Tariq's role in exposing him and Evie, and that was the end of that.

I stared at the scuffed toes of my black leather clogs. The Market's last shoe repair shop had closed, and I had no black polish. I understood why the detectives had questioned Edgar. They are paid to be the suspicious type.

Did they seriously suspect me? Doubtful, but you never know. They hadn't quizzed me closely—at least not yet. I had no motive. And no reason to be in Fremont along the canal early Tuesday morning, but no one could alibi me. Except my dog, currently snoring at my feet in the Spice Shop office. Besides, how would I have known Boz would be there? I didn't even know where he lived, let alone his routine. If otherwise-unemployed drivers had routines.

The detectives had not exactly promised to keep me in the loop, but in the past, when I'd had an inside view of a crime, they'd readily traded information, feeding me crumbs while gobbling up every morsel I served. Most of the time, they got more from the deal than I did, but I got enough to keep me going in the right direction.

But I had not heard from either Spencer or Tracy. Time of death was the key. Estimating the TOD of a body found in water— what they call a floater—is complicated, another factoid I'd picked up while married to a cop. And the lack of a reliable TOD left the field of suspects wide-open.

Ridiculous to think I might be among them. The spice theft hadn't been that big a deal. I'd been acquitted of a broken promise. Edgar had his exclusive spice blend to himself again and was free of his disloyal bartender. I'd helped him find a new employee, a part-timer of mine. Tariq had lost his job but easily replaced it with a much better one.

Tag says everyone is capable of murder in the right circumstances, but most of us never get pushed that far. Or let ourselves teeter over that edge. If Boz's death was murder, someone had plunged headlong over that precipice. Who else had been badly hurt by his behavior? Who had it cost?

Evie, his girlfriend. The restaurant owner or investors, on the hook for the lease and improvements and who knows what other expenses. The landlord? Not likely—raking in the lease payments no matter what.

I dug the note Grace had given me out of my bag and read the address. Evie LeMieux lived in an apartment off Aurora Avenue, north and west of the zoo. An easy hop to Fremont.

She and Boz had broken up, publicly and noisily. But Grace had said that was their pattern. Maybe Evie knew something that could help me figure out whether Boz's death was related to Talia's disappearance.

My thumbs flew as I texted Laurel. *Janine's running the deli at the Fremont co-op, right?* A former employee of hers, a magic hand at soups and salads.

Dot, dot, dot. Then, *Yes, darn it. I miss her! Thanks!*

Then I swapped my apron for my trench coat and grabbed the basket of samples we'd packed for our potential new client.

MY BUSINESS IS built on word of mouth, and I am grateful for every referral. My destination was Belltown, a low-rise neighborhood of leafy streets nestled between the business district and Seattle Center. The bistro was a reincarnation of a much-loved establishment whose longtime chef-owner had retired, and I crossed my fingers that new management saw the past as part of the charm, not as remnants to be painted over.

Near the bistro, I snapped a few shots of the exterior. I'd take a few inside as well, to give my staff a visual. A few feet from the front door, a woman in a black pantsuit stood on the sidewalk, scrolling on her phone. Not an uncommon sight, but my feet slowed and my blood pressure spiked.

She raised her head and spotted me. Slid the phone into her pocket.

"Pepper," she said, her tone steady. When I first met FBI Special Agent Meg Greer, I'd thought she was chill. Ha. More like chilly. Frosty. Icy. I'd thought we might become friends. So wrong.

"Meg," I replied, keeping my voice calm. Cool. My eyes flicked involuntarily toward the front of the restaurant, the paint on the new sign barely dry. Opening was weeks away, the chef busy finalizing his menu and his sources. She wasn't coming from a late lunch or a quick stop for an afternoon espresso.

The door opened, a man in a blue button-down holding it for a man in a dark suit. I snapped another photo. The door closed, and the man in the suit strode toward Greer, adjusting his striped tie as he walked. "I'll get going on the warrant app. Why don't you—" He noticed me at the same time as Meg held out a hand and broke off.

The door opened again, and a shorter, bulkier man in a white chef's jacket appeared, his navy-blue Mariners cap on backward. Marco Dubois. "Pepper! Hey, come on in."

"Good to see you, Meg," I said and nodded to her partner.

Then I put on my pleasant retail expression and strode through the bistro door, ready to do business.

"Oh, this is delightful," I said a minute later. A few tables near the windows were set for future diners, to entice curious passersby. Build a buzz. "You've kept the basics of the space but given it a new feel."

"All it needed was a refresh. You can do a lot with lighting," Dubois said in a conspiratorial tone. "Owner's not big on big changes right now. He got burned at his last place. Redid the whole front of the house and the kitchen, all tailored to the chef's vision." He rubbed his thumb and fingers together in the universal sign of big bucks, then threw his hand into the air. "And kaboom! Place went up in flames. Figuratively. Anyway, he'll join us in a minute. Just wrapped up a meeting with some serious-looking folks. No idea what that was about."

I could guess, and my guess gave me heartburn. Meg Greer investigated financial crimes. What was I walking into? Ordinarily, I work with the chef and rarely meet the owner, but in this case, it might be wise.

Dubois was inspecting the basket of samples. "Ooh, smoked paprika. Caraway. Herbes de Provence." His outstretched hands tapped the edge of the table, the soft lights picking up the reddish-gold tints in the wood. "Two questions. The wine guy in the Market. He good?"

"The best." The goofiest, but the best.

"Great. Second, do you have a source for sweet cicely? I can use the fresh leaves, but what I really want are the unripe seed heads. My produce suppliers roll their eyes."

"I don't think I've ever been asked for that." I opened my shop notebook and jotted down the name. "How will you use it?"

"The leaves are a natural sweetener, perfect in—" Before Dubois could finish, we were interrupted by a kitchen staffer delivering a platter filled with bits and bites.

"Les apéritifs," Dubois said. "To give a taste of what we're planning, get the creative juices flowing."

"And the digestive juices. Beautiful food."

Roasted asparagus tossed in garlic-herb butter. Gougères, crusty puffs starring Gruyère, a mild, nutty cheese. A bowl of mixed olives tossed in oil, minced fresh herbs, and orange zest. Baked Camembert with figs and walnuts, which gave off the heady aroma of a secret honey-and-liquor infusion.

This time I didn't turn down the proffered drink, a Kir Royale. Two days in a row. I was living right.

"We're keeping a few traditional favorites, like boeuf Bourguignon and duck confit, done our own way. People want a restaurant that serves the neighborhood but feels special."

I knew just what he meant.

"Eat. But first—" He raised his flute, the champagne bubbles rising through the reddish-purple liqueur.

I raised mine and we clinked lightly, then sipped. So good.

We dove in, chatting about herbs and spices, blends and flavor profiles, each of us making notes as we talked and ate.

"Oh, good. Glad you didn't wait for me." A tall man in his late forties came to the table, a highball glass in his left hand. Extended his right, the rolled-up sleeve of his light-blue button-down revealing a vine tattooed on the inside of his arm, some leaves inked in reds and yellows, others bare, a few burn scars faintly visible. The man who'd seen the FBI agents out. "Tim Forrester. The man behind the man who makes all this great food."

"It tastes as good as it looks. Pepper Reece. From the Spice Shop, in the Market." I knew Forrester's name—he'd developed several well-known restaurants—but we'd never met. "You don't work in the kitchen yourself?"

"No, no." Forrester set his drink down. Grabbed a chair from an adjacent table and set it at the end of ours. Plucked a slice of bread off the platter and spread it with the warm Camembert. "Once upon a time. Turns out my true talents are behind the scenes. The concept, the property, the chef. Tough business, and it's gotten tougher. You have to hit all the right notes—service, price, location. Atmosphere."

"Food," Dubois interjected.

"And the food," Forrester echoed. "You can think you've got

all the ingredients and still, it doesn't work out. My last venture—"
He blew out a puff of exasperation. "That's why I wanted to meet
you. To make sure there were no hard feelings. And now . . ."

"Hard feelings?"

"I assumed you knew. I'm the idiot who gave Bosworth his
own restaurant." Forrester took a long drink of what I suspected
was the same whiskey used on the Camembert. "Even dead, he's
nothing but trouble. Criminy, that sounds awful, doesn't it?"

No argument from me. Was he the gray-haired man who'd
been searching for Talia? Right. In a city this size, what would be
the odds?

"Never should have hired him," Forrester continued. "When a
guy has a resume that long, it's usually bad news."

Standard HR wisdom. "So why did you hire him?" I picked up
a spear of lightly charred asparagus.

"Simple answer—he passed the test. Made me a meal I couldn't
forget. And I paid for it with a kitchen full of unhappy staff and
an unhappy landlord. Only people who weren't unhappy were the
equipment suppliers. I'd already committed to taking over this
place and a hotel restaurant in Portland when that one tanked, so I
didn't have the bandwidth to try to save it. We didn't need all those
fancy ovens and freezers, so the bulk of the big equipment went
back. For a fraction of what I'd paid."

Ouch.

"Speaking of," Dubois said, his eyes on someone emerging
from the kitchen.

Forrester looked over at the man, in a blue coverall with a
name I couldn't read from this angle embroidered on the left chest
and a ball cap tugged low. He carried a toolbox.

"You're all set," he called. "Walk-in should hold temperature
just fine, now that I've installed better levelers. Did the maintenance check on the other appliances. I've put you down for quar-
terly. The office will bill you."

"Thanks," Dubois said.

"Better levelers," Forrester said when the door had closed behind
the tech. "Better than the ones they sold us when they installed it in
the first place? Better than they used at the old restaurant?"

"I saw the bill for the initial install," Dubois said. "It's practically criminal."

"What happened?" I asked Forrester. "To the other restaurant, I mean?"

"Anybody can make a great meal, but it takes a real chef to do it every night. Like this guy." He tilted his head at Marco Dubois, whose confident smile wobbled a bit.

"Well, this spread is terrific," I said. "So you're not reopening Boz's restaurant?"

"No. It would need a whole new vision and team, and I don't have the drive. Not to mention the cash. I'm on the hook for the base rent until the lease expires, unless the owner finds a new tenant first."

Base rent plus a percentage of sales—same as in the Market.

"But that might not be so easy." Forrester circled the glass with his hand. "Never figured Jason Warwick for trouble with the feds, but hey. Acted like he's rolling in the dough, but what do I know? Owning property doesn't mean you know how to manage it, and having money doesn't mean you don't want more. Or a new Porsche. After that grilling, I deserve a drink." He took a good long sip.

I'd guessed right. Greer and her partner had been questioning Forrester. For some kind of financial crime connected to this Warwick? Not for suspected murder, which was a state crime. If law enforcement thought the two were linked, they'd be working on it together, interviewing witnesses as a tag team. That was how I'd met Greer last fall, in the company of Detective Tracy.

"Wow," I said. "So had you seen Boz since you fired him?"

"Nope. Hadn't heard a peep until the detectives tracked me down, told me he was dead, and raked me over the coals. Not that I could tell them anything. Then the feds called a meeting." Forrester downed his drink and scooted back his chair. "Great to meet you, Pepper. Get this guy what he needs. You need any purchasing info, credit stuff, just call the office."

With that, he left his chef and me alone in the dining room with half a platter of apéritifs meant for four.

"He always says his job is to make it easy to do mine," Dubois said and picked up the cheese knife. "Then stay out of my way."

Strange as my encounter with Tim Forrester had been, in my book, those words made him the best kind of boss.

Fourteen

In The Nutmeg Trail, *British food writer Eleanor Ford says many recipes in the world's first known cookbook,* De Re Culinaria, *published in the first century of the common era, feature pepper, ginger, or cardamom—including a recipe for spiced flamingo.*

OUTSIDE THE BISTRO, THE SPICE SAMPLES IN MY BASKET traded for leftover appetizers, I found myself mimicking Meg Greer, pausing on the sidewalk to scroll through my messages. Nate, sending nothing but heart and fish emojis. I returned them. Fabiola, our graphic designer, confirming that the printer would have the labels for our summer spice blends ready in a few days. An urgent plea from Gabby the designer, begging me to swing by the plumbing supply. The kitchen faucet my mother wanted had been backordered. They had a new model they hoped would do, but a decision had to be made quickly.

I googled the supply company. They closed at four and it was already half past. But they opened at seven, so I let her know I could run up before work in the morning.

The afternoon had turned warm, the skies clear, and I unbuttoned my trench for the walk back to the Market. The chef had given me a small starter order, promising another after he finalized the menu. My task was to provide a detailed price list and source fresh sweet cicely—why Dubois's produce suppliers couldn't get it, who knew. But impossible missions are part of my job.

Forrester was high-octane, the kind of guy who could hold a conversation all by himself then thank you for the chat, certain any issues between you had been resolved. Could he have killed Boz? The man had cost him serious capital and put a dent in his reputation, but Forrester was moving on. Too soon to scratch him off my list of suspects, but he did slip to the bottom.

What about this Warwick fellow? The restaurant's abrupt closure had had an economic impact on him, for sure, but Boz was a step removed.

And it sounded like he had troubles of his own, troubles spelled F-B-I.

Hmm. Had Boz gotten himself tangled up in some kind of mess involving his boss's landlord?

Not that I cared, unless it was connected to Talia. Besides, Greer was not likely to talk to me.

At Virginia, I went down the hill, then took a left into Upper Post Alley. The LED sign outside the Wine Merchant beckoned— Vinny had liked mine so much that he'd commissioned his own version, a wine bottle tipped above a glass.

"The Mistress of Spice!" Vinny called when I crossed the threshold. I hugged him, then Matt.

"Shop looks great." They'd knocked a hole in the wall between Vinny's original layout and the vacant space next door, nearly doubling their square footage. Matt had done much of the carpentry himself, building the stacks of wooden boxes with X-shaped inserts to corral the bottles. A sign above one section read BETH'S PICKS in honor of Matt's sister, gone too soon. "And the bar! A zinc top. Classy!"

"Locking wheels so we can move it for tastings," Matt said. "We didn't have room before."

More of that experiential retail.

"It's terrific. You're going to have more customers than you know what to do with. Speaking of customers." I turned to Vinny. "Marco Dubois at the Belltown Bistro may be calling you. I took him sample spices, and he gave me dinner. And extra dessert." I plucked two lemon tartlets from the basket.

"Mmm," Vinny said barely a minute later. He licked his

fingers, wiped them on his apron, and plucked a bottle from a rack. "Try this. A nice light Oregon pinot noir. Should go perfectly with your dinner, from the smell of that basket."

I kissed him.

In the Spice Shop, I stashed my stuff, then clipped on Arf's leash and took him for a quick spin, promising a longer stroll after work. We both needed it.

When we got back, Sandra was busy ringing up a customer and Vanessa was tidying a display that had gotten too much love. Once Arf was safely tucked in bed in my office with a treat, I joined Cayenne in the nook.

"So, I've been working up a tentative menu for the cooking class," she said. "I've made a list of spices to be featured and what supplies we'll need. Grace thinks they can comfortably manage eighteen in the kitchen. If we set the price right, we can give each student a Spice Shop apron and a gift bag of samples to take home, along with printed copies of the recipes." She slid her handwritten notes across the table to me. "Next, I thought—" She broke off. "Unless you want to handle this."

I remembered the chef's comments about Tim Forrester giving him what he needed, then staying out of his way.

"Nope. This baby's yours."

Cayenne's brown cheeks flushed. "Thank you. I appreciate that so much. There's something else I want to talk to you about. Can we—"

"Pepper, visitors," Sandra called. I glanced over and let out a shriek.

"Tory! Zak! And you brought the baby!" I tumbled out of the nook and rushed to greet my old employees and their adorable little girl, nestled in a sling against her father's broad chest. Both had left the shop more than a year ago, she to focus on her art, he on his band and work as a sound engineer. Now, with a newborn, they didn't get downtown much.

"We had a free afternoon," Zak said, "and a bit of cabin fever. So we decided to introduce Aria to some of our old friends."

"May I?" Cayenne asked. Zak slipped the baby out of her carrier and handed her over. Cayenne and Sandra cooed while the rest of us caught up. Tory slipped into the back room to greet Arf. She'd set me on my life of crime when she became the chief suspect in the murder of a homeless man who died on our doorstep, a sample cup of our tea in his hand. I shuddered at the memory. Real life is hard sometimes.

But babies are soft and sweet, if occasionally stinky and cranky, and we all loved on this one in the brief time before closing. We locked the door behind the new family and surged through the end-of-day tasks before saying good-night, our hearts a little lighter.

I'd promised Arf a long walk, so we strolled north to the Sculpture Park. We entered off Western, between the Ellsworth Kelly piece called "Curve" and the stainless-steel tree. Then we aimed for my favorite of the giant sculptures, Calder's red steel "The Eagle," pointing skyward as if contemplating flight. A pair of seagulls battled for a stray french fry, squawking at all and sundry, but Arf ignored them. Finally, we passed through the glass bridge and headed up Alaskan Way along the waterfront to home. Where the heart is, where the body can let down and the brain can let go of painful thoughts about life, death, and murder.

ARF AND I got going early Thursday.

Supply houses are like candy stores to me. I find tools of the trade fascinating, whether it's art supplies, marine equipment, or the jars, bottles, labels, and other paraphernalia for stocking, selling, and shipping. This one was no exception. But I wasn't here to browse.

It was contractor hour, with men and women in canvas pants picking up pipe and fasteners and whosits and whatsits for the day's work. Arf soaked up all the ear rubs and chin chucks the staff and customers gave him. Despite the press of other business, a sales rep was able to show me the faucet and sprayer combo their supplier had sent in place of the one my mother had ordered.

"So, you see," she summed up, "the difference is in the shape of the aerator and the height of the escutcheon at the base of the body."

"No one would ever notice unless you told them."

She shrugged. "Some customers are picky."

"Put my mother in that category, but I promise, this will be fine. If not, the blame's on me." We finalized the purchase, and I left the faucet with the other items our own contractor would pick up when it was time.

Speaking of time, I had just enough for a detour. I zipped down Stone Way to Northlake, then over to Fremont and the co-op grocery where Laurel's former employee now managed the deli. Outside the grocery, I bought a newspaper and flipped through it until I found a report of the body in the canal. The police had named Boz but provided no cause of death. Anyone with information was asked to call.

"Pepper, what are you doing here?" Janine asked from behind a giant glass case filled with salads and sliced meats and cheeses.

"In the neighborhood," I said, glad it wasn't a fib. "Great to see you. Can I have a word? Oh, and coffee, black. And a raspberry cream–filled croissant."

Three minutes later, she met me at a table with my order and her own coffee. "What's up? Laurel okay?"

"She's fine. Misses you. You were hard to replace."

"And I miss her. Great boss. But it was time for me to be the boss. Deli's only one department in a big store, but it's mine."

"Nothing like being in charge, is there? Hey, it's hard to explain, but I need to talk to a woman I think works for you. Evie LeMieux?"

Janine nodded toward a woman with dark-blond hair in a braid refilling the bread baskets. "Good worker, but—hmm. Prickly."

I sipped my coffee. Liquid courage. "She more likely to talk to me with or without you?"

"I'll stay, if that's okay." Janine raised her own cup. "She walks on eggshells most of the time. She said she'd had a problem with her boss at her last job and got fired, so I guess that makes her nervous. HR confirmed she worked there, but they didn't give any details. Bartender, maybe?"

"Yeah, at a restaurant I supply. A lot of employers make it a policy to not say anything about job performance, good or bad. I get it, but it does complicate hiring."

Janine called Evie over, asked her to sit, and made introductions. She had a heart-shaped face and an almost pointed chin, and I put her in her late twenties.

Her brown eyes flicked rapidly from me to Janine and back.

"First, let me say I'm sorry about Boz's death. I don't know if you two were still involved, but either way, it's got to be hard."

Evie caught her lower lip between her teeth and dropped her gaze to the table.

"I'm looking for a woman named Talia Cook," I continued, deciding to leave out the wherefores and whys. "She's not in any trouble, but I do need to find her. Did Boz mention her?"

"No. Is she—?" She raised her head, then shook it. "No, I don't know her. Did she work for him at the restaurant?"

"I don't think so. I don't know much about his restaurant."

"You knew enough to get him fired. You got us both fired."

I ignored the outburst. Across the table, Janine sipped her coffee with the calm demeanor I'd been counting on.

"Is getting fired connected to his death?"

"I don't know. Seems like it has to be." Evie slumped in her seat. "He said—he said he thought he might be in trouble. But he didn't say what or why. It wasn't until later—" She glanced at Janine before turning to me. "Monday, when that guy came in, and you said I could take five and take it outside. He wanted to find Boz. Said he'd texted, left him voice mails, but Boz wasn't replying. He claimed Boz had something that belonged to him. I asked what it was, but he wouldn't tell me."

The spice heist had been irritating but relatively minor. Had Boz taken something from someone else, something bigger and more valuable?

"I said if he wanted to talk to Boz, fine, but leave me out of it. I was afraid—" She paused, choking back tears. Janine got up and returned with a glass of water. Evie gripped it but didn't drink. Her nails were bitten short, her cuticles ragged. "Then that afternoon, Grace Ramos came in. Edgar's wife. Shopping, but I'd never seen her here before. Made me nervous, like she might tell my new bosses what happened at Speziato."

She drained half the glass. Wiped her mouth with the back of her hand, then told her new boss how she'd lost her last job.

"I was so scared. I didn't want any of that to come out. I need this job. I like this job."

Janine touched her arm.

"Do you know who the man was?" I asked.

"I don't know his name. I think he had some connection to the restaurant, the one Boz used to run."

Tim Forrester? Or this Warwick fellow? But Evie had been

too rattled to notice much about his appearance, and she was too shaken to remember any details now.

"When did Boz tell you he might be in trouble?" I asked.

"Sunday. We were broken up, not broken up." Her hand made a back-and-forth motion. "I wouldn't see him for weeks, then out of the blue, he'd show up. This time he was different. I thought we might make it. And now—"

Now he was dead. The short conversation I'd asked for was running long. Evie sniffled. I dug in my tote and handed her a pack of tissues.

"Evie, do you have any idea who might have wanted to hurt Boz?"

"Lots of people were mad at him after the restaurant failed. And that mess with Edgar. The police asked me about that. Edgar gets mad, but he settles down. No way would he hurt anyone." She wiped her nose with the back of her hand. "Even when he was so mad at me for stealing his special spice blend, I never thought he'd hurt me. He could have kept me from getting this job, but he didn't. Although he did blackball Boz."

"What do you mean?"

"Boz had an interview last month with a restaurant equipment business. Sales. Part-time, but it went great and he was sure he'd get the job. But then he was walking out with the manager and there was Edgar, checking out freezers or whatever. And he didn't get hired. Edgar must have told them what happened."

"You can't be sure," Janine said. "They might have had a better candidate. One with more experience. Could have been a million different reasons."

"Ask Edgar," Evie said. "Or the sous chef, the one who threw Boz under the bus. He was there, too."

Tariq? Was this what he and Edgar had been hiding? Neither of them had said a word about running into Boz.

"I told Boz the whole thing was stupid," she continued. "He wanted to be a hotshot chef, he should blend his own spices. But he always took the shortcut. The easy way." She pressed her lips together, hands steepled in front of them as if to keep the sobs inside. But then her grief turned to anger. "He wrecked it all. I believed him. I believed he was sorry, that he was trying to make things up to me. How could I have been such an idiot?"

Her cheeks flushed. Could she have killed him herself?

"What time do you come to work?" I asked.

"Six. Oh. You think I . . . ? No. No. He dropped me off and said he was going to take a walk. Then—"

And then she pushed back her chair and ran from the table toward the kitchen's big double doors.

Leaving me and her boss staring at each other.

"Sorry," I said.

Janine shrugged. "We got here at the same time that morning. We walked in together, maybe five minutes to six."

"You're sure it was that day? Tuesday?"

"Yeah. I saw her in his SUV, giving him a big, passionate kiss. Surprised me. She'd muttered a bit about him, as you do at work, and I thought they'd split for good. Later, we heard about the body in the canal, and that afternoon, the police came in to give her the bad news."

"They question her?"

"I guess. They talked outside, and I let her go home early. I can't swear that she never left that morning, but the deli staff gets right to work and we have a tight schedule. If she did duck out, she couldn't have been gone long. Work would have been held up and someone would have complained."

I grunted. "Rough all around. So now you know what happened at Speziato. She wouldn't be the first to lie about their job history and turn out to be a perfectly decent employee."

"No, but I am going to have to talk to her." Janine gave me a rueful smile. "Thanks for nothing."

"Any time."

Fifteen

The better I get to know men, the more I find myself loving dogs.

—Charles de Gaulle

SOMETIMES I WISH I WERE MY DOG, STRETCHED OUT PATIENTLY on the back seat of the Saab with no worries except when would I come back and let him out to pee. And give him a treat.

After I left the co-op, Arf and I walked down to the narrow park above the canal. He pooped, I scooped, and we strolled west, well away from the spot near the bridge where Boz had been found. How terrible for Evie, knowing she'd been so close when he died, but unaware and unable to help. Tracy had hinted at a revenge killing, thinking Boz had gone after Talia and she'd fought back. He might have considered Evie for the same scenario, but I didn't. Yes, they'd had a rocky relationship, but going from a passionate kiss to murder in just a few minutes?

I hated the trope, in too many bad books and movies, of a woman, scorned or not, snapping and unleashing a murderous rage against her lover.

I couldn't overlook the possibility. Still, while Evie might have been able to shove him into the water, I had a hard time believing she would have left him to drown.

Who could have been that cold-blooded?

I shuddered.

Edgar had not told me about encountering Boz in the restaurant supply warehouse. Had he torpedoed Boz's chance at the job, as Evie believed? Had he been nursing a grudge—one I hadn't detected—until the opportunity appeared? Over something so petty. I couldn't believe it. But a lot of major crime is petty. Not long ago, in North Seattle, a pair of brothers rigged an explosion at a coffeehouse whose owner called a tow truck on their illegally parked car. They were lucky no one was killed.

Humans. You have to wonder sometimes how the species lasted this long.

At a jog in the path, we turned around. I couldn't imagine Edgar spotting Boz, arguing, and turning murderous—or why he might have been near the canal early on a weekday morning. If I remembered right, he and Grace lived a few neighborhoods north, close enough to shop here but not close enough for a casual stroll. And as he'd said, chefs are night owls, not early risers.

I really needed to know the time of death.

Ha. More than likely Edgar and Tariq feared that if they told me they'd seen Boz, I'd tell the police. Joke was on them. The cops weren't telling me a thing. Because I'd known the victim, though not well, and two of the suspects? Wouldn't be the first time. What was different about this case?

We'd reached the car. "Sit," I told Arf, and he sat while I got a treat out of the glove box.

Would that every male was so cooperative.

I HAD TO FIND TALIA. But before anything else, I had to get to work.

You know how it is when you're in a hurry. I pulled up and the bridge gates went down. I switched off the engine and leaned back, glancing up at the neon princess in the tower window before I closed my eyes.

And woke with a jump when the horn bellowed and the bridge deck creaked into motion. In moments, we were rattling across the decks.

In the Market, I parked in front of the shop. It peeves me when merchants take up spaces meant for shoppers, but it was early and I wouldn't be long.

Inside, Arf went to his bed while I started the morning routine.

One of the Indian silver chandeliers I love so much flickered and my heart lurched. *Please, no.* I sent a quick prayer to the lighting gods. I did not want a repeat of the electrical problems and chaos we'd experienced last year. But then the lights took on a steady glow and my heart returned to a steady rhythm.

I was spooning spice tea into the samovar when I heard a knock on the door.

Not my staff but my ex-husband, who click-clacked his way across the wood floors. Outside, his bike leaned against the stop sign at the corner, his longtime partner straddling his own bike and chatting with a farm stall vendor.

"Everything okay?" Tag asked. "I saw the Saab and figured I ought to check on you. Hey, good boy." Tag had known Arf longer than I had, from the dog's daily wanderings with his previous owner, Sam. A longtime Market dweller, Sam had briefly been a suspect in the same murder as Tory, the former staffer who'd stopped in yesterday. Now, Arf stuck his nose in Tag's hand, and Tag obliged with a good rub and a scratch behind the ear. The dog let out a contented sigh.

Traitor.

"Oh, this remodel my parents are doing—you know my mother. I had to run up to Wallingford to check on a faucet for her. Job should be done soon." I raised both hands and crossed my fingers.

"Right. Then Lena will be back in Seattle and she'll have a whole new list of projects for you."

I made a noise. He wasn't wrong.

"You talk to Vanessa?"

"Yeah. Her version, Logan's a nice guy, she's not sure she's ready or has time. Thing is, I talked with a few vendors who know him. She's not the only girl in his sights. I don't think she knows that. He gave one vendor's daughter such a hard time, they changed locations to limit contact."

"So is he a nice guy looking for a girlfriend, or a pushy love bomber, showering women with attention they don't want? What about the PDA?"

"No one wants to go that route. Not yet. Any chance you could talk to him? Not as a cop, but as a guy?"

He stood there, tall, broad-shouldered, POLICE in big white

letters on the back of his navy-blue uniform. His badge glinted in the light from the chandelier, radio clipped to his vest, baton and Taser on one hip, gun on the other. Whatever else Tag Buhner might be, he was 110 percent cop.

I pushed my luck. "You always say, if you're not interacting with people, you're not doing your job."

"Seriously, Pep? Give a kid I barely know dating advice?"

"Or a lesson in respect for women. In the difference between showing you're interested and ignoring boundaries."

"If that's what he's doing. Guys that age are clueless about women. We think we're cool, but we're acting like idiots. I went way overboard when I met you."

True enough. Flowers, perfume, sappy notes. Dinners and concert tickets he put in overtime to pay for. It had worked.

"You still are clueless," I said. "Maybe you're right. We can't solve this for her. She needs to tell him herself that his behavior is making her uncomfortable and decide whether she wants a relationship or wants to close that door. But would it hurt to make sure he knows you're watching him?"

"I'll see what I can do, Spice Girl. For you." He kissed my cheek and click-clacked back out the door.

The staff arrived, and we breezed through our preopening rituals. Then Arf and I took the car home and walked back to the shop, drinking in the sights and scents and sounds. The farm stalls and high stalls had been up and running for hours, but shops like mine—the stores with doors—open later. Arf and I strolled up the North Arcade. Some craft vendors were ready for the day at their six-foot stretch of the long, built-in wooden tables. Others were unpacking tubs of merchandise hauled up from basement lockers—jewelry, candles, glass art, and more. I caught sight of Logan pushing a hand cart. Was the label *love bomber* unfair? Was I judging the kid too harshly?

The urge to butt in, to tell him to behave, welled up, and I shoved it back down. Part of growing up is learning to fight your own battles. No one Vanessa's age wants a helicopter parent—or a helicopter boss.

The shop was already bustling. I answered questions, refreshed displays, and tried to be useful, but my staff had things well in hand.

I retreated to my office to tackle a few details. After Hayden's heads-up yesterday about the Szechuan pepper supply, I'd reached out to my alternate supplier. No luck. I flipped through my list, trying other sources. Everyone sounded hopeful; no one made any promises.

My concentration was broken by thoughts of Boz and Talia. Visions of the poor bicyclist and Stelle from the bakery, and a drowned body. The wonky wingback sitting with the trash on the curb. Stacks of cash. Images of fear and danger, enough to make a young woman leave behind the things she'd loved and go—where?

Much as I wanted to know what had happened to Boz, my priority remained finding Talia. Should I try the housecleaning service again? I stood and drifted toward the shop floor, debating with myself.

"Oh, Pepper. Geez. So sorry." On her way out of the bathroom, Cayenne practically skidded to a stop in front of me, hands flying into the air like goalposts jerked into place by invisible cranes.

"No, no. My fault. Not paying attention. Are you okay? Ohmygosh. You're pregnant, aren't you? That's what you wanted to tell me."

The space between the office and the bathroom is on the dim side, but no matter. The glow on Cayenne's lovely face lit it up like a spotlight. We shrieked and hugged, then I put my hands on her shoulders.

"No wonder you swooned over Zak and Tory's baby. When are you due?"

"On Halloween! CJ's already calling her his good little witch. And no, we don't know the gender. I'm not sure I want to know. Though Pops is lobbying for a namesake."

"You could go male or female with that." Louis Adams, Cayenne's grandfather, had been a witness to a crime last June involving my parents' circle of friends from more than forty years ago. I still felt terrible about the harm that came his way as a result, but the family had quickly absolved me of any blame. "What about—I hate to ask, but . . ."

"The MS? It's weird. Pregnancy seems to put it in remission, although my symptoms had already calmed down." She'd kept her diagnosis quiet until her symptoms interfered with her work, and we'd all adapted. She got tired easily and occasionally needed time off for appointments. She couldn't lift heavy boxes or climb the rolling ladder. So adapting to the needs of a pregnant employee wouldn't be much of a change.

A few minutes later, I was in my office again when my phone rang.

"Are you looking for cleaning for your home or business?" Claire DaSilva asked.

"Actually, I'm looking for Talia Cook. I understand she works for you, or did. I have something that might belong to her."

The phone went silent, and I wondered if she'd hung up.

"I don't know what's going on," she said after a long pause, her tone sharp, the words abrupt. "I don't know what this game is, but I do not appreciate it."

"No," I said. "No game. What are you talking about?"

"I'm talking about—you are the second woman to call me in a week with that same crazy story about a flake who can't even be bothered to return my phone calls." She gave me no chance to respond. "I'm not sure if you're in this with her, if you're trying to scam me or what, but it's got to stop."

The phone went dead.

Suffering sumac. I had stepped in it, big-time. But what was "it"? Who else was calling Claire DaSilva? And why was she so angry?

I sat back, arms folded, contemplating. Okay, pouting, but pouting while thinking.

Who was the other caller? Why was the caller convinced that Talia had something that didn't belong to her, when Talia herself probably hadn't known?

It had to be the owner of the chair, didn't it? So why call DaSilva? I'd found her through happenstance, the pay stub used as a bookmark. The other caller had also drawn a line from employee to employer. How? What was the connection?

But both Stelle and Talia's neighbor had said the person asking about Talia was a man.

That brought me back to my conversation this morning with Evie. A man had tracked her down, looking for Boz, claiming Boz had something that belonged to him.

The same item? Had to be. Too big a coincidence to be anything else.

Whoever they were, they didn't just know Talia had the chair. They knew Boz had helped her. They didn't care one whit about a ragged wingback. They had no interest in its potential charms and seating opportunities.

They cared only about its hidden value. Cold, hard cash.

Sixteen

*The principal difficulty lay in the fact of there being
too much evidence. What was vital was overlaid
and hidden by what was irrelevant.*

—Arthur Conan Doyle, "The Naval Treaty"

WERE THIS MAN AND WOMAN, WHOEVER THEY WERE AND whatever their connection, responsible for Boz's death and Talia's disappearance?

The problem, as Detective Tracy would be quick to note, was that all I had was supposition based on vague, unrelated facts. That does not a theory make, let alone a sound basis for investigating or probable cause for arrest.

But it sure was interesting. And I try to be a good citizen. I called Tracy and relayed what I'd learned.

"Spice Girl," he said a moment later, "I'll give you points for persistence. But there isn't anything I can tell you."

I showed you mine, you show me yours. "Can you at least tell me when the ME thinks Boz died? And how?"

On the other end of the line, Tracy sighed. "Looks like he went into the canal alive, though the body was pretty beat-up. Head injury. Cuts and abrasions. Looks like he tumbled hard on those rocks on the way in."

How he'd lost the shoe?

"That's just a theory at this point," Tracy continued. "As for when, not long before he was found. Call came in right after six thirty A.M."

Ohmygod. "What about surveillance cameras from the businesses nearby?" I asked when I'd found my voice. "Did you find his phone?"

The silence said what he didn't.

"Okay, but the Uber records will tell you where Boz picked Talia up, right?" I went on. "That will tell you where the chair was."

"And then we're supposed to go on a neighborhood fishing expedition, asking upstanding citizens if they left a chair out for the trash and followed the man who gave a ride to the woman who claimed it, put the fear of God in her, and whacked him?"

"I trust you to be more subtle than that."

"We're working on it," Tracy said, his tone not quite conciliatory but not as combative as it had been. "It's complicated."

I hate when people say that, as an excuse to not explain. On the other hand, sometimes life is complicated.

The call ended, and I returned to the shop floor. Two women came in, clearly mother and daughter.

"Wow. This place is fantastic," the younger woman said, thyme and oregano seedlings from the racks out front in her hands.

"Oh, you know me," her mother replied. "My spices are salt, pepper, and cinnamon."

"And poultry seasoning, twice a year," the daughter added.

I take challenges like that personally. A few minutes later, the daughter had chosen several pure spices as well as the seedlings, and the mother had a jar of our lemon seafood rub and one of Puget Sound sea salt.

"Good job," Kristen said, complimenting me from the floor where she was unpacking a book shipment. We'd ordered several of the latest James Beard award nominees, along with a few new releases and cookbooks for grilling season. What Sandra calls "bad cooking season," reminding everyone within earshot that simply throwing raw meat on a hot grill is not cooking. And that grilling and its cousin, barbecuing, need not be the sole province of the male of the species.

Amen, sister.

"I ordered this one for the girls," Kristen said, holding up a new book on cakes. "They don't squabble nearly as much when they're working in the kitchen. Unless they're washing dishes."

"Happy to help ease the sibling rivalry," I said. Then I spotted the name of a favorite author, Krista Davis. "Oh, a new Domestic Diva mystery. Love them, though they always make me swear I'll never throw another party. Look at everything that can go wrong. And did you get the new book in the series with the gluten-free recipes? A customer was asking about it."

"Libby Klein's Poppy McAllister mysteries. Yep. I took her name and number and I'll let her know it's in."

The Market is home to half a dozen bookstores, most scattered in the lower levels known as Down Under. Each has its own niche and none minds one bit that I'd expanded our book section. Other specialty retailers carry books as well—the kitchen shop, the map store, the Made in Washington shop. If one of us doesn't have what a customer wants, we'll suggest who's likely to have it, or make a phone call to check. The Market was founded on the spirit of cooperation, and it still rules. Most of the time.

Late afternoon, Arf and I drove down to the warehouse to help Hayden and Reed with a special project. We'd been asked by the local Iranian Alliance to create small packages of za'atar and advieh, two of my favorite blends, to distribute at a cultural festival. Without the equipment to fill bags automatically, we were doing it by hand. Call it a labor of love. Health and safety regs meant Arf had to stay in the car, but temperatures were cool and I checked on him often.

Many hands might not make the work light, but they do make it go faster. The bags all filled, labeled, and safely boxed for delivery, I sent the guys home and finished the cleanup. Outside, Arf and I circled the block and I pondered a fishing expedition of my own. Metaphorically speaking.

Google said Cook's Upholstery was closed, but with any luck, I might find the owners. My thumbs punched in a search.

Bingo. A Ruth Cook lived on Southwest 137th, not far from downtown Burien, where the shop had been. Talia's middle name was Ruth. It couldn't be coincidence.

Burien was a straight shot down First Avenue South, over yet another bridge, followed by a jog west. Still early, still light. Nothing urgent waited at home.

"Shall we go exploring, Arf?" I interpreted the look in his golden-brown eyes as yes, and off we went.

I'm a city girl, and some of the outer suburbs, like Renton to the south or Mountlake Terrace to the north, could be the moon for all I knew of them. Burien, near the airport, doesn't feel much different from the rest of working-class Seattle. It had remained affordable longer than many other close-in communities, with the advantage of being near the Sound and waterfront parks.

Finding Ruth Cook's house was not as easy as I'd anticipated. After several turns, some right and some wrong, I found myself on top of a low hill in a block of small, older homes on large lots—built, I guessed, for workers at the long-closed Boeing plant. Most were neat and tidy, the ubiquitous rhodies and azaleas nicely trimmed, but one or two might qualify for a TV fixer-upper show.

I slowed, reading the house numbers. There it was, sandwiched between a blue bungalow and a white clapboard house with a two-story addition. A Hansel-and-Gretel cottage sided in cedar shakes, the trim and arched door brick red. The single garage had been converted, the car door sided over. A breezeway made of mismatched windows and doors connected it to the house.

And surrounding it all, an honest-to-goodness cedar picket fence.

Arf's leash in hand, I unlatched the gate and followed the walkway, a delightful mosaic of aggregate pavers and handmade stepping-stones. A turtle on this one, a dragonfly on the next. Like her neighbors—and almost every homeowner in Seattle—Ruth Cook favored flowering shrubs, fat rosebuds swelling on the thick canes.

A two-tone wooden rocker took up most of the small, covered front porch.

No lights and no bell. I knocked.

No answer.

I walked around to the side of the house and peered in a small window. In the dim evening light, I made out a coffee cup on the kitchen counter, next to a plate holding bread crumbs and the stem of a clump of grapes. A newspaper lay open nearby.

In the breezeway, a cluster of handmade pots on a low bench held orchids and geraniums. Taped to the glass door was a sign not much bigger than a business card. RUTH COOK. THE WOOD WITCH. CUSTOM FURNITURE AND REFINISHING.

Not upholstery. Close enough?

A small figure on the sign drew me, and I leaned in for a closer look. Cackled out loud. A witch, complete with pointy hat and broom, sat in a chair identical to the one on the front porch. I snapped a picture.

I peered in a garage window. The shadow of a tall evergreen obscured the view, but clearly, this was a workshop. A backless chair sat on a worktable, the rest of the pieces ready to be attached. A row of shelves held cans—varnishes and stains, I imagined.

"Are you looking for Ruth?" a man called in the distinctive lilt of a South Asian accent.

"Yes." I turned to see a short, older man in a short-sleeved sport shirt and khakis, a white fringe around his dark, balding head. I gave the leash a quick tug, and Arf sat to heel. "Ruth Cook. She doesn't seem to be at home."

"No-o-o," he said. "Her annual cruise with friends. The Caribbean this year, I believe. I am Pandit Chakravarti."

"I'm Pepper Reece. The Caribbean sounds nice. Blue skies, no rain."

"They are all widow ladies. Good company."

"Oh. I didn't know. When did her husband pass away?" Robert R. Cook, the name on the business card attached to the brown leather valise?

"Some years now." Mr. Chakravarti adjusted his tortoiseshell glasses. "You came about furniture?"

Indirectly, I had. "Yes. I heard she does good work. Upholstery, too? I have a couple of pieces."

"No upholstery, no. That was the expertise of her dear departed husband. Although she did re-cover some dining room chairs for my daughter, as a favor to me. For watching her house."

Had he made himself a cup of coffee and a little breakfast while he was at it?

"How kind of her. And of you. Does she travel a lot? To visit family, along with her cruises?"

"No-o-o. Ruth and her daughter are oil and water." He made a cluck of disapproval. "My wife and I, we feel so sad for her. Our children and grandchildren are the center of our life."

I glanced over his shoulder. The wooden play set in the backyard, complete with a tower and a slide, made his point.

"That's too bad. No one to pass the business along to, then. Does she have grandchildren?"

His bushy brows snaked quickly toward the center of his face, and his mouth tightened. Had I hit home? Had he said something he shouldn't have?

"You should go now." He practically shooed me away, flicking his hands.

"I'll give her a call about the furniture," I said, keeping up the pretense. "When will she be home?"

But the chatty Mr. Chakravarti had gone silent, his lips sealed, his hands fluttering.

Arf and I climbed into the car, and I started the engine but stayed put. After a couple of minutes, the old man left, though I had no doubt he was watching me.

Despite my certainty that Talia was Ruth Cook's granddaughter, explaining my search required an actual conversation. I scribbled a note on the back of a business card—*Please call me—it's about Talia*—then slipped out of the car and stuck it between the breezeway door and jamb. For good measure, I repeated the message on another card and slid it through the mail slot in front, out of the neighbor's line of sight.

My brain was crammed with questions. If Ruth Cook was Talia's grandmother, what kind of relationship did they have? If Talia needed money to cover the rent, had she asked for it? Ruth had a sweet, quirky house in a good neighborhood, but when you make assumptions about finances by what you see, you can be wrong as easily as right. And having enough cash for an annual cruise didn't mean you'd be willing to float a granddaughter the rent money, especially if you were estranged from the child's mother.

Nor would every granddaughter be willing to ask.

A treasured book, a rescued chair, cash in the cushion and none in hand. An acquaintance dead, by murder or a tragic accident. People on the hunt, making calls and asking questions.

With every step, the mystery got deeper.

Where are you, Talia Ruth Cook?

And are you safe?

Seventeen

One of the very nicest things about life is the way
we must regularly stop whatever it is we are doing
and devote our attention to eating.

—Luciano Pavarotti

BURIEN HAS ITS OWN CENTRAL BUSINESS DISTRICT, WITH
shops and restaurants and a still-new public library. I didn't need
books, thanks in part to Talia, but I did need dinner.

Downtown was surprisingly busy for a weekday evening,
diners happy to relax and let others cook for them after a long
workday. And I was happy to do the same. Pizza, fish, Italian,
Mediterranean—so many tasty options. None were my customers
—yet.

A row of bistro tables and chairs sat outside the Mediterranean
restaurant, each set with a candle and a small bottle repurposed
into a flower vase. I poked my head in.

"Okay to keep my dog with me if I sit outside?"

"Oh, yes," the smiling hostess said.

The air was pleasant, if a tad cool, with no scent of rain. I
looped Arf's leash around the arm of my chair, and he stretched
out beside me.

The hostess flicked a switch inside the door and radiant heaters
tucked beneath the awning began to hum, their electric glow
chasing away the chill. Instrumental music played softly through

unseen speakers. Then she emerged and set a bowl on the sidewalk and a goblet on the table.

"Fresh water for your friend, and a glass of our special water for you. Very refreshing. I'll be your server tonight. My husband is the chef." She handed me a menu and ran through the specials. They all sounded fabulous. Maybe Nate and I could make the trek next time he was home. Tonight, light fare sounded best, so I chose the mezze sampler—hummus, tzatziki, and tapenade, served with fresh pita. And a glass of a dry Greek white.

What had I learned? Not much. Pandit Chakravarti had been coy and ushered me away as soon as he sensed my questions going beyond what a potential customer with needy furniture might ask. Hard to blame him—why would a customer stop by in the evening, without calling, in a car not big enough to hold much more than an end table? He'd known I was up to something.

I sipped the wine, crisp and light. That skepticism went both ways. What was the good neighbor hiding? I doubted he was escaping his own home and family to sip coffee and nibble toast in Ruth's kitchen. Was he shielding her from prying eyes? Whose? Why? The male protective streak is an admirable trait, except when it's annoying, but I wasn't sure how much protection a five-foot, four-inch man on the far side of seventy who wore glasses as thick as my little finger could offer.

My dinner came quickly. I dipped a triangle of warm, pillowy pita into the hummus and took a bite. The sumac sprinkled on top gave it a lemony accent, and I detected a pop of flavor that probably came from a dribble of pepperoncini juice.

Or was Pandit Chakravarti protecting someone else? Talia, hiding in her grandmother's house while she was away? It was much nicer than her apartment building, for sure. Did Ruth know?

Had someone else come prowling around, too—that older man with the gray hair I'd heard about but hadn't yet identified?

Ha. Seemed like everyone involved had a touch of gray, including me.

I twirled my glass, the eddy of pale-golden wine tracing patterns that vanished almost as quickly as they appeared. Like my grasp of this case. Now it made more sense that Talia had dragged home a tattered old chair. Her grandparents had been in the business of making furniture new again. Her neighbor had said she spent time with relatives in Seattle as a kid. Maybe she'd learned a few things, or hoped her grandmother would help her refurbish the wingback.

What didn't make sense was leaving the chair behind, even if she hadn't known about the thirty-five grand stuffed inside.

The olive tapenade was rich and chunky, the perfect balance of salty and savory. Like a Greek vacation in my mouth.

Then there was Boz, who'd made a lot of people unhappy. Had it led to murder?

I downed the last swallow of wine, left a healthy tip, and promised to come back. As a diner, not a spice merchant.

As I stood to leave, I checked the restaurant's street address. The Cooks' former shop must have been a block down and around the corner. Arf and I took off.

Midway, we stopped in front of a gallery and stared in the windows. A bright, impressionistic landscape on the white brick wall caught my eye, as did the driftwood mobiles hanging from the ceiling. Beneath them stood a dining table and chairs. Cherry, the design clean and simple.

The gallery owner saw me and opened the door. "Come on in. Oh. I didn't notice your friend."

"You have fragile things and he has a tail. But he'll sit and stay by the door while I peek at that dining set, if that's okay."

He held the door a little wider. I looped Arf's leash through the bike rack outside and walked in.

I ran my hand over the tabletop. Silky smooth, from hours of sanding and rubbing. The chairs were graceful, the back slightly curved, the rails spaced just so. I tried one. No wiggle. The seat fit mine perfectly. I didn't need a new dining set. My salvaged picnic table and wrought iron chairs suited me. A good thing, too—this shop was way too rich for my blood. Although if no one claimed the cash . . .

Perish the thought, I told myself. *You will find Talia, and you'll find the rightful owner of the money, whether it's hers by default or belongs to someone else.*

"Stunning, isn't it?" the owner said. "The tabletop is seamed, so it's easy to move. A leaf and additional chairs would be extra."

"Local maker?" I asked.

"Ruth Cook. She's quite the artist. Not many female furniture makers around."

The name should not have surprised me. Neither did the drawing of a witch on the tag hanging from the knob—or the price.

"She and her late husband had a shop around the corner," he continued. "We're lucky. She's mostly retired, but when she's got new pieces, she brings them to us. Her work goes fast, so if you're interested . . ."

He didn't need to finish his sentence. I've got a good ear for retail puffery, but I believed him.

"I'll let you know. Thanks." After a last look at the table, I left. Untied Arf's leash, murmuring, "Good dog."

We strode on. At the end of the block, we paused to window-shop at the stationery store. This one was all in for Mother's Day and the upcoming wedding season, showing off cards, invitations, and ribbons in all the colors. Plus other paper goods you never knew you needed until you saw how cute they were. Then we rounded the corner and saw—

Nothing. The space where the Cooks' upholstery shop should have been was vacant. I felt deflated, almost bereft. What had I expected? A building that could whisper secrets, give me a sense of the couple who'd made their living in it for so long? Of the daughter now estranged, if I'd gathered right, from both her mother and her own daughter?

Not this. Not a bare lot, scraped almost as smooth as the finish Ruth Cook had laid down on the cherry table.

A metal door clanged shut. A woman stood at the back door of the stationery shop. She tested the lock, then noticed me watching her.

"It's gone," I said. *Brilliant conversation starter, Pep.*

"No tears. Old buildings give a neighborhood character, but that one had long outlived its useful life." An Asian woman a few years older than I, she came toward us, hand out, palm down. Arf sniffed it, then sat and waited for her to pet him. She obliged. "And we can't stand in the way of progress, can we?"

There was a sardonic tone to her words that I quite liked. "What will go up in its place?"

"A four-story apartment building with rents no one can afford and not enough parking."

I glanced at the lot, not nearly big enough for that, then back at her.

"I have no idea," she continued. "But I was born and raised in Burien, and I am not always so sure I like the direction progress has taken. Though it's good for business."

"That I understand. I've got a shop downtown, in the Market."

"Lucky you." She ran a thumb over the magic spot on Arf's forehead. "After Rob died, Ruth kept the business open for a while, but she wanted to cut back and focus on her own designs. She does beautiful work. I've got one of her rockers, lucky me."

If it was like the rocker on Ruth's front porch, lucky indeed. "Sounds like you know the family well. Have you had your shop long? It's super cute."

"Thanks. Twelve years on the Fourth of July. But I've known Ruth since I was a kid. Daisy and I got kicked out of Camp Fire Girls together."

"Oh, right. Talia's mother." Shot in the dark, but it hit home.

"She hated her name. Daisy, I mean, not Talia. What does she go by now? Merrilee? I think that's it."

"Talia never told me."

"Good kid. Hard worker," Arf's new best friend said. She was massaging his ear now, and he was acting like no one had ever petted him before. The faker. But he was helping me keep her talking. "Had she come back to Seattle a few years earlier, she might have taken over the shop. She worked for me one summer, when she was a teenager. Smart, good with her hands. Ruth could have trained her in a heartbeat. But by the time Talia came back to Seattle, Ruth had already closed the business and sold the building."

"That's too bad," I said. "Does Daisy—or Merrilee—live around here?"

"I don't think so. I asked Talia what her mom was up to, but she didn't know. Hadn't talked to her since Christmas." The woman straightened and wiped her hand on her coat. "Good dog."

"When did you see her? Talia, I mean." I was pushing past casual conversation and into prying.

"Oh, gosh. In the grocery store, with Ruth. Before Easter. I swear, I live my life by the next holiday and the one after that. I'm ordering for Christmas, if you can believe it."

Easter. Two and a half weeks ago.

"Good to chat. Stop by when the shop is open. I'd love to show you around." She tugged Arf's ear one last time and aimed her keys, pressing the fob with her thumb. Down the street, a white Prius blinked its lights.

"Arf, my boy," I told my furry sidekick, "I think you've just earned your keep."

We returned to the Saab. Arf jumped in the back seat, and I closed the door. That's when I noticed the car parked in front of mine, one not there earlier. A shiny, dark-blue, all-electric Ford Mustang.

No exaggeration, my heart skipped a beat before settling into a nice, sweet purr. I reached out, jerked back. *Hands off. It's not yours.* I circled it, peering enviously at the interior. It wasn't a carbon—no pun intended—copy of the classic sports car, but unmistakably its descendant. I'd heard the electric engine was surprisingly powerful. Plenty of room inside for passengers and the dog, plus the tubs of spice I often haul around.

Big price tag, too, I bet. But thirty-five grand would go a long way.

Oh, shut up, I told myself. *It may not be Talia's money, but it isn't yours.* I opened my door, climbed in, and turned the key.

The Saab fired right up, no doubt terrified by my flirtation with a younger model.

I steered into traffic, then backtracked to Ruth Cook's house. I didn't care if Mr. Chakravarti tried to stop me. If Talia was there, I was going to talk to her.

Still dark. Had I been wrong? Or was Talia out? She didn't have a car, but presumably Ruth did, and she wouldn't have parked at the airport—talk about the proverbial arm and a leg, if you could manage to find a space. Living so close, it would be easy to get a ride.

I got out and marched up to the front door. Knocked. Waited. Knocked a second time. Tried to see inside, to see if my card had been picked up, but no luck. The card I'd left in the breezeway door was gone, but I credited that to the watchful Mr. Chakravarti.

No reason Talia should think I was on her side. If she was hiding out, caution was wise. But I was on her trail now, and I was not going to let her shake me off.

She needed me, even if she had no idea.

Eighteen

In town for the 1962 World's Fair, Elvis rode the Monorail, an elevated train running from downtown to Seattle Center, site of the fair. The original trains still carry tourists and convention goers and are especially popular with fans of the Kraken, the city's new hockey team.

AT TEN O'CLOCK FRIDAY MORNING, I TURNED ON THE LIGHTED saltshaker and flipped the sign in the door to OPEN. I'd stopped for flowers, and fragrant bouquets now bloomed on the front counter and in the nook: Tulips dressed for the spring formal in fringe, in white with red and purple streaks, in colors the rainbow only imagined. Daffodils in cocktail dresses, their petals ranging from the palest cream to the deepest yellow, the cups juicy orange, lip-puckering lemon, and ruby grapefruit. Their dates were stems of statice and branches of forsythia and pussy willow, the corsages and boutonnieres hyacinths on steroids, the radiant purple of the mountains just after sunset. No wallflowers here.

Dang, I love this place.

As I worked, I considered all I'd learned yesterday. I'd been convinced that Talia's disappearance was linked to Boz's death, but what if I was wrong? What if she really had flaked out on job and rent, leaving the wingback behind despite all the trouble she'd gone through to get it home? Both Pandit Chakravarti and the stationer had described three generations of a disconnected family. The stationer had called Talia a hard worker, one who, according to her neighbor in Fremont, was juggling the low-paying jobs that were the lot of too many these days. Vernon Phan, the building manager, had painted an unflattering portrait, but I wasn't sure I trusted his judgment. Stelle and Blue Hair liked her. Boz had called her a sweet kid. And despite his own misdeeds, he wasn't necessarily wrong.

On the other hand, she'd sold her grandfather's valise at the Vintage Mall and who knows what else. To raise cash, or break the bonds? I don't consider myself sentimental, but if all I had left of my late grandfather was his suitcase, his business card still in the bag tag, I'd be lugging it everywhere.

I nearly dropped a jar of white pepper, and trust me, that stuff makes you sneeze every bit as much as the black. And it's a lot harder to clean up. What if I had it the wrong way around? What if Spencer and Tracy were keeping mum with me because they *did* believe Talia's disappearance was connected to Boz's death, and I stood to benefit if she was out of the picture or unable to claim the money?

But that was backward. I was trying to find her, not blame her for murder.

I tucked the white pepper safely on the shelf and sped to my office. Sergeant Reyes was in charge of the found-property investigation. If the detectives wouldn't share more than the barest of details, maybe he would.

"Very interesting," he said when I explained how I'd connected Talia to her grandmother in Burien and given him Ruth's phone number. "You're saying no one's seen her since she put the chair out for the taking and took off?"

"Yes, but that's not the point. It makes no sense that she put the chair out," I said, for what had to be the tenth time. Then I tried fishing for the info Tracy wouldn't give me. "Any luck tracking down where the Uber picked her up?"

But the blue wall was made of stone. He told me nothing.

My desk chair squeaked as I leaned back, arms folded. Yes, I had an interest in the matter—I'd made the claim. Why didn't they get that I wasn't trying to establish my claim? I was trying to defeat it. I wanted to know where the chair and its secret stash had come from so the money could go to its rightful owner.

Having an interest didn't make me a person of interest in all connected crimes.

And it sure as sugar didn't make me a suspect.

Right. I'd been married to a cop for thirteen years. I'd solved half a dozen homicides and assorted other crimes. But try as I might, I could not pretend to think like a cop.

All that made me more determined to find Talia. Sooner rather than later. I snatched my phone off the desk and punched in another search. Claire DaSilva was the only lead I had left. No physical address listed for Queen Anne Cleaning. I couldn't assume from the name that the owner lived on Queen Anne Hill, one of the city's more prosperous neighborhoods, but it was a decent bet that most of her clientele lived there.

And Queen Anne is just across the canal from Fremont.

Vinny owns a duplex on Queen Anne. He lives on the main level and rents out the second floor. I'd been to wine tastings in his postage-stamp garden and heard him talk about scrubbing the toilet and mopping the floors in anticipation. My brother and sister-in-law live on the hill, too. They were more likely than he was to know DaSilva, but they didn't have the budget for hired help. If I asked Carl, he'd say, "Ask Andrea," so I thumbed a text to her. *Do you know Claire DaSilva? She runs QA Cleaning. Any info helpful!* My finger froze above the SEND button. Andrea can be a bit guarded—uptight, Kristen would say—especially if she suspects someone is not being completely open with her. Besides, she teaches middle school, and it might be hours before she got back to me.

As Vanessa had said, don't be afraid to ask for what you need.

But you have to ask the right people. Andrea would know in a heartbeat that I was, as she would say, "up to something." *Putting yourself in danger, again.* And then maybe she'd say this or just think it, but I would hear the message loud and clear, laden with layers of disapproval: *I suppose it's okay, since you don't have children.*

I x-ed out the unfinished message and moved on.

There were ways to find out the registered address of a business. I texted an old law firm staffer who occasionally digs up details for me.

Next, I contemplated another puzzle. From everything I'd

heard, Talia was short on money. She'd made a big move, and starting over can be expensive. Not much chance of getting help from her family. But then, this hard-up, hardworking young woman had quit a job. Ghosted an employer. Cleaning houses for other people couldn't be fun, but at least it paid.

Had she disappeared to avoid the caller who'd so upset Claire DaSilva? Or the gray-haired man who'd been prowling her neighborhood?

My phone pinged. My researcher pal. That was fast.

Sorry, Pepper, her text read. *Wish I could help, but I'm in Spokane with my mom. More treatment . . . Cross your fingers this round works.*

I crossed my fingers and sent a sympathetic reply.

Another idea and another phone call. Success. She could squeeze me in at noon, if that would work. It would. In fact, it felt like fate.

Out front, the door chimes played their sweet tune. Footsteps and hellos followed. My staff had arrived. Time to get spicy.

WHILE VANESSA WAS OUT making deliveries, I filled Cayenne and Sandra in on what Tag and I had discovered about her would-be suitor.

"I told myself I wouldn't say anything to her, but now I'm not so sure."

"If she were my daughter," Sandra said, "I'd tell her. Even if she didn't want to hear."

"But she's not our daughter. She's my employee. And I'm not sure where the line between responsibility and interference is."

"He thinks he can do whatever he wants," Cayenne said. "So far, he's right."

Then the door opened and a gaggle of women entered, led by a semiregular customer.

"Hey, Pepper! My cousins are in town and we're doing the Market. First, coffee and croissants. And now spice!"

The coffee onboard—from the volume of the chatter, double or triple espressos—did not stop any of the five from trying sample cups of spice tea. They fed off each other, calling, "Come see this," and suggesting a spice this one would like, a book one should pick up for a daughter or a sister-in-law, tea for the cousin who hadn't been able to make the trip. I hated to leave them—and itched to see the credit card charges—but Sandra would take good care of them.

I swapped my apron for my coat. Powered up the hill, my tote slung over my shoulder, then trotted up Pike.

On the way, I passed buildings better known for what they used to be than what they were now. The downtown JCPenney had transformed into a City Target, a lifeline for downtown residents. The old Macy's—still the Bon Marché to me, famous for the collection of Santa Claus and St. Nicholas figures from around the world that filled its big corner window at the holidays—had become an Amazon office building, and who knows what now. New businesses were filling in the storefronts that had sat empty for too long, victims of the pandemic, of crime, of changes in buying habits and changes in the downtown workforce and plain old change. The city was rearranging itself yet again.

I dashed across Third and around the Westlake Mall to the monorail station. Swiped my ORCA card and hopped on for the short ride. Seattle Center was fairly quiet on a misty Friday, though the Armory food court would be busy at lunch time. I sprinted past the glass wonders of the Chihuly Garden and out of the Center, reaching my destination two minutes after the appointed time.

"So," the stylist formerly known as Lavender Fields said once I'd gotten seated and she'd swiveled the chair to face the mirror, framed in a zebra-striped molding that matched the cape she swept over me. In the few months she's been cutting my hair, she'd gone from renting a chair to owning the salon, and in the process had decided to reclaim the name her parents gave her, Olivia. Liv. She'd kept the lavender streak in her pale-blond hair, and purple accents had begun to crop up around the salon.

"Same cut, or something new? Not that we can change your look much unless you're willing to grow it out."

"No. I like the finger-in-the-light-socket look."

"Your cut is darling," the woman in the next chair told my reflection. "It shows off those fabulous cheekbones and flawless skin."

"And your perfectly symmetrical features," her stylist said.

"Oh." I studied my features, never having given their symmetry much thought, a blush rising on those cheekbones. *Fabulous* cheekbones. "Thank you. But—" I spread my fingers and used them to lift the hair above my right temple, exposing the gray.

Liv's soft cluck reminded me of the tiny sparrows that sometimes line up on the railing of my veranda.

"A little salt to go with your pepper." She smiled at her own joke. "I tell all my older ladies to think of it as sparkle and glitter. But if you're not into the glam, we can certainly focus on the roots. You don't need all-over color."

Not yet, she was too kind to say.

"I'll match your natural tone, then add gloss and pull it all through for a soft sheen. Sound good?" She waggled her fingers, the tips of her nails glittery purple, a trendy update of the French manicure. At my nod, she said, "Good. Give me a minute to mix up some magic."

She was back in a flash with a small bowl and brush.

"You know everyone on Queen Anne, right?" I asked as she painted my hair. "Do you know Claire DaSilva? Queen Anne Cleaning?"

"Name's not ringing any bells." She leaned close, dabbing the cold, thick liquid on my roots. The unfamiliar chemical smell stung my nostrils. "What does she look like? Her hair—I know everybody by their hair."

"It's long and dark and quite thick," the woman in the next chair said. "She pulls it back when she's working. She's cleaned for me for years. I ran into her one Sunday out for brunch and almost didn't recognize her with her hair down." The other stylist was busy wrapping strips of foil around the woman's hair, and she pointed. "Working on my radio reception."

I smiled, our gazes meeting in the mirror. "My brother and sister-in-law live on the hill. They need someone and I'd heard her name, so I'm asking around."

A tiny lie, in pursuit of the truth.

"Oh, they'll love her. So thorough. Not sure if she's taking any new clients. She just lost a girl who did a great job. I can ask her for you." She leaned forward, stretching her hand toward the black leather bag hanging from a hook under the mirror.

"No, that's okay. I'll let my sister-in-law call her. The employee you liked," I said. "Was that Tina? Tanya? I heard the name, but I can't remember."

"Talia," she said. "A sweetheart. Hardworking. But then,

poof! Apparently, she didn't bother giving notice—just stopped showing up. Better offer came along, I suppose. Claire wanted me to reschedule this week, but it was impossible. We're throwing a dinner party Saturday for my husband's sixty-fifth birthday. She understood—said she'd fill in herself. They work in pairs. They're at the house right now. I don't like to be underfoot."

"Now that's service," I said.

"Claire cleans for half the block. I don't know what Cynthia Warwick's problem with her is."

Warwick. I'd just heard that name. Where?

"Across the street," she said by way of explanation. "Cynthia and Jason."

That was it. Jason Warwick, the man who'd brought the FBI agents to Tim Forrester's door. The man who owned the building housing Boz's restaurant. Small world, in the middle of the big city.

"How are your new hires working out?" Liv asked as she moved to the front of my chair, blocking my view of the mirror. "Pepper runs the Spice Shop in the Market."

"Oh, the Market. I haven't been there in years. Too crowded."

"Um, good, thanks." I was trying to figure out how to steer the conversation back to Talia when Antenna Woman piped up again. Quite the broadcast channel.

"Talia even scored a chair. Beat-up old wingback. She loved it. Said her grandmother would help her re-cover it."

"Nice," I said, hoping she couldn't hear my heart thumping. "I should swing by your block myself."

"Any time. Second, off McGraw," she said. "You never know what you'll find."

Then it was time for her stylist to tuck her under the heat hood. As she changed seats, she chatted about her azaleas—she'd put in several new bushes last year, and the white blossoms with coral starburst centers were simply stunning—and the opportunity to mine for more conversational gold was lost.

Liv was tending to her schedule book while my color soaked in, no foil or heat lamp required, so I dug out my phone. I replied to a couple of text messages, scrolled through the shop's socials, then decided to clean out my camera roll. In the photos of the Belltown Bistro, I'd captured both Meg Greer and her partner. What were they up to?

Then it was my turn for the rinse and snip. Not much later, I walked out, my hair gleaming. Amazing how even the merest trim—a nibble, as Liv called it—can make you feel lighter and springier. The skies were clearing, the air warming. Excellent weather for following up on what I'd learned about Talia and Claire DaSilva. Who'd been calling the cleaning woman or why, I had no idea, but it had to be connected to the chair and its hidden treasure. I needed to get to the top of the counterbalance and scout around before Antenna Woman got home. I liked my ears—my perfectly symmetrical ears—and didn't want her to talk them off.

But my stomach was sending out noises I didn't need antennae to hear. Passersby could probably hear them. The food court in the Center was fast and fun, and I adore the fish tacos.

A bus pulled up. Coincidence—or another stroke of fate? The doors opened and in I went.

When the Universe talks, listen. No matter what your stomach says.

Nineteen

The steep slope of Queen Anne Avenue is often called "the counterbalance," referring to the electric trolley system that ran from 1901 to 1940, using heavy weights in a pair of tunnels beneath the tracks to counterweight the cars above. The tunnels still exist, tempting urban explorers.

MY CHATTY SALON FRIEND LIVED ON A LOVELY BLOCK. MOSTLY four-squares and oversize bungalows, a few with Craftsman leanings. Lots of front porches, gables, dormers, and very high price tags.

I knew in an instant which was hers. The soft gray clapboard in the style known as the Seattle box, its front yard split by a narrow walkway lined with flowering shrubs. Coral-pink azaleas with starburst centers, if I was not mistaken.

And the white van in the driveway, *Queen Anne Cleaning* written tastefully on the open slider.

So which house had the chair come from? "Across the street," I'd been told, but the lots were different widths, the houses not lined up face-to-face. The redbrick with trim in need of paint? The sunny yellow bungalow or the 1930s mock Tudor?

I was too busy checking out the prospects to watch where I was going and tripped over a crack in the sidewalk. Caught myself before I fell in front of a car pulling into the driveway of the redbrick. An older, black Mercedes-Benz two-seater, as classic as my dad's Mustang and a lot more expensive. The door of a modern garage opened, and the Benz drove in. But not before I saw the personalized plate—JAWCAW2.

Jason and Cynthia Warwick.

Was this where Talia's chair had come from? Boz had said the man who gave Talia the chair had been cleaning out the garage. I could see the corner of a second, smaller garage, likely the original, opening onto the alley. Boz hadn't mentioned Warwick to me, but why would he?

Then I heard a door slam. I desperately wished I'd brought Arf—no one ever questions a stranger's presence when there's a dog involved. A blonde with one of those intentionally messy topknots stalked down the driveway. The wide legs of her cropped linen pants swung, the heels of her hard-soled leather slip-ons rapping on the old cement sidewalk. She crossed the street without a glance.

The object of her ire was Claire DaSilva, given away by the dark ponytail her client had described in the salon. She stood beside her van, dressed for work in a white T-shirt, tan cargo pants cuffed above the ankle, and gleaming white tennis shoes. Her face hardened as the blonde approached.

Without foil wraps to improve my reception, I had no chance of hearing their conversation from here. I ducked behind a parked car, then sprinted across the street to the other side of DaSilva's van. This yard had no fancy flowering shrubs to fake an interest in. I'd have to hope the women were too focused on each other to notice me.

"Claire," the blonde said. "I beg you. You have to help me."

"I don't have to help you with anything, Cynthia. Remember, you owe me, not the other way around."

"I explained about that." Cynthia Warwick, wife of Jason, driver of the fancy car. "We're going through a difficult time. We'll be able to pay you shortly. I promise."

I peered through the van window. Not tinted, thank goodness. I had to be careful—being tall enough to see through the window and the open door meant I was tall enough to be seen.

"If I had a dollar for every time you've told me that," Claire DaSilva said. "I told you two weeks ago, that was the end. You could pay me every penny you owe me and tip my staff and I still would not so much as sweep your front hallway again, let alone scrub your toilets."

What on earth had happened? Nonpayment, but what else?

"Claire, please. Just give me her phone number."

Whose number? Was Cynthia the caller looking for Talia? DaSilva hadn't actually said she didn't know the other caller, had she? No, she'd only asked what kind of game we were playing. Anxiety was written all over Cynthia's face, resistance on DaSilva's.

"Why? You said she left a bracelet. I said give it to me and I'll make sure she gets it back. You said no, you wanted to talk to her yourself. If you're trying to poach my employee and cut me out of the deal, then leave her in the lurch—no. I will not be part of that."

Ohhh. DaSilva thought Talia had left and planned to take clients with her. Was that why she was so angry over Talia not calling her back?

"Please, Claire." Cynthia's rose-pink nails flashed as she pleaded her case. "If Jason knew—"

"If Jason knew what?" DaSilva threw her hands in the air. "I don't know what kind of game you're playing, but I'm done. You're trespassing on my client's property. Now leave." She gave the other woman a glare so intense I could almost feel the sparks from ten feet away with a van in between.

Me, I stood stock-still, though my head was spinning. The housecleaner had used the same phrase with me—*what kind of game?* That convinced me. Cynthia Warwick had been the other caller.

But what did Cynthia not want her husband to know?

I watched as she whipped her head so hard that her hair fell loose. She spun on an expensive heel and marched blindly into the street. A silver Audi slammed on its brakes, the driver sounding the horn. She jerked to a stop just in time, then staggered to the safety of the sidewalk and her own front door.

Wow.

I'd come to the top of Queen Anne hoping to figure out which neighbor had given Talia Cook the wingback. Instead, I'd stumbled into a whole different mess. One that had nothing to do with me but that clearly did involve Talia. Claire DaSilva had fired Cynthia as a client. Was that a factor in Talia's disappearance?

Curiouser and curiouser.

DaSilva thrust the mop into the van, where it landed with a clatter. Then she surprised me. She slumped against the edge of the open door and buried her face in her hands.

I took a deep breath. Before I left, I needed to know for sure where that wingback had come from. I needed names. I needed details. How weird was it that Talia had called an Uber from a house she'd been cleaning, and the driver just happened to have a beef with the homeowner? The driver who was now dead, and Talia out of sight.

I couldn't wait for the police to follow up on the found cash—yes, thirty-five grand was a lot of money, but they had life-or-death matters to tend to. And I could never accept that money if I didn't think I had done everything I could to find its rightful owner, whether the law said that was Talia, who used spare change to buy scones, or someone sitting on a million-dollar property who drove a fancy car and took expensive vacations but stiffed her house-cleaner.

Ask for what you want, my young employee had said. I wanted information. And you don't get it by keeping your mouth shut.

I glanced across the street. No sign of Cynthia Warwick or anyone else, the redbrick house closed tight. I put my shoulders back and stepped into Antenna Woman's driveway.

"Are you Claire?" I called. "Claire DaSilva?"

She quickly put on a businesslike smile, no doubt assuming I was a neighbor in need of a housecleaner.

"I'm Pepper Reece." I extended my hand. "We spoke briefly on the phone, when I called you about Talia Cook."

Her expression immediately darkened. She held up her hands, warding me off. "Look, I told you. I don't know what this is about or why you're following me, but—"

I decided on the truth, or some of it. "Hear me out. Please. It won't take long."

A young Black woman emerged from the side door, holding the screen door with her hip as she juggled a plastic tote of cleaning supplies with one hand and a vacuum with the other.

DaSilva glanced at her employee, who was watching us with wide eyes, then gave me an almost-imperceptible nod.

"Last weekend," I said, "in Fremont, I found a chair put out for the trash. When I got it home, I found something connected to Talia inside, something I knew she would want back. Like you, I haven't been able to reach her. She moved out, on the spur of the moment, and no one seems to know where she is."

DaSilva studied me cautiously. "I'm listening."

"I met your client"—I pointed to the house where she'd been working—"in the salon, and she told me you'd be here today. She also told me Talia was a sweet kid and a good worker who quit without notice. It doesn't add up."

"Claire, should I lock up?" the employee asked. DaSilva put out a hand, not replying.

"Yesterday," I continued, "you said I was the second person claiming to have something that belonged to Talia. It was clear you didn't believe me. I couldn't figure out why, but then I heard the neighbor pleading with you for help finding her."

DaSilva flicked her gaze across the street, then back at me. Her expression had shifted, as though she'd decided to trust me. To a point.

"Cynthia Warwick," she said. "I cleaned for her for ages. Every so often, she'd be short on money, but she'd always catch me up quickly, with a bonus. I could never understand it. She drives a Mercedes, he drives a Porsche. She goes off on these spa vacations two or three times a year. Once it was a spa cruise."

The second person to mention a cruise in two days. A sign that I should take one? Ha.

"But they can't pay 'the help.'" DaSilva put it in quotes. "And it got worse the last few months. She'd pay one time, beg off the next. Her husband's business was slow to recover after the pandemic, they had a cash shortfall, yada yada. One excuse after another. I've got my own bills, employees to pay. Finally, two weeks ago . . ." She drew a finger across her throat, signaling the end.

"Two weeks ago," I said. "The last time Talia worked for you."

"I have issues with Talia, but I'm not going to let the two of them cause her trouble."

"Do you honestly think Talia intended to steal your clients? I run a retail business myself. I know what poaching is like."

"Talia would never," the employee said, her voice rising with indignation. She was still holding the vacuum and carryall.

"No, not really. I mostly said that to get rid of Cynthia. Her story about finding Talia's bracelet sounded like BS. But I don't know whether to believe you, either."

"I'm telling you the truth," I said. "I think Talia is in danger. And I need to know everything you know to help me find her."

"Claire," the younger woman said in a tone that demanded we pay attention. She set down her load. "She's right about the chair. We'd done this house and were finishing up at the Warwicks'. Talia was putting the stuff in the van while I did the walk-through, and when I came out, she was standing on the sidewalk with this ratty old wingback. She said the guy was cleaning out the garage and told her if she liked it to take it."

"What guy?" DaSilva and I asked at the same time.

"I don't know. Cynthia's husband, or a neighbor? She didn't say and I didn't see him. She asked me to take her and the chair home in the van," the employee continued, "but I was supposed to meet you at that new job down on Bigelow. So she called an Uber. The driver got here in, like, minutes. He pulled up right as I was leaving. I didn't strand her, I promise. She told me to go."

"Did you see the driver?" I asked. "What was he driving?"

"White SUV, kinda newish. White guy, I think. I wasn't paying attention."

"Did Cynthia see any of that?"

"She left a few minutes after we got here," the employee said. "Pilates. She's super into exercise."

"I bet she never stiffed her gym," DaSilva said. "She didn't leave a check, no surprise, so I came up after we estimated the new job. She was home by then but full of excuses, and that's when I told her we were done."

"You said Talia dropped off the radar, didn't return your calls for jobs," I said. "When did you last see or talk to her?"

DaSilva scrolled through her phone, checking her calendar. "That was a Friday, two weeks ago. She wasn't scheduled again until midweek, but I called her several times over the weekend to see if she could work a last-minute job on Monday. She never called back. Didn't show for the other jobs. I figured she'd blown me off, so I sent her final paycheck a day or two ago." She shoved her phone back in her pocket. "A lot of employees come and go. Nature of the business. I did think Talia would stick. But . . ." She raised her hands in a "who knows?" gesture.

"She never said anything to me about quitting," the employee said. "Or starting her own cleaning service."

"First Cynthia started calling," DaSilva continued, "rambling about needing to find Talia and talking about her husband, and I didn't know what was up. Then you called. I had no idea what was going on, but it all sounded like trouble."

"Thanks," I said, holding out my hand again. This time, DaSilva took it. "And please, let me know if you hear anything from Talia."

"You, too," she said.

"Oh, one last question. Can you describe Jason Warwick?"

"I dealt with her," DaSilva said. "Never met him."

"Me, neither," the employee said. "I always assumed he was at work."

So if he was the man who gave Talia the chair, why had he been home that day?

I watched as they finished loading their gear. DaSilva backed the van into the narrow street and drove away.

I glanced at the redbrick. Cynthia stood in the open door. Her glare could have cut glass.

Time to go. I'd be able to get a bite and a bus on Queen Anne Avenue. I hadn't gone far when a nondescript gray car crept down the block toward me.

If I was not mistaken, the driver was none other than federal agent Meg Greer.

The plot was getting thicker.

Twenty

*Sometimes I sits and thinks,
and sometimes I just sits.*

—Anonymous, no doubt a woman baffled by the world

MY STOMACH GOT THE BEST OF ME. AT THE TOP OF THE HILL, I found a casual lunch spot, ordered, and took a seat. Could not find my phone. It needed a leash, like Arf. Found it and texted Sandra to make sure all was well at the shop. I'd be back soon, but could she ask Kristen or Vanessa to take Arf for a walk? *Yes*, she replied almost instantly.

A trusted employee is a treasure. Keeping them is harder in some lines of work, and housecleaning is often a job people—women—take when they have few other options. And Claire DaSilva did not seem like the easiest of bosses. Why had she been ghosted? Was Talia hiding out at her grandmother's house while Ruth was on vacation, trying to map out her next steps while avoiding trouble?

Why? No one except the building manager had described Talia as flighty or opportunistic, and he wanted her gone to eliminate an illegal sublet. There was that business of selling the things the boyfriend in San Diego had left behind, though after what he'd done, I almost admired her gumption. She'd sold her grandfather's leather suitcase—her loss, my gain.

Had someone forced her out of the picture? No evidence. But as I'd told DaSilva, none of this added up.

I got a shiver. No one had seen her in more than a week. At least, no one I'd tracked down. Was there another body in the canal?

The server delivered my lunch—a chicken curry wrap—and I dove in. Delish, the curry full flavored but not overwhelming. Slivered almonds, diced celery, and halved green grapes added crunch. After three bites, I forced myself to slow down. Eating too fast is never a good idea, though good luck convincing my dog.

I took a swig of mineral water. What was Meg Greer doing, driving down Jason Warwick's block? Tim Forrester had said his meeting with the feds was related to Warwick, but he'd given no details. Boz made the third man in the triangle. What was at the apex?

I tried to picture Greer's partner, the man I'd glimpsed on the sidewalk. Tall, navy suit, striped tie. Dark hair. Was it graying? Were the feds looking for Talia?

But why? She hadn't known Forrester. She'd met Boz once, if he was to be believed. Her coworker did say he'd showed up quickly, but that's the rideshare model. Didn't mean they already knew each other. She'd cleaned for Cynthia Warwick. And I'd bet it had been Jason who gave her the chair.

Had he stashed ill-gotten gains—whatever that means—in the cushion and now they needed them back, to avoid making a federal case of it?

Except that Cynthia hadn't said boo about the chair. Did she know about the FBI investigation?

To borrow DaSilva's phrase, what game was she playing?

Talia's disappearance meant there was more to this. What, I had no blooming idea—or what any of it had to do with Boz's death. But Tracy always says that if odd things keep happening around the same circle of people, it isn't just coincidence. It means something.

Slow down, Pepper. Jumping to conclusions may be good exercise, but it isn't good investigation.

According to DaSilva, Talia had last cleaned for Antenna Woman and the Warwicks two weeks ago, just days before her neighbor, the building manager, and the bakery staff last saw her. The pay stub I'd found dated back a few weeks. It was not her last paycheck from DaSilva, which she might not have gotten yet. As far as I knew, her only connection to Boz was that he'd given her and that stupid chair a ride. He'd been a hothead whose blowup cost decent people their livelihoods and Tim Forrester a chunk of change. Maybe Jason Warwick, too. So why did I believe he had not harmed her? Why did I believe anything he'd had to say?

Good question. But even douchebags can do the right thing now and then.

I'd refused to help him find her, then decided that was my mistake and I had to get involved. I would have told him, eventually, except that he'd turned up dead.

My stomach now more unsettled than before, I wrapped up my sandwich and headed for the bus stop. Minutes later, I was riding down the counterbalance, making a list on my phone of all the things I wanted to ask my detective pals and the details that might pique their interest.

Had they found Boz's phone? Narrowed down the time of death? What more could they tell me about the cause of death? Did they still think it looked merely suspicious? Or had they taken the next step, as I had, and concluded that it had to be murder?

Surely they'd searched his apartment and interviewed friends and family, besides Evie. He'd been difficult in his professional life and had a tumultuous love life. But that cast little light on his interior motives.

What about those Uber records? Less important now that I knew Talia had called him from the Warwicks' house and that he'd driven along the canal to drop Evie off at work. But if the police hadn't found his phone, those records could help them recreate his movements. Build a timeline of his last days.

Ohhh. What if the killer had taken his phone so it couldn't be easily tracked?

The police wouldn't be able to get a warrant to trace Talia's phone records, not even location pings, without facts establishing that evidence related to a crime was likely to be found on it. Probable cause. Which they didn't have. Did I?

Could they get location evidence if they had good reason to believe she was missing? I'd been so sure of it until finding her grandmother's house and meeting Mr. Chakravarti.

As my list of questions grew, so did my determination. The bus rolled down Third Avenue, and I did not get off at Pine. Or Pike.

Or Union or University, despite the rain beginning to dot the bus windows. At Cherry, I hopped off and dashed up the hill, my hood drawn close, to Seattle Police Department headquarters.

If the detectives weren't calling me and weren't dropping by for tea and talk, I would have to go to them.

"Pepper, nice to see you." Detective Cheryl Spencer strode across the lobby toward me a few minutes later, then showed me to a small interview room. That in itself was unusual. In the past, they'd given the okay for me to ride the elevator up to their secret lair. They'd let me sip stale coffee in Tracy's cramped office and study the whiteboard and pictures hung on the wall. For some reason, in this case, I was persona keep-her-at-a-distance, though now I had a decent guess why.

I laid my damp coat over one of the heavy metal chairs and found my phone. "I have questions. And I might have answers to some of your questions."

"Let's start there," she said, laying a notebook on the table.

I told her about tracing Talia to her grandmother's house in Burien. "I know they've been in touch since Talia moved to Seattle, though I don't know if she's there now. You two aren't convinced that her disappearance, if that's what it is, is related to Boz Bosworth's death."

A twitch in Spencer's normally placid features confirmed my suspicion that they might have changed their minds about that.

"But here's why I think it is connected. You talked to Evie LeMieux. She says Boz came to see her Sunday, after he saw the chair on the sidewalk and discovered that Talia was gone. He didn't mention Talia, but he was worried. He knew he might be in trouble. A man came to see Evie at work. I don't know if it was Jason Warwick, Tim Forrester, or Agent Greer's partner." Spencer's eyes widened ever so slightly. I had surprised her. "And I don't know if it's the same person trying to find Talia. But the odds are good."

"I'm not sure I want to know how you—" Spencer stopped herself.

"I'm looking for Talia." I chopped the air with one hand. "I'm looking for her because I found the cash in the chair and it might belong to her. Legally and morally, even if she didn't know it was there. But everywhere I go, I run into these guys. Well, not literally, since Boz is dead and Warwick I haven't met yet. And I don't know what to think of Tim Forrester. Point is—" I leaned forward, nearly knocking my water bottle off the table. "Point is, searching for her leads me to them. It has to be connected. How? Why?"

"Always the question." She brushed a strand of hair off her temple.

I told her what I'd learned from Claire DaSilva and her employee. Spencer made a note. Had I found a link or a lead they didn't have?

"No one has seen her in more than a week," I said. "At least not anyone who admits it. She may not know what happened to Boz—she disappeared before he was found. But clearly, she is not following her usual routine in her usual places. And she might have information."

"We never said we weren't worried about her. And yes, the address is helpful. Thank you."

"Good. Did you find Boz's phone? Or pin down the time of death? Obviously, when and how he was killed shortens the suspect list."

Spencer gave me a hard look, calculating how much to tell me.

"All the ME can confirm at this point," she said, "is that he suffered a head wound, either in the canal or on his way in, along with other injuries, and drowned not long before he was found."

That I already knew.

"You don't think he took his own life, do you?" There had been talk at the scene about a jumper. I hadn't thought it likely, given the height of the bridge, the currents, and where the body surfaced. Had I dismissed the possibility too soon? Boz had lost a career he'd loved through his own fault. Couldn't get a job.

But he'd made up with Evie and bought himself time with the rideshare gig. Had that been enough to pay the rent and keep the proverbial wolf from the door?

When I was ten or twelve, a man my dad taught with had been diagnosed with cancer, back when treatment options were limited, and chose suicide to spare his family the ordeal and financial ruin. My dad had been wrecked. A lawyer in my old firm, facing disbarment and possible arrest, had done the same. I'd been part of the HR team that arranged counseling for anyone who wanted it, but few lawyers took the offer, the stigma too strong. Not long after, the firm imploded, the dead man's mistakes only one weakness in a house of cards.

And last year, a Market vendor's wife, outwardly cheerful and happy, had swallowed a bottle of painkillers and not woken up.

But despite all the trouble Boz was facing, the facts—at least the ones I knew—did not point that direction. He'd been found upstream of the lower bridge, his car nearby. If he'd left a note in his car or his apartment, the police would have found it and closed the case.

"No," Spencer said. "The buildings north of the canal all have high-tech cameras with great resolution, though there are always gaps. The security footage shows him park the rig, right where we found it, and get out. No passengers. That's consistent with Ms. LeMieux's account. But then he walked out of view and the cameras didn't pick him up again."

"No footage of a confrontation."

"Nothing so far. We've asked anyone in the area who might have seen anything useful to contact us, but no one's come forward yet."

As I'd seen in the paper. I bit my lower lip. "So unless the pool of suspects widens, you're asking questions and checking alibis. But that's your job, not Meg Greer's. Why was she quizzing Tim Forrester and driving by Jason Warwick's house?"

"I can't tell you anything about that, Pepper. Even if I knew."

Oh, she knew. On TV, the feds and the local cops are sworn enemies, defending their territory and their investigations, but Tag had always scoffed at that. They had their own targets and their jurisdictional boundaries, but they talked. Joint task forces were common. And no officer wanted to walk into trouble and get shot by an officer from another agency who hadn't known who was who.

"Well, Evie LeMieux was at work when Boz died. We don't know where Talia was, but probably not Fremont. I don't know what Warwick or Forrester were up to, but restaurant guys like Edgar Ramos aren't early risers." Though I knew he hadn't been working late Monday night. And Forrester was a restaurant business guy, not a kitchen guy. But Edgar hadn't told me the whole truth. What had he told the police?

"Ah, yes. Mr. Ramos." Spencer closed her notebook and laid

the pen on top of it. "Tuesday morning, he says, he was home in bed. But according to his wife, the little girl woke up screaming, from a nightmare. She went to comfort her and stayed with her the rest of the night, until it was time to get her up and ready for school."

I couldn't believe it. The police doubted Edgar's alibi?

"What motive did he have? How would he have known Boz would be at that exact spot at that exact time?" A grudge is one thing—I'm still irritated with Mary Jane Mahoney for nudging me out of the eighth-grade spelling bee—and murder quite another.

"Now you know the questions that keep me awake at night." She pushed back her chair and we stood. "If you find the answers, let me know."

Twenty-One

The humble cumin seed sprouts off the end of a weedy grass, and is nearly as universal a seasoning as black pepper. Pungent and earthy, the savory base of cumin is surrounded by the lightest hints of citrus and pine, giving it a well-rounded and pleasing flavor.

—Amanda Bevill and Julie Kramis Hearne,
World Spice At Home

OUTSIDE, THE RAIN HAD STOPPED. I FISHED FOR MY ORCA card, eyes out for a bus stop, then decided the air and exercise would do me good. I walked down Cherry to First. Paused at the corner to reply to a text from my mother about the substitute faucet and dropped my phone in my tote as I stepped off the curb. Then something—or someone—slammed into me. I staggered sideways and one foot landed in a puddle, cold water splashing into my clog and up my leg as I tried to catch my balance. In that odd way the senses have of recalibrating to cope with danger, my vision whirled and sharpened, while my hearing became both dulled and more acute.

A small woman in a lime-green slicker stood beside me, her arm outstretched.

"That motorcycle almost hit you."

Instinctively, we both eyed the steep slope I'd just come down, the roar of an engine trailing behind the bike as it disappeared from view.

"Thank you," I told my guardian angel. "My mind was on something else."

"Idiot, revving around the corner like that. Matter of time before he lays that bike down. Stay safe," she said and strode off.

I followed slowly, checking both ways twice before crossing. I was soaked. The encounter demonstrated how little force it took to knock someone off-balance. My guardian had been small, her touch not much more than a good nudge. If a runner or a cyclist had thrown Boz off-balance, they'd have noticed, and if he'd gone into the canal, they'd have stopped to help him.

Bottom line, size didn't matter. Boz's attacker didn't have to be big, or male. I'd pretty much ruled out Evie, certain she couldn't have left her lover to drown and gone back to work without completely falling apart.

As for Talia, I had to admit, I didn't know her. I had no idea what she was capable of. But I also could not place her in the vicinity or give her a reason to kill the driver who'd helped her out, no matter what trouble he might accidentally have set on her tail.

I strolled up First, watching for traffic and puddles at every corner. Spencer had trusted me enough to confirm a few details, but I wasn't convinced that the detectives would follow up on my tip about Talia and her grandmother.

A flash of red in the street sent my heart rate spiking. Not danger, but an electric Mustang cruising up First. Fire-engine red. Dang, they were pretty.

Safely in my loft a few minutes later, wet pants swapped for dry, I perched on the bedroom chair to put on clean socks. Caught sight of Talia's book on my nightstand. Well loved, clearly, the pages much thumbed. Hard to believe she'd left the box of books behind voluntarily. A reader—and Talia clearly was one—always kept a few treasured volumes with her, no matter how lightly she traveled.

And what about the chair and the suitcase? Why hadn't Talia stored her things at her grandmother's house? Or I'd guessed wrong and she'd left Seattle altogether, leaving behind what wasn't essential.

The suitcase. The Vintage Mall. On my phone, I scrolled back to the photos of the desks I'd seen. Compared the cherry model with the tapered legs to the picture I'd taken of Ruth Cook's dining set in the gallery in Burien.

So similar. Had the desk belonged to Talia, too? Why sell it? All she had of value?

I left my damp clogs to dry out and slipped my feet into a comfy pair of rubber-soled Mary Janes. I'd grabbed the mail on my way in and flipped through it, recycling everything but an outdoor furniture catalog that might interest my parents. Then it was back into the raincoat and out into the mist.

On my way through the Main Arcade, I stopped to see Herb the Herb Man. "Special request. New customer wants sweet cicely. I've never seen that on your table. I barely know what it looks like—a cross between carrot greens and parsley?"

"Good description. I don't grow it," Herb said. He spread his hands, indicating his seedlings and cut fresh herbs. "Not enough call. And frankly, for one customer, I don't want the bother."

"Fair enough. Thanks anyway."

Next, I stopped to see a longtime vendor who created her own screen-printed designs. Stacks of T-shirts in every color in the crayon box filled her table, a few of the most popular designs hanging behind her. She'd made our shop aprons and Cayenne had called her to discuss a new design for our cooking class students. We figured out the price and delivery date, then I added a special request.

"Oh my gosh," she said. "That will be so much fun. I'll shoot you a couple of images."

"You rock."

Down the Arcade, Logan was handing out samples of mountain-grown honey. I walked away. He was Vanessa's problem, not mine.

In the shop, I greeted Arf, deep into his afternoon nap after a walk with Kristen. She was on her way out—weekdays, she leaves early to beat her girls home—and waved off my thanks.

"He was the perfect gentleman, as always," she said.

"And you are the perfect friend. As always."

"Don't you forget it," she said, and our grins matched. She was born two weeks before me and she's been giving me grief pretty much ever since, mostly in fun.

Finally, I had a chance to sit in the nook and finish my lunch.

Propped up my tablet and scrolled through our socials while I ate. Cayenne had added a recipe for asparagus braised in butter with herbs to our blog. I hoped it got the same hearts and stars as our asparagus soup.

I printed out my feta and beet salad recipe, the one with cumin dressing, and asked her and Sandra to try it. My wrap reminded me that we didn't have a good chicken curry on the blog, so I made a note to ask my staff for their favorites.

Another prospect for the sweet cicely occurred to me, and I sent a message to Tara Novak, owner of Terra Nova Farm on San Juan Island. I was putting in a lot of work to source a product that wasn't going to earn me a penny, but the name of the game is connection. If I linked a reliable grower to a dependable customer, neither would forget. And doing an unexpected favor is always a good thing, for business and for the soul.

Well, almost always. I was starting to regret nabbing the wingback on the sidewalk last weekend. What we do for our mothers.

And they for us.

"Boss?" Sandra called. I slipped my phone in my apron pocket and slid out of the nook. Cayenne was busy guiding a couple through our bridal registry, and Sandra had a three-customer pileup, two more than we like to see. People shouldn't have to wait for great flavor.

When the sales were rung up, the bags packed, and the customers out the door, I straightened the displays on the front counter. I'd just scooped up a stray tulip petal when my phone buzzed. A reply from Tara Novak. Yes, she grew sweet cicely. Did I want fresh herbs or dried?

Fresh, I replied. *Leaves and seed pods. I'll tell my customer and let you two work out the details.* My thumbs flew, sending Marco Dubois the good news and Tara's contact card.

Almost the moment I finished, my phone buzzed again. This time, it was the man at the Vintage Mall.

Still thinking about that little desk? It's capturing eyeballs— could go fast!

Was he being helpful or pushy? Impossible to tell. If it was a Ruth Cook piece, he was probably right.

Thanks! I texted back. *Will decide soon!*

Time to close. I muscled the rolling rack of seedlings over the threshold. We raced through our end-of-day routine, and Arf and I headed home.

On the way up the stairs to the loft, I made a new plan.

"Arf, my boy," I said after I'd filled his supper dish and changed out of my shop clothes, "hold down the fort. I've got a lead to follow and a suspect to scratch off my list. If I can."

With the Mariners away, traffic moved quickly past the stadium. Funny not to stop at the warehouse, but I had no reason. The crew would be gone now anyway. That made me think about summer hiring. Time to ramp up the search.

Would Cayenne keep working after the baby came? I couldn't ask—major legal minefield. I trusted her to bring it up sooner rather than later, giving us both plenty of time to plan.

Once again, I drove down First Avenue, over the bridge, and into Burien. This time I drove straight to Ruth Cook's house, moving slowly down her block. Pandit Chakravarti had said Ruth was away on a cruise, though I'd thought it strange that she hadn't left her car at home.

She was back. Sitting in the driveway was a gray and black truck-van mashup, about as ugly as could be. The low back end and cargo area were made for hauling big, bulky items. Like furniture.

I pulled to the curb two houses up. I was about to shut off the engine when the side door of Ruth's house opened. Out came a slender young white woman, her dark hair brushing the shoulders of her black leather jacket. Then she got in the boxy rig.

Talia?

She backed out of the driveway into the street, giving me a clear view of the plate. WOODWCH.

Wood Witch. The business name on Ruth's card. That was her vehicle. And the driver had to be her granddaughter. Not missing after all.

A flash of movement to the right caught my eye.

I'd been spotted. Pandit Chakravarti came shuffling down the sidewalk toward me, shaking his fist.

The WOODWCH moved down the street. I put the Saab in gear and followed. At long last, I had Talia Cook in my sights, and I was not going to let her get away.

Twenty-Two

The only thing I like better than talking about food is eating.

—John Walters, aka the Food Dude

DUSK SETTLED QUICKLY OVER THE HOSPITAL PARKING LOT.

I'd followed the WOODWCH down Fourth to Sylvester, keeping the distinctive vehicle in sight while trying to be discreet. Where we might be going, I had no clue. Then the hospital came into view and Talia turned into the main parking lot.

Who was she here to see?

I'd driven past, banking on a second entrance. Took it and doubled back, creeping down the row parallel to the one Talia had chosen. On First Hill, the medical corridor where many of Seattle's hospitals and clinics are clustered, parking is always hard to find, but this lot was half-empty. After dinner, I imagined, evening visitors would fill it up.

I found a spot facing Talia's row in time to see her climb out, sling a small bag over her shoulder, and march toward the bright lights of the main entrance. She tugged the hem of her skirt, a flouncy sunflower print that clashed sweetly with the leather jacket, a small box in her other hand.

Goth up top and flower power below, much as her Fremont neighbor had described. I loved it. The black-and-white Chuck Taylor high-tops were the perfect finishing touch.

She did not glance my way.

Now what? I couldn't go inside. Hospital security would not take stalking lightly.

Waiting was my only option. It would be stupid to lose her after all this, though at least now I was fairly sure she was staying at her grandmother's house. Was she visiting Ruth, who was not on a cruise, as Mr. Chakravarti had claimed, but in the hospital? A good reason for Talia to come down here. How that meshed with what I'd learned earlier, I didn't know.

WOODWCH. Too funny. You had to like a furniture maker who called herself the Wood Witch and gave her delivery truck the same name, minus a couple of letters.

If I got a new car, what kind of personalized plate could I put on it? I played with the possibilities as I watched for signs of my target on the move.

SPYCGRL. PURRFCT.

Roughly thirty minutes after she went inside, Talia came out. No box.

I left my car, closing the door quietly. Stood between a Prius and a pickup and waited as she approached, watching her feet and not her surroundings.

"Talia!" I called.

She jerked her head up, scanning the lot for the source of the voice. In the blue-pink glow of the parking lot lights, I saw her clutch her bag close to her side and fumble in her pocket. Metal glinted in her raised fist. Women of all ages have been taught to thread their keys between their knuckles to fight off an attacker, a maneuver Tag says only tears up a woman's hand. You can't get a real grip that way—or do any real damage.

"Talia," I repeated, extending my hands in the universal sign that I came in peace.

"Who are you? Stay away from me."

"My name is Pepper Reece. I run the Spice Shop in Pike Place Market. It's hard to explain, but I know you're in trouble. Let me help."

"You left your card." Her chin and shoulders were raised, but she did not back away. "Who sent you?"

"No one." My stomach growled. The air felt heavy with impending rain. "Listen, can we go somewhere to talk? Grab a bite? I promise, I'm not here to hurt you."

She hesitated, sizing me up.

"My treat," I said. That did the trick.

If only she knew how much money she'd been sitting on.

I followed her downtown, to a pub I'd walked by the other night.

"This okay?" she asked after we'd parked and met on the sidewalk. "I've been craving a burger and a beer."

"Always in good taste."

Inside, we found a high-top table near the window. A redheaded server with a matching beard and a fire-breathing dragon tattooed on his forearm delivered our menus, his words aimed at both of us but his eyes targeting Talia.

I was the older generation now.

"Is it your grandmother who's in the hospital?" I asked when he'd left. "Ruth Cook?"

"Lung problems, from all the sawdust and varnishes. She's been doing woodwork for more than fifty years. Since she was a teenager. Before they knew to wear respirators, or even a mask. It created scar tissue." She ran a hand up and down her chest, over her own lungs. "She has trouble breathing sometimes, and they had to put her on meds—bronchodilators, they're called—to open up her lungs."

"That sounds awful," I said. "Like black lung, the miners' disease. Will she be okay?"

"They can't cure it, but they can treat it." She paused as Red Beard delivered our beer, then returned the smile he flashed her. "She says she's too stubborn to let it stop her, and I believe her. How did you know about her, anyway? How did you find me?"

"Like I said, it's complicated." Dang, I hate that phrase. I reached for my glass. An old Soundgarden tune sang through the airwaves. "You know a guy named Boz—Boz Bosworth? I think you met him when you were doing a housecleaning job on Queen Anne a couple of weeks ago."

Her eyes widened, and I went on.

"I ran into him last Sunday in Fremont, outside your apartment building. He got pretty frantic when he couldn't find you."

"I saw the guy looking for me," she blurted out. "Not Boz. The other guy. It's not me they want. It's him. I don't think he did anything, but he knows stuff."

"I hate to say this, especially so bluntly, but—"

"I know, I know." Her chin wobbled. "He's dead. I saw it in the paper. I'm staying at my grandmother's so I can visit her in the hospital and help out when she comes home. I almost called the cops, but what if the people who were after him found me first?"

Like I had. "Do you know who would be after him, or why?"

"No. Maybe."

"Talia, tell me the truth. I don't know what's going on, but you could get seriously hurt."

"Uh, 'scuse me." Red Beard with our dinners. How much had he heard?

"Look. I know Boz through the food business," I said after the server left. "I think he may have stumbled across evidence of illegal activity, possibly involving Jason Warwick. Why anyone thinks you might be part of it, I don't know. But let me help you figure it out."

Our plates looked fabulous, my burger nestled between glistening fries and a pretty little salad, the top of the bun slightly askew like a jaunty French beret.

The smell of the fries was overwhelming. I picked one up, despite knowing it would be too hot. I waved the potato around to cool it down, then bit off the end. Seriously tasty blend of salt and seasonings.

Talia focused on her plate. She picked up her fork and stabbed a cherry tomato, juice squirting out, then rested her fork on the plate without eating. "At first, I thought he was just a chatty cabdriver. Well, rideshare, but same thing, right? Anyway, then he said he knew them. The Warwicks. Jason mainly, but Cynthia, too. For me it was the other way around. Jason was never home when I cleaned, except that one time."

"The Friday when he gave you the wingback?" At her look of surprise, I clarified. "Boz told me that's how he met you. When the homeowner gave you the chair and you needed a ride."

"Right. I'd taken the trash out to the bin behind the house, and Jason was in the garage. One of those tiny old ones that you can't actually fit a car in."

Too funny. The chair had gone from one Model A garage to another.

"He said he was digging for some old files from his business and he was tired of moving this stupid chair in and out of the garage every time he needed to get in there. Like Cynthia—and he said this, not me. He said, like she would ever reupholster it herself no matter how many times she said she would—you can break a nail doing that." Her eyes glinted wickedly. "Cynthia did have a nice manicure."

I'd noticed.

"Anyway, I said it was a great chair and he said I could have it, but Danika couldn't give me a ride—that's who I was cleaning with—so I called an Uber and Boz came."

"Eat," I said. "The food is terrific." I'd ordered the Cumin Nature burger, the beef mixed with ground cumin and other good stuff, topped with crisp, peppery bacon and a mayo guac. I love seeing what real cooks in real kitchens do with spices. So far, my venture into the wilds of Burien's food scene had been delish.

Talia took a bite—she'd ordered a mushroom burger—and immediately bobbed her head in approval. We ate in silence for a few minutes. Then she wiped her mouth with her paper napkin.

"Cynthia didn't usually stick around—most homeowners leave after they tell you any special requests. Some clients are super nitpicky and talk down to you. But she was nice enough."

"Wait. Did you leave a bracelet there?"

"No. Why do you ask?"

"No reason." Telling her how I'd found Claire and heard about Cynthia's call might spook her. Bits and pieces were flying around in my head like free radicals searching for each other, programmed to bond but not yet knowing what facts went where.

"But this was weird." She set her napkin down. "Cynthia hadn't come back yet when Jason gave me the chair. When the driver arrived—Boz—it was obvious they recognized each other. You know how, in the comics, the artists draw sparks between the characters?" She held up both hands, flicking the fingertips toward each other. "We got the chair loaded and took off. I had to sit up front with Boz, and he asked me how I knew them. I said I was just cleaning, I didn't really know them. That's when he said—" She broke off as Red Beard appeared at our table.

"How are your dinners, ladies? Another beer?" Red Beard aimed his high beams at my new friend. We agreed that the burgers were great, the fries were fabulous, and one beer was enough. She watched him leave out of the corners of her eyes. As if I wouldn't notice. I sipped my beer, and she turned back to me.

"So, Boz said he'd been clearing out his stuff at the restaurant, whatever that meant, and overheard Jason and Cynthia arguing."

"Boz cooked in a restaurant that occupied a building Warwick owns. He did a dumb thing and lost his job. But I don't think Warwick had anything to do with that. Go on."

"Boz said Jason said he was tired of all the lies and wanted to come clean. Cynthia said she'd told him—Jason—not to get involved in the first place. In what, Boz didn't say. Jason said yeah, but she hadn't had any trouble living the good life all these years, and what did she think paid for that?"

"How strange."

"Then she said," Talia continued, "that he could end up in prison, and was that what he wanted? Stupid question. Who wants to go to prison?"

I remembered my friend Hot Dog saying he knew some men who'd had so much trouble keeping it together on the outside that they committed minor crimes so they'd get sent back. Three squares, a bed, and a roof. All the tough decisions made for you. And fewer temptations. But that was a whole other thing.

"Did Boz say anything else?" I asked.

"Just that Jason wanted to clear his conscience, and Cynthia said she understood that, admired him for it, but it was too late. Boz told me their conversation made him realize he had some amends to make himself, but you had to be ready for the consequences."

"Truth to that." I swiveled the stool away from the table and stood. "And one of the consequences of beer is a visit to the bathroom."

My thoughts darted madly hither and yon as I made my way to the back of the pub. Warwick had had nothing to do with Boz getting fired, I was sure. The way Tim Forrester described the business, the two men would barely have known each other.

Boz had gone back to clean out his stuff, Talia had said, and overheard the Warwicks talking. Jason must have suspected he'd heard their conversation.

But what was Jason involved in? And what, if anything, did it have to do with the old wingback?

Twenty-Three

Vanity plates are a popular form of personal expression, but officials have banned more than 13,000 letter and number combinations for violating Washington state law against messages that are "offensive to good taste and decency."

WHEN I RETURNED TO THE TABLE, RED BEARD AND TALIA were deep in conversation.

"Hey, there," I said. Red Beard straightened and stepped back, gesturing toward my empty seat.

"You two hit it off," I said to Talia when we were alone.

"We knew each other ages ago," she said. "I spent summers with my grandparents, from about eight to fifteen. Jonah lived close by. He was skinny and geeky, and so was I. I doubt we ever said more than a few words to each other all summer."

"Things have changed."

Tiny pink spots bloomed on her cheeks. Her bag buzzed, and she pulled out her phone.

"It might be Gran." She read the screen. "Oh, too funny. It's her neighbor, Mr. Chakravarti. He wanted me to know 'that woman' came back. To Gran's. I guess that's you."

"He knows Ruth is in the hospital, right? He told me she was away on a cruise, but I didn't believe him."

"He's very protective." Talia picked up her beer glass, still half-full. "After my grandfather died, about ten years ago, Gran kept the business going for a while, then set up a workshop at home. Upholstery was his thing. She's a furniture maker."

"I saw her work in the gallery down the street. It's amazing."

"I loved helping out in the shop. I'd sweep, organize the samples—whatever they needed. When I was little, I'd make pretend furniture for my dolls with wood scraps and bits of left-over fabric. I loved it." She swirled the glass, took a sip, made a face. The beer had to be warm by now. "I adored my grandparents. Their first date was to see the movie *Rocky*—"

"Are you named for Talia Shire? She played Adrian, Rocky's girlfriend."

"Yep. Gran suggested it when my mom was pregnant." Talia's face turned wistful, then sad. "After Grandpa died, Mom and Gran had a huge fight. Anyway, I was horrible to my grandmother. She wrote, she called, and I wouldn't have anything to do with her."

"How did your mother respond?"

"She didn't. I mean, she knew how I was behaving and she didn't stop me. She didn't talk to Gran, either. My mom is—she's always right, even when she's not. She never changes her mind. Gran never stopped trying, and I didn't stop being an absolute brat. I mean, she sent presents for Christmas and my birthday and I gave them away. Except when she sent money. That I kept." She bowed her head, ashamed.

"You kept one gift," I said. At her puzzled expression, I explained. "The building manager, Vernon Phan? Apparently you left some things in the basement hallway—"

"Everybody left extra things out. I was subletting from a woman I met through a friend. And yes, I know he claims it violates the terms of the lease, but she says it doesn't. He was trying to force me to rent a place on my own. No way. Even if I did have the money. Too many problems with that building and he doesn't care."

"Why leave the desk and chair downstairs?"

"No room in the apartment and her storage locker was packed. She's practically a hoarder. You're not saying—he didn't."

"He did. He put the chair and a box of books and a few other things I'm not sure were yours out on the curb. That's where I found them, Sunday morning. It's kind of hilarious that you called an Uber to get the chair home—my friend and I had this big debate over doing that." I waved it away; it was funny, but it didn't matter. "Anyway, I took the chair and the box of books. That's how I discovered your full name and where you worked, from the inscription inside a book and a pay stub."

She pressed her hands together in front of her mouth.

"I'd found the chair and decided to take it when Boz showed up. After all the trouble you'd gone to getting it home, he was certain you wouldn't have gotten rid of it."

"Why was he looking for me?"

"It must have had something to do with Jason Warwick."

Behind her fixed gaze, I could almost see the swirl of emotions.

"Hey," I said, stretching a hand across the table. "Don't be too hard on yourself about the way you treated your grandmother. You had to protect your relationship with your mother, because you loved her and lived with her. You needed her. You were just a kid. But you grew up, and you grew out of it."

"I know, but . . ." Her voice trembled, then trailed off. "When I moved to Seattle, Gran would have happily let me live with her. But I needed to repair things first. If that makes sense. I've been coming down here on weekends, if I wasn't working. My mother doesn't know. I did call to tell her Gran's in the hospital. Not sure I can mend that breach."

"One problem at a time," I said. "At your building, after Boz left, I talked to one of your neighbors. Tall woman, red raincoat, says she chatted with you when you were doing laundry."

"Danae," Talia said. "Second-floor studio."

"She said you got ditched by a boyfriend in San Diego, who stuck you with high-priced rent you couldn't pay. And you sold some of the things he'd left to get the money to move up here."

"I'm not proud of that."

"You were carrying a box when you went into the hospital."

"Lemon scones. Gran loves them. I made them myself. They're not as good as the ones at the Fremont bakery, but they weren't bad. For a first try."

"I've had those scones. They are worth every calorie." I let out a deep breath and made a decision. "I think you need to talk to the police," I said at the same moment that she asked, "Why were you looking for me?"

"I don't know what Jason Warwick did," I said. "But I think—

and it's complicated, so please, trust me on this—I think he's the subject of a federal investigation. By the FBI."

"Oh, wow. Did he kill Boz?"

"Maybe. I don't know. Other people may be involved."

"I can't talk to the cops," she said. "My ex may have reported me. Besides, if I do, the real killer might come after me."

I couldn't say she was wrong. And I wasn't sure whether to tell her what I'd found in the chair. For now, she might be better off not knowing.

Red Beard brought our check and I paid, then we walked outside.

"Thanks for dinner, Pepper," Talia said. "How stupid was I, walking away from a job I liked? But I can't ask Claire to take me back now, not after ghosting her, let alone ask for my last paycheck."

"I worked HR for ages," I said. "She owes you and she knows it. She told me she mailed you your check a couple of days ago."

"That's great. I need to go get it," she said. "But not if they're watching me."

"What if I went with you?"

She hesitated, then agreed. We made a plan to meet at the bakery late the next morning, after her visit to Ruth, then we'd get her mail and a few things from her apartment. I'd take her the valise and her box of books.

"See you tomorrow. If you need anything, you have my number."

"You've already done a lot, Pepper. Thank you."

As I climbed into my car, I saw Talia go back inside the pub. Had she forgotten something?

Ah, no. She wanted the chance to chat with Red Beard, away from the watchful eyes of a woman old enough to be her mother.

"Good for you, girl," I said. Go after what you want.

DID I TRUST HER? I replayed our conversation on the drive home.

The real question was whether she trusted me enough to let me help her. Although I had not been ready to tell her about the cash in the cushion. Not that I was trying to keep it to myself. No. I did not doubt my own motives, or my sincerity in trying to return it to its rightful owner.

But I wasn't going to assume everyone else who knew about the money would feel the same way. Thirty-five grand is serious ka-ching.

Did it belong to the Warwicks? If it did, why stash it in the cushion? That would explain why Cynthia insisted on keeping the chair, despite its condition and her lack of interest in DIY.

And clearly, her husband had not known, or he'd never have given the chair to the household help.

'Twas a puzzle.

"YEOW," I SAID, swatting at my ear. After talking with Nate, I'd picked up Talia's fantasy novel and fallen asleep on the couch well after midnight. Right now, I wanted nothing more than another hour of sweet, dreamless sleep. And for whatever fly was buzzing me to go away.

I swatted again and brushed a warm coat. A fur coat.

Pooh. Or more precisely, pee.

Arf is patient in the mornings, but I knew not to press my luck. Three minutes in the bathroom. Feet in shoes. Raincoat on, hood up. Phone and keys in my pocket, leash in hand, off we went.

The skies were that mix of not-still-dark and not-yet-light that suggested the day could go either way. That was certainly how I felt about it.

We reached the end of the block and I tugged on the leash, ready to head home, but Arf wasn't having it. He never seems to mind spending most of the day in the shop—"must love dogs" was an informal job requirement, and the staff adored and spoiled him. So did customers. I tried to make up for his hours as a shop dog by letting him walk as much as he wanted.

At ten minutes to six in the morning, I was rethinking that.

We passed one of my favorite restaurants, dark but for the soft glow of a brass downlight on the host stand. If the FBI's investigation of Jason Warwick had brought them to Tim Forrester, a well-known player on the local restaurant scene, was it connected to Warwick's ownership of restaurant spaces? With his leasing arrangements or business partnerships? I knew very little about all that. Alex Howard, my onetime sort-of beau, had owned his flagship restaurant building, keeping a corporate office on the second floor and a fabulous apartment on the third. He'd leased space for his other restaurants. The couple who own Speziato own the whole block, including Aimee's vintage shop and the apartments above it, where she and Seetha live. As Grace had said, they were hands-off landlords, but I had seen them eating there regularly. Showed their good taste.

What did the FBI think Warwick was up to? Had Boz been involved?

Arf decided he'd gone halfway and we could go home. No point trying to get any more sleep. If I went to the shop early, I could finish a few projects before meeting Talia.

Back in the loft, I made a cup of coffee and sat at my dining table, one foot tucked beneath me. With its warm wood and clean lines, Ruth Cook's table and chairs would look right at home here. Her style was both modern and classic. Grown-up, unlike my weathered cedar table with its pink wrought iron chairs and flamingo-print cushions.

This was me. This was my style. A tansu chest in the bedroom and a pair of neon lips on the wall above it, an antique black-and-white quilt, a packing-crate coffee table, an old mint-green Dr Pepper cooler. Aimee says the things you love always go together because they are a reflection of yourself, and she is a professional decorator. She is also my friend. One who'd given me a lava lamp as a thank-you gift, so maybe her judgment was suspect.

At half past six in the morning, everybody's judgment is suspect. I picked up the steaming mug. But coffee helps.

Twenty-Four

Furniture historians say the iconic design of the wingback chair, with sides that curve outward above the armrest, originated to keep drafts away from the sitter's head in the era when homes were heated by fireplaces, when modern amenities like double-paned windows and weather stripping weren't even the stuff of dreams.

"I KNEW IT," SANDRA SAID AS WE WATCHED CAYENNE MAKE another dash for the bathroom. "Baby on board."

"She told me earlier this week," I said. "She didn't ask me to keep it quiet until she was ready, like with the MS diagnosis, but it's probably wise not to let on. Let her tell you."

Sandra drew a finger across her lips and mimed turning a key in a lock, but the glint in her eyes betrayed her. She was eager for grandchildren, now that the daughter she proudly called her one and only was married, but the new bride had also just started grad school and told Sandra to cool her jets.

"We can hold a double baby shower at my house," Kristen added. "For Cayenne and Hayden. When the time gets closer."

Our warehouse manager and his wife were expecting this summer. "I'll leave the party planning to you. But I do have the perfect gift in the works."

I did a last-minute scan of the shop, so warm and welcoming, then unlocked the door. Saturdays in the Market are always busy, especially in spring, when the first kiss of sunshine lures damp Seattleites from our cocoons.

A few minutes later, Vanessa and I were behind the counter, wrapping up the first sale of the day. The customer left and Vanessa beamed at me, a spark in her eyes that I had not seen all week.

"I did it, Pepper. I did what you said. I texted Logan and asked him to meet me after work last night. I told him I like him, but with school and work and getting to know Seattle, I'm not ready for a boyfriend."

"And?"

"And—it went okay. His face got red and he was super fidgety—but I kept it together. I knew what I wanted, and I remembered what you said about not backing down when it gets uncomfortable. After a couple of minutes, he said he understood, I had a lot going on, and maybe he'd been a little pushy." She gave me a probing look. "You didn't talk to him, did you?"

"Me? Nope. Not a word." I sent Tag a silent thank-you.

"Guys are kinda clueless sometimes, aren't they?"

"Oh, we're all clueless now and then."

"Not you, Pepper. You always know the right thing to say."

Ha. If only that were true.

Late morning, I kissed the dog goodbye and promised him a special treat later. I had a stop to make on the way to my rendezvous with Talia.

I parked across Eastlake from Speziato and crossed the street, glancing at Aimee's shop, Rainy Day Vintage. Earlier in the week, Cayenne had mentioned wanting to look for something there, but we'd run into Tariq and never made it. What had she hoped to find?

Ohhh, I bet I knew. Aimee had dedicated a corner of the shop to vintage children's things—clothing, decor, baby-safe toys, and furniture. And crib quilts. I stopped in once when she was unpacking a collection of quilts and throws and crocheted baby caps she'd bought from a woman cleaning out her late mother's house. Whatever drives people to hold on to things like that, to make or acquire far more than they'll ever use long after they'll use them, I don't know. But I find it fascinating. Before the baby shower, I'd pick up gift certificates for both my expectant employees.

Meanwhile, I was on a mission. Edgar was sitting at his

favorite two-top, a tablet propped up in front of him. The day's specials, reservations, staff list? The restaurant business was built on moving pieces.

I rapped on the door. He glanced over, the preoccupation on his broad face quickly disappearing.

"Pepper! What brings you to this arm of the woods?" He paused to think about the right word. "No. Lakes have arms. Woods have necks. Cappuccino?"

For half a second, I mistook his offer of espresso for the pseudo-Italian "capiche?" meaning "understand?"

"That would be great."

He busied himself behind the bar and I surveyed the room, picturing happy student diners savoring food they'd created, spiced to perfection. Taking home recipes, memories, and a new level of kitchen confidence.

I remembered Vanessa's compliment and how well she'd solved her problem with Logan. My young employee, who my ex claimed looked up to me, was turning out to be full of her own brand of inspiration. I took a hint from her. Be subtle. Ease into the tough conversations.

"Cayenne is super excited about our spice dinner collaboration," I said when we were seated with our coffee. "She's got ideas from here to Vancouver and a spreadsheet to track it all. She sent you a few menu suggestions, based on our conversation. When we work that out and you tell us your cost, we can add in our costs and decide what to charge."

Edgar opened a screen on his tablet and showed me the list he and Grace had put together, incorporating several of Cayenne's recommendations. We chose seven items to price—two appetizers, three main courses, and two desserts. The final menu would depend on the figures. And the flavors.

"This will be great," I said when we'd finished. "I heard you've been eyeing new kitchen equipment. I hope everything's working okay. Replacing commercial equipment sounds like a major pain in the anise, not to mention the wallet."

"The walk-in freezer has cold spots and not-so-cold spots. Repairman say nothing more he can do. Owner say buy new." His brow darkened. "But how did you know?"

I told him about my conversation with Evie LeMieux and her

belief that Edgar had cost Boz a job with the restaurant supply company. "Why didn't you tell me you'd seen Boz?"

"I tell no one. You I trust, but you talk to those cops. If I keep him from getting a job—and I did not—that would be one more reason to suspect me of killing him. No." Edgar punched the air with one finger. "No. I keep quiet. I said nothing about his theft from me of my intelligent property. I see him on my way out, but the past is behind me."

So why hadn't Boz gotten the job? As Janine had said in our conversation in the deli, there could have been a million reasons. But Evie was convinced it was tied to the restaurant he'd run for Tim Forrester in the building owned by Jason Warwick. The spice theft and the temper tantrum that had led the staff to quit en masse? Reason aplenty.

"There is something not right about that place," Edgar continued.

"The supply company?"

"You call, say what you need. They say they have it. You go to see, but no. They have this thing and this other thing—" His right hand went one way, his left the opposite. "And not what you want. They can get it, they say, for more money, but when you need, you need now. I have heard others say the same. I go to a different company, one that deals in no nonsense. Boz, he was better off not working there."

"Sounds like it."

"I am sorry he is dead," Edgar said. "But I did not kill him. I am emotional, I am demanding, but I am not a—well, you are polite. I don't want to say the word."

I was flattered to be considered polite company.

He went on. "Your friends the detectives, they ask me where I was Tuesday morning, and they ask Gracie, too. They think she was asleep with Ana, so she cannot be sure I did not leave. But did they ask her? No. They make a leap." He made a bouncing motion with his hand.

"What would she have said?"

"The truth. She did not sleep. She sat up, watching, worried. If I left, she would have heard, and she would never lie. Besides, we have the one car only. Even if I had known Boz would be on the canal that morning, and how could I have known? I could not drive. She pick me up Sunday and I leave my keys in the restaurant by mistake."

"You could have taken hers."

"No, never. I never touch my wife's purse. That is hers. Sacred."

"Hey, boss." A voice broke in. Tariq, the ever-present earbuds around his neck, the aquamarine in his earlobe catching the light. "Hey, Pepper."

I stood for a quick hug. "Edgar was telling me he had a bad feeling when you two went to the restaurant supply business. Where you saw Boz."

"Yeah. Sorry I didn't tell you about that. I figured—" He blew out a breath. "I knew the cops would zero in on Edgar, and I figured it was better if we hadn't seen the guy. Shoulda known it would come out. But nothing happened. We said hey and he said hey and that was it."

"You didn't tell anyone at the supply house about your run-ins with Boz?"

"No. Why would we?" He narrowed his eyes, shaking his head. "To blackball him? Nah. He got his reputation as trouble all on his own, without any help from us."

Made sense. "Thanks, guys. Edgar, you'll send me the prices for the menu items? Then you and Cayenne can narrow it down and we'll finalize the plan."

"Si." Edgar stood. "Pepper, you saw Evie? She is okay?"

"She's okay. Upset about Boz, of course. Sounds like it was a volatile relationship, but this was a rotten way for it to end. Grace was right about her new job, in the grocery deli. I know her boss. She's in good hands."

"Good, good."

Outside, I checked my phone. Nothing from the shop, but a text from Talia.

So sorry. Gran had a setback this morning and I don't want to leave her. Can we reschedule?

Did I believe her? No reason not to.

Plenty of reason, my less kind self said.

Sure, my thumbs wrote. *Same time tomorrow? I hope she's okay.*

Yes, thanks! came the almost-instant answer. *She's breathing easier and so am I.*

Texting. Love it or hate it, it has its moments. Since I had unexpected extra time, I texted Marco Dubois to ask if he could see me and go over my quote for the herbs and spices he'd requested. His reply was fast: *Great!*

I merged into traffic, intending to circle around and head back downtown. In the next block was the yoga studio. I hadn't been in ages. A sign out front read NOW OFFERING PILATES. I was probably the only woman over forty who'd never been to a Pilates class.

At the bistro in Belltown, the chef let me in and offered cappuccino.

"I'm caffeinated enough, thanks. Sparkling water?"

It came with a hefty dose of fruit salad—an orange slice on the rim and a bamboo spear holding a chunk of pineapple sandwiched between two cherries. I bit one off and let the flavor explode in my mouth.

"I talked to Tara, the herb farmer you told me about. Everything sounds great," he said. "I'm considering her for my other fresh herbs, too. Might be risky to depend on a supplier on an island—she can't be more reliable than the ferry system, and we all know what trouble it's had."

Between staffing shortages, maintenance issues, and a spike in groundings and other accidents, the system that links Seattle to the islands dotting Puget Sound had been strained.

"If there's a way, Tara will find it. About our prices, we buy as fresh as we can, and that means we're subject to market fluctuations."

"You and everyone else. Makes it hard to hold the bottom line. Plus staffing, equipment. It's enough to drive a man to drink." He raised his own glass of water and fruit. "But not quite this early."

We made a mock toast.

"I wanted to ask you about equipment," I said. "The other day, you told me Tim outfitted the kitchen in Madrona with all-new equipment. One piece came here and the rest went back to the supplier."

"Right. A walk-in cooler. We—Tim—owned it, but you can't just toss those things in the back of your pickup and move them. Everything is specialized and proprietary. Electronic. Motherboards and control switches and whatever."

"Is that what the service tech was working on when I was here?

You two were complaining about the bill before he was out the door."

"I don't know if it's actually a scam," Dubois said, "but it feels like one. The equipment is exclusive to them. You can't repair anything yourself, even if you knew how. You can't buy the tools or parts, and the repair manuals are top secret. A fifty-cent screw, they charge thirty-five bucks. Then they tack on a trip charge and a mileage fee, and their hourly rate would make a lawyer blush. If I understood right, the building owner had signed the contract, and it was binding. Tim couldn't get out of the deal."

What had Tim done to try to end the arrangement? I wondered.

"Part of the reason we know it's fishy," Dubois continued, "is the new place in Portland. The equipment dealer there is completely legit. None of these overcharges or dirty tricks. Tim just got back from a visit, and he's raving about the service and how good and fair and affordable they are."

"When did he get back?"

"They did a soft opening Monday night and a second one Tuesday. He drove home Wednesday morning, in time for his meeting. Well, the cops first, from SPD. Then the meeting."

Boz died Tuesday morning. Tim Forrester had been out of town.

But the building owner, Jason Warwick?

Everything I heard about the man made him sound more and more like a killer.

Twenty-Five

*Never underestimate the value of having friends
who cook well.*

"HAVE YOU EVER CONSIDERED COOKING PROFESSIONALLY?"
I twirled my wineglass. My plate, once an artful display of coquilles
Saint-Jacques topped with tarragon, now looked so clean you'd be
forgiven for thinking Arf had licked it. Although I don't know if
he eats scallops.

Who am I kidding? He's a dog. He'll eat anything.

"Perish the thought," Other Nate said. His husband, Glenn, a
city councilman I'd first met when I bought my loft, simply smiled.
Glenn and I had both been single then and often commiserated
over dinner and good wine. I have decent taste in wine, largely
due to Vinny. But Glenn has exquisite taste and the knowledge and
budget to go with it.

Their remodel had combined their loft, formerly a mirror
image of mine, and the one below. They'd kept the main
entrance on the top floor, where the three of us sat at a glass
table with a curved wooden base beneath a trio of mismatched
bubble pendant lights, gazing out at Elliott Bay. Despite all
the changes, their sense of style remained intact. Mid-century
modern with a touch of glam. Like the Jetsons ate breakfast at
Tiffany's.

Happily, they'd recreated Arf's corner, with a comfy new bed and a shiny new set of bowls. He often spends a few hours or a weekend with them if I'm out.

"Let's have dessert downstairs," Glenn said. "Though we've probably missed the first pitch."

The lower level includes their bedroom, Glenn's office, and an entertainment space to envy. Glenn aimed a remote at the wall and panels opened to reveal a giant TV screen. The picture was so sharp that we might almost have been in the park. Except that the Mariners were on the road and the seats were much too comfortable. What ballpark can compete with an Eames lounger?

The guys' last-minute invitation had saved me from an evening of ruminating. We cheered our team, groaned at a missed double play, opened a second bottle, and scraped up every last bite of Nate's divine crème brûlée. Arf had a new bone Edgar had sent with me. It was Saturday night, I didn't have far to go to get home, and I didn't have to get up early for work.

But the questions surrounding Boz's death and everything I'd heard today rattled in my brain. Fortunately, despite their devotion to the game, the guys never mind conversing as we watch.

"When you redid the kitchen, you bought commercial appliances, right?"

"Yep. Best way to get what we wanted," Nate said. "More powerful and more reliable."

"Did you hear any scuttle about the business, like dealers salvaging appliances from commercial kitchens and selling them as new, or insisting on exclusive service contracts, then overcharging?" Nate is a former journalist working on his first novel. He loves scuttle.

"Not that specific issue, but I wouldn't be surprised," he said. "That's one reason we used a professional kitchen designer. All kinds of scams out there."

"I know nothing." Glenn raised his hands. "Yes, I chair council's public safety committee, and people always think I've got the inside scoop on every crime, but we focus on policy and oversight. Structural stuff, not the day-to-day police work. Besides, the scammers' ability to think up new tricks far exceeds my ability to keep track of them."

"Hmm. Okay, thanks."

Despite the great food, wine, and friends, I couldn't quite

relax. I was still struggling to make the connections that would make the whole Boz-Talia-Warwick thing make sense.

Then it was the bottom of the ninth, the Mariners leading by two.

We held our breaths as the Ms' ace reliever wound up for a three-two count, two out, runners at the corners. The players' coiled energy was almost palpable.

Strike! The inning and the game were over, and we cheered for our team.

But my brain was working extra innings.

I WOKE SUNDAY MORNING with a dry mouth and a teeny little headache. A wine and sugar headache.

After a quick walk, Arf and I settled in the living room, he on his bed with his bone and me on the couch with black coffee and the newspaper, my Nate's favorite jazz playlist on the air. Most Sundays, unless Nate is home, Laurel and I meet for brunch and a long walk. Our plans are flexible, though, so when she'd said she wanted to meet up with an old college friend in town for the weekend, I didn't mind. It also freed me to swing by the house and check on the appliances, as my mother had requested, before going to Fremont.

I'd packed up Talia's books and her grandfather's valise yesterday and had left them in the car. Now I sliced a banana into a bowl of yogurt and carried it to my dining table.

It was perfect for me, the way Glenn and Other Nate's two-level showcase was perfect for them. And Ruth Cook's cherry dining set would be perfect for someone else. Aimee was right: my things go together because I love them. And if anyone thinks they don't, then they don't know me very well, do they?

My whole life is like that: Mix and match. Salt and pepper. Spice and spying.

Okay, but what about the appliances? Not mine, or the new French-door fridge my mother had ordered. What Edgar and Marco Dubois had said, along with Other Nate's comment about corruption in the business. I put down my spoon and picked up my phone. I didn't know my mother's designer well enough to ask, but Aimee might have heard a few things.

Or not. She answered my text from her own kitchen table.

Sorry. I'm clueless about the commercial appliance business. I can ask???

Thanks. No need.

A little while later, I dropped Arf off with the guys—they had an outing planned that would involve plenty of fresh air and opportunities for him to run. Then it was up to Montlake.

In my parents' garage—a real garage, not a Model A version—I carefully cut open the front of the refrigerator-shaped box. It held a refrigerator, all right, but was this the one my mother had ordered? The finish was darker than I'd expected. Texting to the rescue. I snapped a pic.

Is this right? I thought you said stainless steel.

Then I waited, but not long.

Oh, it's beautiful! Black stainless. So sleek with the black lower cabinets and white uppers. Thank you, darling!

As if I'd had anything to do with it.

I checked the other boxes, opening a corner to confirm the finish. The project was coming along nicely. I'd been happy to help, but I'd be happier when it was done. When my parents were here to see to the last-minute details and this house was once again our home base. Our anchor.

When the Nate-shaped space in my life would be full again. A fisherman's schedule was part of the deal, and most of the time, I didn't mind. His absence gave me plenty of room to obsess about my own work and help my friends. Like now.

But his presence brought such joy.

Love the life you have, Pepper. Don't go wishing things you can't change were different.

I locked up and got in the car. Luck and the bridge gods were on my side, and in minutes, I was zipping toward Fremont.

Until all of a sudden I wasn't. I'd forgotten about the Sunday Market.

An SUV pulled away from the curb, and I swooped in, despite the long walk I'd have to the bakery and apartment building. Talia's things could stay in the car for now. Should I text her a traffic reminder? No. She lived here. She knew about the Sunday crowds. I was the scatterbrain. Besides, I didn't want to tempt her to check her phone while driving, especially in that awkward rig of her grandmother's.

I was teetering on the edge of what Laurel calls Universal Mother. Best to stop myself before I went over.

Fremont's second motto, in addition to being the Center of the Universe, is "where everybody's creative," and that was on full display. Traffic was blocked on the street above the canal, which was lined with booths offering food, art, and crafts of all kinds. A trio of men in helmets, body paint, and little else raced past me on Rollerblades. At the corner, a pair of young teenagers played old-time fiddle. I stopped to listen and dropped a couple of singles in the open violin case.

Then I made my way toward the appointed meeting spot, outside the bakery. As I neared the corner, my phone buzzed. Pooh. Was Talia canceling again?

Sunday Market! she'd written. *How could I forget? Give me twenty minutes!*

No worries. That gave me time for another dose of caffeine.

Inside, Blue Hair greeted me like we were old friends—fair enough, considering that this was my third visit in a week. I ordered a cappuccino and sat in the window, an eye out.

Stelle delivered my drink. "I'm glad to see you," she said. "I wanted to thank you for your kindness the other day."

"Stumbling across tragedy can be rough," I said. "How are you doing?"

She gripped the back of the empty chair next to me. "The first couple of nights, I couldn't sleep. I kept picturing him floating in the water, even though the bicyclist had already laid him on the grass by the time I got there. I couldn't even tell if it was a man or a woman. But in my dream, I turned him over and it wasn't him. It was my daughter, or my partner."

"I am so sorry." I knew the situation, and the nightmares, too well. But Tag had always said water deaths were especially terrible.

"So I've been reading mysteries. It's weird. There's a murder, but it's not really about that. I read a few chapters and I can sleep without nightmares. I love the women in them. They take charge."

"Right? They face their fears and solve their problems. I love that, too. I run the Spice Shop in the Market, and we sell some foodie fiction, including mysteries. Cozies, they're called. Big hit with the customers."

"My favorites are the ones set in bakeries. As if I don't get enough sugar and spice all day."

We compared notes—she loved V. M. Burns and Ellie Alex-ander, and I thought she would enjoy the Secret, Book, and Scone Society series by Ellery Adams.

"Since you like the take-charge aspect," I said, "you might try Misha Popp's Pies Before Guys series. Classic cozy main character, but with a twist. I don't dare say any more. And a customer was telling me about one set in an old house in New England, at a baking contest, but I can't remember the name."

"*The Golden Spoon*," Stelle said. "I loved it. Sweet revenge."

Then my phone buzzed. Talia. *Almost there. Two minutes!*

"Gotta go," I told Stelle. "Be back later. I promise."

Talia came rushing up the street just as I reached the corner.

"I can't believe Phan put my stuff out for the trash," she said on our way up the block. "The scumbag."

"Anything else going on? Was he trying to pressure you in some way?"

She stopped. "You mean like sex?"

That was exactly what I meant.

"No," she said. "I never got that feeling."

At the building, the FOR RENT sign was gone. Talia unlocked the front door and we went inside.

"The apartment first," she said. "I need to grab some clothes and other things."

Vernon Phan hadn't been far off when he called the legal tenant a borderline hoarder. Tall bookcases, all double shelved, made the compact living room look even smaller. Books and magazines were stacked on and beneath the glass-topped coffee table, twin to one in the vacant apartment I'd seen a few days ago. Framed art covered the few patches of open wall. An elliptical trainer took up one corner, the chair that might have fit there instead blocking the slider that opened onto the tiny deck. Naturally, it was too crammed with chairs, a table, and a grill for anyone to sit outside.

"Pepper, can you water the plants while I pack?" Talia handed me a small metal watering can. I filled it in the kitchen, as crowded as the rest of the place. Made sense that the tenant didn't want the commitment of a bigger space if she traveled a lot for work, but she needed it. The occasional short-term sublet would help with the rent. And more room would make it easier to attract tenants. No way could Talia have fit the wingback and desk in this overstuffed space.

"Got what I need for now." Talia emerged from the bathroom, one bulging canvas tote in hand and another slung over her shoulder. "Let's go downstairs and see if Phan left any of my stuff."

I set the watering can in the sink where it had been, took a bag from Talia, and followed her down the stairs. At the bottom was the laundry room, if you can call a space without a door a room. The lights were on, and a wicker basket sat on top of a dryer.

"The storage lockers are this way." She unlocked a steel door and flicked a light switch. A shady place, the walls and floor dark-gray concrete. The lockers were about the size of a standard refrigerator, framed in four-by-fours, the walls chicken wire. The few I could see were packed with boxes and the odd lamp or pair of crutches.

"It's gone," Talia said, gesturing to the corner behind the door. Aside from a few flattened cardboard boxes propped against the wall, the space was empty. "It's all gone."

"That's where you put the chair?"

"And my books. My grandfather's suitcase and the desk my grandmother made when I was a kid. She kept it all these years. I thought for sure I could make room for it in the apartment, or I never would have taken it from her house. I never imagined . . ."

I didn't have to imagine. I knew where her treasures were and how they'd gotten there.

"At first, Phan said it would be okay," she said. "But then he started pressuring me about the lease."

"He after you to rent the apartment across the hall from yours?" I asked. "He showed it to me Sunday."

"No. That vacancy's new. There was a two-bedroom open on the second floor, and I forget what else. I never would have passed the credit check. Why waste money applying, not to mention the fees he tacks on? When I said no, he made a couple of comments about my stuff being in the way, but he never said he would get rid of it." She sniffed back tears, holding the back of her hand to her face, then walked out. I followed.

In the laundry room, a door slammed shut with a tinny clang. A washer or dryer, by the sound of it. A woman emerged, the wicker basket I'd seen earlier in her arms. The neighbor I'd met last Sunday at the bus stop. Danae, Talia had called her.

"Talia!" The woman glanced between us, trying to place me, frustration on her flushed face. "You're back. Now both dryers are on the fritz. Again. And I have a load full of wet towels. Again." She set her basket on the floor.

"Does this happen often?" I asked.

"Often enough," Talia said.

"The laundry's not the half of it," Danae said. "Deliveries go missing. Repairs take forever. When anyone moves out, Phan finds the tiniest excuse not to refund the damage deposit. Like I said, I'd move if I could, but I'd lose my deposit, get a ding on my record, and have to scrounge to find a new place."

"There are legal remedies, you know," I said.

"We can't sue," Danae said. "It's in the lease. And yeah, you can invoke regulations and the city Renter's Handbook and all that, but when you do, it's like things get worse. The guy across the hall from me broke his lease and left. Told me he hated to forfeit his deposit, but he couldn't put up with it anymore."

"Bet Phan had a new tenant the next day," Talia said. "And jacked the rent."

"You know it. Housing market's so tight, anything with four walls and a toilet goes in about ten minutes."

Weird. I hadn't liked Vernon Phan or his attitude toward Talia and her things, but now I wondered what else he was up to.

"Wherever you've been," Danae said, "stay there. Now I'll have to drive this stuff up to the Laundromat and plug quarters all afternoon." She picked up her basket and led the way up the stairs.

"Good luck," I called.

"Thanks. I need it."

We trudged up, Danae continuing to an upper floor. In the entry, Talia unlocked the mailbox. Drew out a stack of mail and quickly flipped through it. Stopped when she got to a standard white envelope.

"Claire kept her word." She slit it open with a finger and peeked inside, then stuffed the envelope into her quilted baguette bag and reached inside the box a second time. Twisted and wriggled. No luck. She frowned and dipped her shoulder to let the tote slide to the floor, then tried with two hands. Bent the sides of a manila envelope toward each other to slide it out.

"What's this?" she asked. "Can you read that?"

The envelope was addressed to Talia, no last name. The hand-written return address was hard to decipher, but I squinted and made it out.

W. A. Bosworth.

Boz.

Twenty-Six

*Dogs know who to trust.
Why is it so hard for humans?*

"WHAT THE—" TALIA SAID. SHE UNDID THE METAL CLASP ON the back of the envelope and unsealed the flap. She slid out a short stack of photocopies and photographs, topped with a handwritten note.

> *Talia,*
> *So sorry to involve you in this. I have to get this in the hands of someone who will do something about it. Evie will not know what to do, but I know I can trust you.*

"How can he know that?" Talia asked. "We spent less than an hour together."

"You were a good listener. He needed someone who wasn't going to be pushed around by—by whoever is doing whatever this is." Boz had known knew how pliable Evie was—he'd manipulated her himself.

We flipped through the paperwork, Talia scanning each page and handing it to me. Copies of invoices, many of them from the restaurant supply company where Boz had run into Edgar

and Tariq, addressed to JAWCAW Holdings. Jason and Cynthia
Warwick. Photos of the kitchen and dining room at his Madrona
restaurant during construction, while operating, and after.

I flipped back to the invoices, then to the photographs. The
documents would need expert help to interpret, but I had a good
idea they illustrated the deception and swindle Edgar and Tim
Forrester had described.

What if Boz hadn't gone to the supply company to apply for
a job, even if that's what he'd led Evie to believe, but to gather
evidence of overcharging, fraud, and other wrongdoing?

I put the papers back in order, Boz's note on top.

I've hurt people, he'd written, *and I need to make amends.
This is one way. I will make it up to you, I promise.*

But he hadn't gotten the chance.

I skimmed the rest of his account. When he saw Warwick that
day on Queen Anne, he'd been sure the man realized he was on to
him.

You never know what's going on behind the scenes of what
seem like solid businesses. Warwick owned commercial property and lived in fine style, or so it appeared. So why was he out
of money? If he was—as Tim Forrester had said, having plenty
doesn't stop some people from wanting more.

"I know the detectives investigating his death," I said. "We
have to give them these documents."

"Well, if it isn't the missing Ms. Cook. I was about to think
you'd abandoned your apartment," a man said from behind us.
Vernon Phan. "The apartment you have no right to occupy."

"And you have no right to give away my things," Talia retorted.

"People leave stuff where it's not supposed to be. That doesn't
make it my responsibility. You're turning out to be quite the trou-
blemaker, Ms. Cook. People, police, coming for you. I could evict
you for half a dozen reasons."

"Do you really want to do that?" I stepped into view. Phan
hadn't seen me, standing next to the artificial ficus. I wondered
which tenant had left it behind. "Just so you can make a few bucks
selling what they leave behind at the Vintage Mall?"

Talia gasped.

"I did no such thing," Phan said.

"You did," I said. "I bought her grandfather's suitcase there.

That's what gave me the clue I needed to find her. Do you want the tenants to report how you manufacture reasons to force them to leave? To break their leases, forfeiting deposits? Deposits I'm guessing you keep, hiding from the owners the real reason this building has such high turnover. Every building you manage, I suspect. It could get ugly."

"You." He spat out the word, then pointed to the door. "Off the premises. You're trespassing."

"She's with me," Talia said. "I invited her into the building, and you can't make us leave."

He fixed her with a long glare, then stalked away.

"Let's get out of here." I slid Boz's papers into the manila envelope and grabbed the bulging tote. Talia scooped the other bag into her arms and out we went. I had to tell her about the money in the chair cushion. She could easily afford a place of her own, even if she didn't want to live with her grandmother. Though she might balk at giving Phan the satisfaction of driving her off.

By unspoken agreement, we carried our burdens and our questions to the bakery. The moment I opened the door and Talia walked in, Stelle shrieked with delight and surged toward us. They threw their arms around each other. Behind the counter, Blue Hair grinned.

"Lemon scone sales haven't been the same without you," he said.

"My gran was so desperate for them, I tried baking my own. They turned out okay, but nothing like yours."

Oh, duh. That's why she'd been buying up the scones on Fridays, before her weekend visits to Ruth. And though we didn't order scones to go with our afternoon coffee, I knew without a doubt that a plate of them would show up.

Blue Hair cleaned a corner table for us, and we spread out the papers. When we went over them again, reading between the lines of Boz's notes, it was clear that he'd uncovered a scam and that Jason Warwick was part of it. Tim Forrester, I was convinced, was another victim.

Where had all the money gone?

I pulled out my phone and texted Detective Tracy.

I found Talia, along with evidence that might be related to Boz's death. We're at the bakery in Fremont.

It was Sunday. He was a family man. But he was also a Major

Crimes detective, and if anything is a major crime, it's a body in the canal not of its own accord.

On my way, came the answer.

"Funny," Talia said, sipping her macchiato, "how someone you meet once can change your life in ways you never could have imagined."

As Stelle had said of her. Talia meant Boz, I was sure, but it was equally true of Jason Warwick. "Listen, I have to tell you something." I put out my hand, but she was on a roll and sped right past me.

"All this"—she pointed at the papers—"is this why that man was trying to find me? Because Boz got caught up in some scam— scheme—whatever it is, and led them to me? I know he says he was sorry for involving me, but you ever notice when somebody says they're sorry for something they haven't done yet, they go ahead and do it anyway?"

What had Boz said to me in the Market? That there was stuff going on, and it might cause trouble for her. How did that mesh with his note, which he must have sent before rushing to Talia's apartment on Sunday? He might have regretted making her a witness and asking her to solve a problem that had nothing to do with her. But I was sure he hadn't meant to put a target on her back.

"You've got a point. I wondered at first if he'd known about the scam all along and decided this was his chance for revenge disguised as justice. But the more I learn, the more convinced I am that he wasn't involved. He discovered it by accident, like he told you in the car, and thought he could make things right by exposing it to the right people. But—"

"Ohmygod. They killed him? Is that why they're after me?" She sat bolt upright, ready to take flight.

"Hold on," I said. "We need to figure out who and work out the timeline." Clearly it hadn't been Jason Warwick following her—she'd have recognized him.

"Is this the man?" I held up my phone, showing her a photo of Tim Forrester standing in the doorway of the French bistro after seeing his visitors out.

"That one," she said, pointing. Not Forrester or someone from the restaurant supply company. Someone else entirely.

"Lemon cream scones," Stelle said as she set a plate on the table. "On the house. Oh. That's the man who was asking about you."

They were both pointing to the same person. The FBI agent in the blue suit. Agent Greer's anonymous partner.

Well. That put a different spin on things.

As it had been last Sunday, the bakery buzzed with folks grateful to sit and relax after the whirlwind along the canal. I won't say a lone man stood out, but when Detective Michael Tracy arrived—well, he stood out. Even without his trusty camel hair sport coat and a visible badge, he screamed "cop."

And a cop was exactly what we needed at the moment.

"Coffee, black," Tracy told Blue Hair, then spoke to Talia. "Ms. Cook, I presume. Good to see you are alive and well."

A flush crawled up her cheeks.

"She's been staying at her grandmother's place," I said. "I told Detective Spencer I had an idea that's where she was."

"Yes. Our colleagues in Burien confirmed it with a drive-by."

So they had believed me. They just hadn't bothered to tell me.

I rested my hands on the paperwork spread out on the table. "Here's what we found. Boz seems to have stumbled into a conspiracy involving commercial restaurant appliances. We think Jason Warwick was part of it. Boz's restaurant was in a building Warwick owns, and after his boss, Tim Forrester, fired him, he went back to get his stuff."

Talia picked up the story. "I had a job cleaning houses, and we were at the Warwicks'. Jason, I guess his name is, was messing around in his garage and put out an old chair I liked—"

"Ah, the infamous wingback," Tracy mused.

"How do you know about that?" Talia asked, but she didn't wait for an answer. "I called an Uber to help me get it home, and that's when Boz showed up. Crazy that he knew Jason, but he did, and in the car on the way to my apartment, he told me that he heard Jason and Cynthia, his wife, arguing over what Jason had done. In the restaurant he used to run. Boz got the impression that Jason wanted to pull the plug on the scheme. Cynthia was upset that he'd ever gotten involved at all, but if he admitted it now, they'd be ruined. He would go to jail, and maybe she would, too."

"Prison," Tracy said, automatically correcting her.

"So," I said, "after the Warwicks left the restaurant, Boz stuck around and documented what he'd heard. He made copies of invoices that show billings for new appliances, but the serial numbers show the same pieces being sold over and over. He printed out pictures of some of the equipment. I'm sure the originals are on his phone, along with pictures from other kitchens. You still haven't found his phone, have you? Can you get a warrant and check his cloud?"

"Did you know," Tracy said, "that if your cloud is full, none of your data backs up?"

They were half a step ahead of me. "How much of this do you already know?"

"Not much. I know that's a thing you cook on—" He pointed to a photo of a giant stove.

"That," Blue Hair said as he delivered Tracy's coffee and a plate with a scone of his own, "is an eight-burner, gas-fired professional kitchen range. Top-of-the-line and a total pain. It's like they're designed to break. What?" he said, noticing all of us staring at him. "I used to run a full-service restaurant. Baking is a lot more fun."

"Thanks," I said. He left our table, but he didn't go far. We'd piqued his curiosity.

"But what does it have to do with Boz's death?" Talia asked. "Hard to imagine killing someone over freezers and stoves."

"Sadly, not hard at all," Tracy said. He reached into an inner pocket of his blue fleece jacket and brought out a small notebook and pen. No cheap department-issue Bic for him. He wrote with a refillable fountain pen and, as I had learned, lent it to a witness in need begrudgingly and never took his eyes off it.

"So," I said. "Is that why the FBI is involved? Some kind of interstate commerce? I saw Meg Greer and her partner coming out of Forrester's new place."

"Of course you did," Tracy said.

"His chef needed spice. Greer's partner even came here, trying to track down Talia." At that, Tracy grunted. "Though how they knew about her, I can't imagine. Unless they were following Boz."

"Mighta been," Tracy said. "But it's not my case. And you know how closemouthed Meg Greer can be."

In other words, I'd guessed right.

"Wait," Talia said. "Are you saying the FBI is after Jason Warwick? And they think I know something?"

"Well, you do, don't you?" Tracy asked. "And now you know even more."

"Did Jason honestly want to confess, or was he feeling the heat?" I asked. "Did he change his mind when he found out what Boz knew? He was looking for him. Even tried browbeating Evie LeMieux into telling him where Boz was."

"So he found him, knocked him unconscious, and shoved him in the canal to drown?" Tracy bit off the tip of his scone and spoke with his mouth full. "It's as good a guess as any."

Twenty-Seven

Nearly fifty women-led farms sell at Pike Place Market, offering fresh flowers, herbs, fruit and vegetables, jams and jellies, and more.

I WAS READY TO GET THE HECK OUT OF FREMONT, TO GET Talia to safety and get back to my own dull, quiet life where appliances occasionally caused problems but were never a cause for murder.

But Tracy had his own agenda.

"Did you know, Ms. Cook, when you called the Uber, that you were using your ex-boyfriend's account without his permission? That's part of why we had trouble finding you. We knew Mr. Bosworth made a pickup near the Warwicks' and where he went, but we didn't know who his passenger was. You cost us a lot of phone calls and door knocking."

Ahh. That's what Phan meant when he accused Talia of bringing the police to the door. He'd had good reason to worry.

"I'm going to pay him back, I swear. I have money now." She patted the purse sitting on the table, where she'd deposited her paycheck.

Tracy shot me a meaningful glance.

"There's something I need to tell you," I said. "About the chair."

"Keep it." Talia gestured with both hands, as if pushing the troublesome wingback away. "I never want to see it again. Not after all this."

"No," I said. "There's something else." I told her how my friends and I had detected a lump in the cushion, torn into it, and found the cash.

"Thirty-five thousand dollars?" She paused between each word, as if not sure she'd heard right.

"You and Boz stashed the chair in the basement storage room," I said. "You weren't sitting on it, so you didn't notice the lumpy cushion."

"Thirty-five thousand dollars?" she repeated.

I looked at Tracy, then at the papers Boz had sent Talia. "This changes the found-property claim, doesn't it? That money could belong to anybody Warwick and his pals scammed."

"No," Talia said. "Jason didn't know the money was in the chair. He couldn't have, or he wouldn't have been so irritated that his wife insisted on keeping it. And he wouldn't have given it to me."

"True enough," Tracy said. He drained his coffee and stood. "Gotta call my pals in Burien. And the FBI. They've got their sights on my killer, and I want first crack."

In my younger days, I'd regularly closed down bars. Now, in my mature days, I close down coffee shops. While we'd been focused on untangling the webs of theft and deception, the place had all but emptied out.

"I've got to get to the hospital." Talia gathered up her totes and the bag of scones Blue Hair had given her. I was relieved to know Tracy would arrange for drive-by patrols of Ruth Cook's house. "Boz thought he could trust me to solve all this. But I didn't. I couldn't. I'm not the person he thought I was."

"You can be," I said.

Too late, I remembered her things stashed in the Saab. No problem. I was certain we would meet again.

GLENN TEXTED A PHOTO of my dog, his fur wet, his feet crusted with sand, a giant driftwood stick in his mouth. So much for his recent grooming. Obviously they were all having a blast at the beach.

We'll get him home by dinnertime.

His, theirs, or mine, he didn't say. But that meant I had time to chase a stick of my own.

At the foot of the stairs inside the Vintage Mall, the traffic light beckoned. I inspected the power cord. Not that I'm any kind of expert, but I'd learned a few things a while back about frayed cords and shorts in wires. And about making sure your fire insurance is paid up. No visible damage. It even had a roller switch you could operate with your thumb. Red, yellow, green, off.

I checked the price tag. No need for the money in the chair cushion, not if I truly wanted it. I unplugged it carefully. Bulky but not heavy. Where would I put it? I'd decide later.

"Anything I can—oh, it's you." Chopstick Woman, once again dressed formally, once again with her hair piled high and held with utensils. Convenient if you got hungry.

"I owe you an apology," she continued. "When you were here last weekend, I was upset. It had nothing to do with you, but I was rude and snapped, and I'm sorry."

"Thanks. I appreciate that."

"There was a person I was interested in. Romantically."

She paused. I waited.

"Too interested, apparently," she said. "I got pushy. When you came in, I'd just discovered she'd started blocking my texts."

"Ouch," I said.

"But there was no excuse for taking it out on you." She sniffed and wiped a tear off her cheek. "That traffic light is one of my finds. Let me mark it down 10 percent. No, let's do fifteen."

"Sold," I said and hoisted the light onto the counter. "After I talked with you, the shop owner showed me a small cherry desk, and I bought a little brown leather suitcase. I wonder if you can tell me who brought them in. Same person, I think." I held out a photo of the valise and the price tag, with some kind of numerical code.

"Oh, sure. We can check." She plucked an electronic tablet off a stand on the counter. "Show me the desk."

I led the way, fingers crossed that it hadn't sold.

But there it was, right where I'd last seen it. And as lovely as I remembered.

Chopstick Woman flipped the paper tag and checked the numbers. Keyed them into the tablet. "Okay. Here it is. Same source as your little suitcase. A regular—Vernon Phan, with a *p-h*. I don't know him."

"Trust me. You don't want to."

Her sculpted brows rose. "Got it. I'm surprised this desk hasn't sold yet."

"Can I put a hold on it? A deposit? I'm not sure it will fit the space I have in mind." What I really wanted was to get it back to Talia. "Plus, it won't fit in my car."

"No need for a deposit." She returned the tablet to the front counter and came back with a red SOLD tag. I filled in my name and phone number, then she tied the tag to the drawer knob. "If you decide no, call us within the week, and we'll just rip this off."

"It's a plan." Last weekend's rudeness forgiven and forgotten, I handed her my credit card and she rang up my purchase.

Outside, shoppers streamed north on the sidewalks, toting bags filled with fresh produce, new pottery, old doorknobs, and other lucky finds. Balloons tied to children's wrists bobbed along above the crowd.

And Fremont being its funky self, no one gave a second glance to a woman carrying a vintage traffic light.

As I made my way back to my car, I wondered what to do about Vernon Phan. Weren't property managers licensed and regulated? The property owners needed to know what he was up to. Unless they were involved, too. I'd only been speculating that he was keeping the forcibly forfeited deposits. This might be one rogue creep—or another complicated scam, like whatever Jason Warwick was party to.

So Warwick had been feeling contrite, either from an attack of conscience or the fear of federal prison, when Boz overheard him and Cynthia talking in his office. But the chef had gone further and done his own investigation, scrounging up the invoices and photographs to prove it. And I was sure it had cost him his life.

How the chair fit in, I didn't know. I suspected now that Cynthia Warwick had made up the story of the lost bracelet to cover her tracks and pry Talia's phone number out of Claire DaSilva. It was anybody's guess whether the bad guys following Boz knew who Talia was or where to find her—the reason for Tracy's concern—but I was reasonably sure Cynthia and Jason had not known where she'd lived. Where she'd taken the chair.

Or where I'd taken it.

But I was equally sure I knew why they wanted it back. Jason might not have known about the money hidden inside when he gave it away, but he knew now.

According to Boz, Cynthia had protested Jason's plans to come clean, preferring to keep living the good life. Had she known about the scam all along or discovered it when the FBI investigators targeted her husband? How big a player was he? Did the feds hope he'd turn and spill the beans on his coconspirators in exchange for leniency?

I unlocked my trunk and laid the traffic light on an old blanket of Arf's. Cynthia was only a coconspirator if she'd known the cash was stolen when she hid it.

Why else would you hide that much money? Yes, I keep a few bills in the glove compartment just in case, and a lot of people tuck emergency cash in a sock drawer. But thirty-five grand?

What was she thinking?

With the foot traffic mostly gone, I drove west along the canal. The last of the artists and craftspeople were packing their rigs, stuffing bulky tent canopies into Subarus and loading plastic tubs and wooden crates of unsold wares into pickup beds. Volunteers in reflective safety vests swept up the inevitable dropped cups and ice cream–smeared napkins.

I had an urge to visit the spot where Boz was killed, reversing the route he'd had taken after dropping Evie at work. Sometimes it's helpful to look at things from another direction—literally.

Often, when a person is killed, a makeshift memorial springs up. It had happened in January outside the Gold Rush Hotel in the Chinatown–International District, as it had outside the Spice Shop a while back. Nothing similar marked this tragedy, but I could honor the place anyway. I drove past the chaos and parked, then climbed out of the Saab. Turned to lock it—the clicker had died years ago—when the sign on the nearest building nearly made my heart stop.

Tracy and Spencer had been checking alibis on their main suspects—Edgar, Evie, Tim Forrester. Even Talia. But they would have had no reason to check up on the real killer. To imagine she might be involved, let alone that she'd been here Tuesday morning for the sunrise Pilates class.

But knowing who didn't tell me why.

Why had Cynthia Warwick killed Boz?

Twenty-Eight

To err is human. To forgive takes thyme.

I STOOD ON THE SIDEWALK ABOVE THE CANAL, ROUGHLY where I'd seen the divers and CSU officers searching last Tuesday. An acrid odor of diesel mixed with decay wafted off the water. Before I called Tracy, I needed to know how this might have worked.

Cynthia was strong—all that Pilates. I'd seen it myself the other day in the way she'd marched across the street, then punched the air. Though I knew from my experience being knocked out of the way of a motorcycle that it didn't take much to throw an unsuspecting moving target off-balance. I'd only been pushed into a puddle, out of the path of real danger.

Unlike Boz.

I acted it out, stepping this way and that, raising an arm, pretending to stagger sideways. It was possible. She could have done it.

But why? To shut him up? To keep him from taking the evidence he'd gathered to the FBI?

Oh. Boz had said in his note to Talia that he had more evidence on his phone and would text it to her. Evidence proving what Jason had done. And Cynthia's own involvement, and where the cash had come from? More questions.

So why hadn't Boz sent Talia the rest of the documents? Maybe he'd been waiting to hear from her, to confirm that she was willing to be the go-between. But she hadn't gotten back to him. She'd been away taking care of her grandmother and hadn't picked up her mail. She hadn't known a thing about it.

Or maybe he had sent them to the number on the Uber account. Her ex-boyfriend's number. I hoped he hadn't decided it was all spam and swiped it into the great big cyber trash bag.

"So what did she want?" I muttered out loud. "She wanted to know where Boz took Talia and the chair. And the thirty-five grand. Her safety cushion."

"That money was mine and I want it back."

I whirled toward the source of the demand, almost twisting my ankle. Seriously? Was Cynthia Warwick standing in front of me in the flesh, or had my addled brain conjured her up?

She held up a phone. I recognized it right away—the same phone with the custom tie-dye case that Boz had waved in my face in the Market, when he begged me to help him find Talia. Had he already known he had the wrong number? He hadn't said.

This was no figment of my imagination. This was an angry woman. A killer. Did she know I was on to her? How could she know?

"I saw you," she said. "Sneaking around my house, then prying gossip out of Claire DaSilva. The witch. I thought you were that female FBI agent Jason mentioned—"

Ha. Meg Greer would not like that one bit.

"—until she showed up at my house, right on your heels, to quiz me about my husband. So who are you?"

"I'm Talia's friend," I said. "And Boz's. He made a lot of mistakes, but he was doing his best to make up for them. And I am not going to let you get away with his murder."

"That's what you think," she said, stepping closer.

I steeled myself not to back away from her. Into the water.

"You made up that story about the bracelet to trick Claire DaSilva into telling you where Talia lived. You thought if you showed up on her doorstep, you could worm your way inside and get the money back. Claire didn't know what you were up to, but she didn't trust you. And she was right."

"It was mine. My money." She raised the hand that gripped Boz's phone. She'd taken it from him, that I was sure, but why did she have it now?

"It didn't belong to Jason," she continued. "Not to his criminal buddies or that sniveling Tim Forrester, whining about getting used ovens and being overcharged. What did he think he was getting for that kind of money?"

He thought he was getting what he'd ordered. As anyone would.

"You spotted Boz on your way to Pilates. You grabbed his phone and shoved him in the canal, then stashed it in the studio." I waved a hand across the street. "You're a regular. I bet you have a locker. You turned off the tracking and hid it for safekeeping."

Behind me, I heard the clang of the warning bells, stopping traffic on the Fremont Bridge. I shifted my shoulders, hoping she wouldn't see my bag slip down my arm as I slid my hand inside and dug for my phone.

"I loved him," she said, her voice breaking, and nothing could have surprised me more. She couldn't mean Boz, could she? "He promised me everything I wanted, but he was in over his head. I trusted him."

My fingers found my wallet, a pen, a pack of tissues. A bag of dog biscuits. But no phone.

"My mistake. Jason Warwick is the emperor of nothing. It's all gone now." She choked back a sob. "Can you blame me for keeping something for myself while I watched everything disappear?"

I'd joked about a safety cushion, but it was no joke to her.

Cynthia straightened her shoulders, broad and buff from all that exercise. She raised her arm, still clutching the phone. She wasn't going to throw it in the water, was she?

No. She had a different target in mind.

She lunged toward me. I might not go to class and I wouldn't know a reformer from a revolver, but I lift boxes and bags. I push a hand truck over cobbled stones and uneven thresholds. I climb stairs all over the Market, and I was not going into that canal. I swung my bag at her head and shoulders, hoping the phone buried in its depths made contact with a critical part. She ducked, and my momentum swung me around. As I whirled, I caught a glimpse of Neon Rapunzel in the bridge tower, yellow hair flowing.

You always know what to do, Vanessa had told me.

I was facing the water, Cynthia behind me. Ready to push.

I dropped to a crouch just as her palms hit my shoulders. My feet slipped on the grass and I pitched forward, landing on my knees. Cynthia tumbled over me and kept on tumbling. Down the slope. Over the rocks and into the water, just as Boz had done. She must have screamed, but the squeal and clank of the bridge deck going up blocked out every sound, including my own thoughts.

In the water, Cynthia bobbed and flailed. Her head surfaced, hair pasted to her skull, then slipped under the water again. Could the poster child for fitness after forty not swim?

Either that, or she was putting on an Oscar-worthy show.

Off came my clogs, and I scrabbled down the slope. The skanky cold of the water hit me like a polar bear, but I couldn't stop. The currents were stronger than I'd expected. We didn't have much time.

I reached her in two long strokes. But while I'm a decent swimmer, I'd never rescued anyone. Especially not someone so full of fight and anger. I hooked my right arm under her left and slid it across her back, holding on tight. She kicked and wriggled, her head barely bobbing above the water.

"Stop it," I shouted. "Stop fighting me."

I wasn't sure she heard. Wasn't sure she cared.

Then an unseen force pulled me down, the cold water rushing up my nose, my vision blurring, fear swarming my senses. *This is what it's like. This is what drowning is like.*

She'd wrapped her lower leg around mine and was grabbing at my waist with her free arm. Now I knew. She was trying to drown us. In her twisted mind, killing us both was the next best thing to victory.

I'd give my life for a lot. For Nate, for my parents and my brother and his family, for my friends and my staff. For a stranger in crisis.

But I was not dying for Cynthia Warwick.

We plunged farther down. How deep was this canal? I had no idea. My feet struck a hard surface. I flexed both knees and pushed up, one arm gripping Cynthia. Keeping hold of her was getting harder and making less sense. I stroked with my free arm as if I was swimming. I was—but vertically. I broke through the surface and gasped for air.

"There she is. There they are." Voices pierced the waterlogged haze in my brain. "Two of them."

I dog-paddled toward shore with one arm. My load grew heavier as the rocks grew closer. My feet hit ground. So did my knee.

"We've got you. We've got her." Hands stretched toward us.

My eyes weren't working right—water in them? The arms were green and blue.

"Take her," I said, gasping. "She's hurt. I can get out on my own."

I could have, I'm sure, but I was grateful for the help they gave me anyway. Eternally grateful.

Safe on the grass, I drank in the air. My vision had not been wrong after all. The man hauling Cynthia out of the mucky water was blue and yellow, like a Van Gogh sky. His friend, hovering near me, wore green. Body suits?

No. I started laughing. Or choking—hard to tell which. Their bicycles lay on the grass a few feet away. They weren't wearing wet suits. They weren't wearing anything at all except paint and little tiny G-strings.

That's when I saw my bag on the grass. And a few feet away, a phone.

"Oh, your phone," Green Man said, bending to pick it up.

"No," I shouted, instinctively lunging forward. "Don't touch it. It's evidence." Nonsensical words that made me sound like a crazy woman, but it was Boz's phone. His prints were on it, and so were Cynthia's.

Someone handed me a small towel, the kind bicyclists use to mop off sweat. Instead of wiping my face, I crawled to the phone and wrapped it carefully in the towel.

I had never been so wet. When you've plunged fully clothed into a frigid canal and make it to the safety of a cool April afternoon, you stay cold and wet. Someone wrapped a jacket around my shoulders. A police jacket. Patrol units had already arrived on the scene.

My knee screamed with pain. A few feet away, Cynthia lay face down on the grass, Blue Paint patting her back like a baby's.

In the distance, I heard more sirens. "Don't let her go," I told the nearest officer, pointing at Cynthia. "She tried to kill me. The man who died here last week? She killed him. Call Detective Tracy."

Turned out Tracy had stuck around after coffee, prowling the neighborhood and asking questions.

"I was in the line for the bridge when I heard the call about a woman, maybe two, in the water," he said to me. "How did I know it would be you?"

"Lucky guess?"

"And her lucky day," he said, nodding at Cynthia sitting on the grass, an EMT checking her out. Two patrol officers in full uniform, gleaming handcuffs at the ready, had relieved the painted men of guard duty. Both now stood by their bicycles, giving their accounts to another officer.

"She won't see it that way," I said. "I don't know where the money came from—whether it was genuinely, legally hers or part of the spoils. She killed Boz to get his phone. I'm not sure she meant to kill him, but she was desperate. She may have suspected he had more evidence of Jason's fraud on his phone, or maybe she just wanted to find out where he'd taken Talia so she could get the chair back. And the money."

"How did she know Boz was involved?"

"From Jason. His business was failing—I suspect he was in debt to the restaurant supply company and they used that as leverage to rope him into the equipment scam. How far back that goes, I couldn't guess. When she told him she'd stashed her safety net in the chair, they both went on the hunt. If any other Uber driver had taken the call, they'd have been up a creek, but they knew Boz. When he showed up, Jason was sure it was no coincidence and that he'd figured out everything. She only cared about getting the chair back."

"Quite the pair, those Warwicks."

"I think she loved him. Jason, I mean. But he lost everything they had. He humiliated her."

"So he might have been next," Tracy said, "if Greer and her partner hadn't taken him into custody this morning."

"Oh." I dug in my bag for my water bottle and spotted my phone sitting in its pocket, so innocent, as if I hadn't been desperately searching for it. I twisted the cap off and took a long swallow. Wiped my mouth with the back of my grubby, scraped hand. I was going to be covered in cuts and bruises. "That's why she came back to the studio, to get the phone she'd stashed in her locker. Her last chance."

She'd almost made this day my last.

No way, baby. No way.

Twenty-Nine

*Forget the old proverb about teaching a man
to fish and feeding him for life. Teach someone
to bake, and you'll feed the hearts of everyone
they know.*

I'D PUT ON MY TUESDAY BEST FOR A SUMMONS TO THE Seattle office of the FBI. Talia had done the same, though her denim-on-denim look was not quite as somber as my black pants and checked jacket. Black-and-blue checks, to match my left eye and much of the rest of my body. Even half drowned, Cynthia Warwick had packed a punch. I'd put on a pair of black Mary Janes. My black clogs had been spared a second dousing Sunday at the Ship Canal, but I thought they deserved a few days off.

"Agent Greer," I said. "Meg." Our first encounter, last fall, had not ended well, and I had no confidence that this one would go any more smoothly, though seeing Detectives Spencer and Tracy at the table in the small conference room eased my anxiety a smidge.

But she surprised me. "Pepper, I want to thank you. By finding Ms. Cook and getting that last bit of evidence from the late Mr. Bosworth, you allowed us to make the final connections linking Jason Warwick to a conspiracy we've been trying to unravel for months."

"Wait," Talia said. "I know who you are, and the detectives.

But who are you?" She stared at the man in the navy suit standing by the window, arms folded. A white man with dark hair, flecks of gray at the temples. "And why were you following me?"

"Steven Miller," he said. "Special Agent, FBI."

"My partner," Greer said.

"Did you think she was involved in all this?" I asked. "That a twenty-three-year-old housecleaner who'd been in Seattle—what, three months?—and sublets an apartment the size of this office had anything to do with a ring of crooked appliance dealers?"

"We didn't know who was involved," Greer replied. "We've been taking a hard look at everyone who bought or sold commercial restaurant equipment from the dealer up north. Mr. Bosworth and Mr. Forrester, your Mr. Ramos—"

"Edgar? You thought Edgar was part of this fraud?"

"And Jason Warwick," she finished. Who I still hadn't seen, though I was sure he too had dark hair graying at the temples. So glad I'd gotten mine colored.

"What I don't get about Warwick," I said, "is why he's broke, if he's got all these buildings leased out, plus money from this scam. Yes, his wife has expensive tastes, but diamonds and spa vacations only add up to so much. Slim margins, coupled with rent concessions from the pandemic? And if most are restaurants, I suppose some never recovered and are sitting empty."

"That's part of it," Miller said. "He'd been hemorrhaging money the last few years. Bad investments, mostly—some in the restaurant business, others in crypto. When that failed, he tried to get a little back the wrong way. We think he was a minor player, his share of the take plunging as his ability to recruit new suckers collapsed."

"You can see," Detective Spencer said, "that the FBI's investigation had substantial overlap with our homicide investigation. Any person involved in one case had to be considered for the other."

"I wasn't involved in anything," Talia said. "A guy I didn't know gave me a cool chair. That my landlord decided to give away. Thank goodness Pepper nabbed it. Anybody else would have stashed it in their garage to rot. Years later, they'd have tossed it in a dumpster. Nobody ever would have known about the fortune hidden in the stuffing."

"And we need to know who that money belongs to," I said.

"But whatever Jason Warwick was up to, I don't think Boz and Forrester were part of it. And you're never going to convince me that Edgar knew what was going on."

"We're not finished looking at Bosworth and Forrester." Miller took a seat at the table. "The unfortunately deceased Mr. Bosworth. Your Mr. Ramos appears to be as clean as his kitchen counters. His only link to anyone else was his beef with Bosworth and the girlfriend, Ms. LeMieux. And a brief visit to the appliance dealership."

"Warwick went to see Evie at the deli," I said. "But she didn't know what Boz was up to or that he had documents Warwick wanted."

"We followed him," Miller said. "Your spices must be pretty special. Bosworth unearthed some damning evidence against Warwick and the dealership. More arrests are in the works."

"After he overheard Jason and Cynthia arguing," I said. This all fit with Detective Tracy's theory, shared Sunday afternoon in the shadow of the bridge. "If I understand right, you're saying there's an organized ring operating around the region and you wanted to turn Warwick into an informant. Had you already talked to him?"

"That was the plan," Miller said. "We were waiting on a search warrant. Didn't get it in time to keep Bosworth alive."

I heard genuine regret in his voice and saw it on Meg Greer's face.

"Now we have the evidence," she said, "from Warwick's files and computer. But we needed to know what Bosworth knew and what he'd tried to do with it. We knew from Evie LeMieux that Bosworth had gone to the appliance dealership."

"Job hunting," I said. "Or so he said. He didn't get hired, and she blamed Edgar. But that's not what he was really up to. He was protecting her."

"Part of that new policy of making up for the harm he'd caused," Tracy said.

As Boz had written in his note to Talia.

"He was spying," I said. "Trying to get more evidence of this price-gouging, bait-and-switch stuff."

"We think so," Greer said. "And we thought that was why he was killed, though we couldn't put anyone with a motive near the Ship Canal at six A.M. last Tuesday morning."

"No one but Cynthia Warwick," I said.

"Who didn't show up on the security footage," Greer said. "Blocked by the cars and the angle. We wouldn't have known about her without you."

"But this conspiracy thing isn't the reason she was after Boz, is it?" Talia asked. "Pepper filled me in Sunday night, on the phone. Cynthia was after the money in the chair."

"Seems right," Greer said. "We searched Mr. Bosworth's apartment, but we didn't find any additional documents. We needed his phone, which Ms. Warwick had taken."

"Couldn't you track it?" Talia asked.

Spencer answered. "Cell-tower pings put the phone in Fremont that morning, probably after he was killed. We suspect she was trying to figure out where he'd gone after picking up Talia, but he had wiped that data. Then she switched off the location settings and shut down the phone. Soon as she turned it on again, we'd have picked up the signals, but until then, we were stymied."

"That woman likes to hide things," I said, and a murmur of amusement rippled through the room.

Boz's phone had been thoroughly examined. As Evie had said, Jason and Cynthia had sent him repeated texts and voice mails, each more threatening. That's what had sent him to the police last Monday, and to me, fearful for Talia. The messages had stopped when Cynthia grabbed his phone, shoved him in the canal, and ran. Would she have stayed to help him had she realized he'd hit his head on the way down the slope? No way to know.

"One more thread," Spencer said. "Boz did in fact send you additional documents, Talia, that clearly establish the conspiracy. It had several layers, ranging from selling used appliances as new, jacking up parts prices, refusing to provide repair manuals or sell parts, and more. But the only phone number he had belonged to your ex."

Talia's hands flew to her mouth. I had suspected as much.

"He knew you were in Seattle, from the Uber charge," Spencer continued. "When he saw the area code, he was suspicious enough to hang on to the documents. Then we called."

"He hates me," Talia said through closed fingers.

"Don't know about that," Spencer said. "But now we know for sure that neither of you were involved in Boz's death or in the fraud ring."

"I know Cynthia killed Boz," I said, "and she would have killed me. But I almost feel sorry for her."

The charged silence in the room told me no one shared my sympathy.

"No, seriously," I said. "She kept saying she loved him. Jason, that is. I don't think she knew much about his business or how he lost the money. She trusted him, until she finally understood he'd been lying to her. She finally understood she had to take care of herself. Although cash in a cushion is a funny way to do that."

"If I'd been Cynthia," Talia said, "and I discovered Jason gave away my safety net, I'd have killed him, not Boz."

That gave us all a laugh. And brought us back to the question of ownership. The answer might be weeks or months in coming. I'd made the original claim, and Talia had filed one, too, at my urging. Cynthia's claim would depend on the results of a forensic examination of the couple's finances, as well as the outcome of the criminal case. Thirty-five grand had seemed like so much money, but it was a fraction of what the restaurant equipment scam had cost Tim Forrester and the other victims. Then there were restitution payments and court costs and legal fees.

In all likelihood, we'd never see a cent.

No matter. I had other things of value, including a good relationship with two of the hardest-working police officers I'd ever known. I had a chance at a decent relationship with Greer.

And I'd been right when I told Cynthia that Boz and Talia were my friends. Only one of them was alive, but I had kept the promise to help her. The promise I hadn't gotten to share with Boz. I had to trust that wherever he was now, on some other plane, he knew.

TALIA AND I left the federal building knowing a lot more than when we went in, but with more to discuss. We crossed the street, rode the escalators up to Third, and crossed to the forty-seven-story Black Box where I'd worked for years and rode more escalators. My knee appreciated the respite from Seattle's hills. At Ripe, Laurel's Fourth Avenue deli, Laurel served us herself.

Cappuccino and muffins. Not lemon cream scones, but I knew from experience that Laurel's rhubarb-almond muffins were pretty darned tasty.

"So, tell me the latest on Vernon Phan," I said.

The tenants, including Talia, had met Sunday evening to compare notes. Danae, the upstairs neighbor with the wet laundry, had been chosen as spokesperson and met with the owners first thing Monday morning, laying out the tenants' complaints with as much documentation as they'd been able to assemble on short notice. The owners were suitably horrified. Phan was now unemployed, and the owners had scheduled an all-tenant meeting at each building he managed to apologize, gather facts, and declare their intent to make it right.

"Some of the tenants he scammed had already moved out," she said. "So they've hired a lawyer and a CPA to track them down and account for security deposits and fees he took."

"Good to hear of a corporation taking responsibility for its employees' actions," I said, "despite what it's going to cost them. Will he face criminal charges?"

"They've made a report. I guess it will depend on how much he stole. If he has any of it left." She bit into her muffin. "Mmm. These are good."

"Might be harder for the tenants to get back the personal items he sold." I'd told her I'd bought the valise and would get it and the books back to her. And that I would go with her to the Vintage Mall. The cost of the desk would swallow most of her paycheck from Claire DaSilva. I hoped I could talk the dealer into giving it to me for what he'd paid Phan. Then I'd give it back to her.

"The owners promised to fix everything. They also said the tenants could terminate their leases early, without penalty. The woman who leases my apartment hasn't decided. But either way, I'm out of there."

"Where will you go?" I had an idea and hoped I was right.

I was. Ruth was scheduled to be released from the hospital on Wednesday, and Talia planned to move in with her.

"She insists she doesn't need a babysitter," Talia said. "Even though Pandit disagrees."

Ah, yes. The ever-watchful Mr. Chakravarti.

"So does my mother," my new young friend continued. "Who is actually planning to visit. What Gran needs is an apprentice. Grandpa taught me a little about upholstery—how to do a chair seat, and I did a footstool for my mom, but I don't know much about woodworking. Now I have a chance to learn from Gran.

And I wouldn't be doing any of this if it weren't for you. How can I repay you?"

I sipped my cappuccino. "By making the most of it. And by not being a stranger."

"And with this?" She held up her phone, showing a swath of fabric, red floral shapes dancing on an off-white background. "I have plenty for the wingback and a throw pillow."

"Just right," I said and picked up my muffin.

Thirty

The mountain is out. The mountain is out!

—Seattleites, celebrating a sunny day

Two weeks later

I SWITCHED ON THE SHOP LIGHTS. THE PSEUDO-SAMOVAR was perking away with the day's first batch of tea, and I drank in the familiar aroma. Almost time for the weekly Wednesday morning staff meeting. Would we all fit in the nook? Yes. Like the human heart, it expands to hold those who need it.

"It'll be good to see everybody, right, Arf?" My canine companion did not respond, his attention on his chew bone.

My scrapes had turned to scabs, my bruises faded to yellow. Almost every night for the last two weeks, my Nate and I had talked late and long about everything from fishing to food—he was looking forward to trying that cumin burger I'd raved about—to the dog and the new furniture and the boat and the shop. Not about the future. Our future.

And that was okay. I trusted in it, even if I didn't know what turns it might take.

My parents' new-old house was almost done. Last night, Kristen and I had met Talia and Ruth at the house and unloaded the old wingback from the WOODWCH. It scarcely resembled its former self. Talia had done most of the work, under Ruth's careful supervision. They'd made a new leg, and the chair was solid and comfortable. I'd sent my mother pictures of the dining table and chairs in the Burien gallery, and she wanted to buy them. Ruth planned to make a desk for the wingback, with Talia's help.

Everything old is new again. Change is the only constant. Food is love.

Ask for what you need. Welcome strangers. Eschew trite proverbs.

The staff arrived. Kristen brought a glazed chai spice coffee cake the girls had made, using a recipe in the book she'd taken home for them.

"The mountain is out!" Vanessa exclaimed. "It's like this giant ice cream cone in the sky."

"You're a true Seattleite now," I said. Her love bomber had kept his word to back off, and she was her bright-eyed self again. I'd seen him leaning over the table of a young potter, flirting hard, and suspected he hadn't learned his lesson. Some of us need more time than others to get a clue. Hopefully, we don't do irreparable damage along the way.

Sandra and I had gone to a memorial service and potluck reception for Boz, where nearly everyone had worn tie-dye T-shirts in his honor. To my surprise, Tariq and Edgar had come, as had Tim Forrester and others who knew Boz from the food biz. It had been quite touching, a fitting tribute to a chef who, in the end, had given his life in the effort to be a better man.

"I am so excited," Cayenne said as she slid into the booth. "This dinner is going to be the most fabulous ever."

"Before we go over the last-minute plans," I said, "I have a little token for you, and one for you, Hayden."

I handed them each a gift bag. She'd already shared her big news with the staff, so I wasn't spilling any beans. "From me. Open them at the same time."

Out came two tiny T-shirts, each showing a stork catching a baby dropped from a saltshaker and proclaiming the wearer "Spice Baby." And two larger versions, reading "Spice Baby Mama" and "Spice Baby Daddy."

"Perfect," everyone said, and as I looked around the nook, overflowing with joy and happiness, I had to agree.

THAT EVENING, Edgar and I stood inside the entrance to Speziato, greeting our guests. Our students. Bouquets of peonies, lupine, iris, and other flowers from the Market graced the bar. Smaller arrangements of lilacs and sweet peas sat on each table.

Cayenne and Sandra stood nearby, wearing Spice Shop aprons. Hayden, who had trained in Edgar's kitchen, was in back with Tariq, making final preparations.

Once the students were seated, I let Cayenne do the honors of introducing the Spice Shop. She'd coiled her braids on top of her head, wrapped in a glittery red stretchy thing, but it was her face that glowed. She was good at experiential retail. Very good.

I wiped a bit of pride from one eye, hoping no one noticed.

We divided the students into groups and showed them their workspaces, the kitchen's stainless-steel wheeled tables reconfigured for the occasion. Edgar introduced the menu, and the students spent the next hour chopping, slicing, stirring, and spicing. Laughter seasoned the air. An older woman was delighted to learn the right way to chop onions after decades of cutting them wrong and ending up in tears. Two older men, one as tall as the other was short, each claiming to not know a thing about cooking, browned the chicken beautifully and beamed at the compliments. A teenager stuck her finger in her tiramisu parfait so no one else would eat it, and everyone promised to oblige.

Then it was back to the dining room. Wine flowed. Tariq and Hayden served while Cayenne and Sandra circulated, answering questions. Behind the gleaming mahogany bar, Edgar beamed, and I tried not to cry. Then we sat at our own table and toasted an evening that far exceeded all our expectations.

This, I thought, I *knew*, is what we all hunger for. Brother Cadfael knew it, and so did I. To cherish our time with friends and strangers, learning new skills and adding new stories to our personal libraries. To nourish ourselves and each other, so that we can all better weather the storms of this world.

Recipes and Spice Notes

The Seattle Spice Shop Recommends . . .

Find the recipe for the Spice Shop's custom tea blend in *Between a Wok and a Dead Place*. The recipe for Carrot Soup with Toasted Spices and Pecans, which the staff shares with customers, originally appeared in *The Solace of Bay Leaves*. The recipes for Glazed Chai Spice Coffee Cake and Edgar's Baked Paprika Cheese come from *Chai Another Day*.

Toasting spices, especially seeds, adds a depth of flavor and brings out their earthiness. Toast in a small sauté pan on the stove top, keeping the pan moving or using a spatula to prevent sticking and burning. As Pepper says, use your nose and watch the color of the lighter spices. Most will be fully toasted in 3–5 minutes. As with nuts, spices continue to cook as they cool, so remove the pan from the heat and let experience and your taste buds be your teacher.

COOKING ASPARAGUS:

Pepper's a fan of two classic methods for cooking asparagus. First, wash the spears and snap off the woody ends.

To cook in water: Fill a large sauté pan with cold water, about 2/3 full, and bring to a boil. Lay in the spears and cook 2–3 minutes. Remove spears with tongs and give them a quick cold rinse to stop the cooking and preserve the bright-green color. Serve with melted butter or good olive oil and your favorite fresh herbs or seasonings.

To roast: Heat oven to 425 degrees. Line a baking sheet with a silicon sheet or parchment paper. Lay out the spears in a single row. Drizzle with olive oil, salt, and fresh black pepper and toss with tongs. Roast 10–12 minutes. Don't worry if the thinner spears appear to be slightly charred; that only adds to the flavor and the rustic appeal.

CREAMY ASPARAGUS SOUP WITH CUMIN

As sure a sign of spring as tulips, asparagus is one of Pepper's favorite veggies—and a hit at every produce and farm stall in the Market. A few asparagus tips or spears make a terrific garnish for this soup. Buy cumin seeds toasted or raw.

> 2 pounds green asparagus, rinsed, woody ends snapped off
> 3 tablespoons butter
> 1 large white onion, chopped
> 1–2 cloves garlic, minced
> kosher salt
> fresh ground black pepper
> 5 cups chicken broth
> 1 teaspoon ground cumin, or more to taste
> 1 teaspoon ground coriander, or more to taste
> ½ cup sour cream, crème fraîche, or heavy cream, plus more
>   for garnish
> ¼ teaspoon fresh lemon juice, or to taste
> toasted cumin seeds, for garnish

Cut 1-1/2 inch off the tips of 12 asparagus stalks and set aside for garnish. If the stalks are thick, slice them in half. Cut into 1-inch pieces.

Melt the butter in a stockpot over medium-low heat. Add onion and garlic and sauté until just soft, about 5 minutes. Add asparagus pieces and salt and pepper to taste, then cook, stirring, 5 minutes. When the asparagus is tender-crisp and still bright green, add the broth, cumin, and coriander, and simmer, covered, until asparagus is very tender, 15-20 minutes.

Meanwhile, bring a cup or two of salted water to a boil and blanch the asparagus tips until just tender, 3-4 minutes. Drain and set aside. If your cumin seeds are raw, toast lightly in a sauté pan on the stove top, about 3-5 minutes.

When the asparagus in the soup mixture is tender, taste and adjust spices. Purée with an immersion blender or in batches in a standard blender until smooth. (Use caution when blending hot liquids.) Return to pan if you're using a standard blender and reheat if necessary. Stir in sour cream, crème fraîche, or heavy cream. Adjust seasonings and add lemon juice.

Serve, garnished with asparagus tips, additional sour cream, and toasted cumin seeds.

Serves 4.

ASPARAGUS BRAISED WITH BUTTER AND HERBS

Use any combination of fresh herbs you have. Oregano, chives, and parsley are a particularly good combo—no coincidence that all three grow nicely in pots on a deck or in a windowsill, perfect for the urban gardener!

> 1½ pounds asparagus
> 6 tablespoons butter
> kosher salt
> fresh ground pepper
> ½ to 1 tablespoon lemon juice
> ½ teaspoon lemon zest
> 1 tablespoon chives, scallion greens, ramps, or shallot, finely chopped
> 2 tablespoons fresh herbs, finely chopped
> 1 tablespoon or more pine nuts or sliced almonds, toasted (for optional garnish)

Rinse the asparagus spears and snap off the woody ends.

Place butter in a large skillet and turn heat to medium. When butter is melted, add the asparagus and sprinkle with salt and pepper to taste. Add ½ cup water and simmer. Check at 3 minutes. You want the spears to be a bright green, firm but beginning to soften. Move them around with a pair of tongs and cook another minute; fat spears might need 2 more minutes. Move to a serving platter, leaving the buttery sauce in the pan.

Increase heat to medium high. Add the chives and cook, stirring, until most of the liquid has evaporated, leaving a thin sauce. Turn off the heat. Add the lemon juice and zest and the fresh herbs. Taste and adjust the seasonings and lemon. Pour sauce over the asparagus and garnish. Serve immediately.

Serves 4. Unless you really love asparagus, then it serves 2.

At Home with Pepper

ROASTED BEET AND FETA SALAD WITH CUMIN DRESSING

Beets are often thought of as a winter vegetable, but this is a tasty salad any time of year! Pepper varies the dressing now and then, substituting walnut oil and balsamic vinegar for the olive oil and lemon juice and topping with toasted walnuts.

For the beets:

1 pound red or golden beets, or a mix (3-4 medium beets)
½ teaspoon salt
1 teaspoon extra-virgin olive oil

For the salad:

4 ounces feta, crumbled
1 tablespoon extra-virgin olive oil
1 tablespoon lemon juice
1 tablespoon cumin seeds (raw or toasted)
½ teaspoon ground cumin
salad greens, washed and cut or torn
parsley or cilantro leaves (for optional garnish)

To roast beets: Heat oven to 375 degrees. Trim and wash the beets. Place the beets on a piece of foil. Sprinkle with salt and drizzle with 1 teaspoon olive oil. Wrap the foil over the beets and place on a baking sheet. Roast until tender when poked with a fork or knife, 30-45 minutes. Let sit until cool enough to handle, about 20 minutes, then slip off skins and dice the beets into bite-sized pieces.

In a medium bowl, combine the diced beets, feta, 1 tablespoon olive oil, lemon juice, cumin seeds, and ground cumin. Serve on a bed of mixed greens, with parsley or cilantro leaves as optional garnish. Taste and adjust seasonings, adding more oil, lemon juice, and a dash of salt if needed.

Serves 4 as a side salad.

Treats from Seattle's Bakeries

LEMON CREAM SCONES WITH LEMON GLAZE

One bite of these fluffy lemon beauties and you'll know why Talia scrimped and saved to buy them! Using cold butter and cream helps the scones rise and stay fluffy.

For the scones:

3 cups all-purpose flour
⅔ cup granulated sugar
4 teaspoons baking powder
¼ teaspoon salt
1 cup (2 sticks) butter, cubed, very cold
1 large egg
¾ cup heavy cream, plus more as needed
1½ tablespoon lemon zest (1 large lemon)
1 teaspoon fresh lemon juice
1 teaspoon vanilla

For the glaze:

1¼ cups powdered sugar
¼ cup heavy cream
1 tablespoon lemon zest
1 teaspoon fresh lemon juice
¼ teaspoon vanilla extract
additional lemon zest, for topping

To make the scones: Heat the oven to 350 degrees. Line two baking sheets with parchment paper or silicon sheets.

Using a stand mixer or a large food processor, whisk the flour, granulated sugar, baking powder, and salt. Add the butter and mix or pulse until fully combined and the texture is that of coarse crumbs. Do not overmix.

In a small bowl, combine the egg, cream, lemon zest, lemon juice, and vanilla. Add to the flour mixture and mix or pulse until the dough comes together, adding more cream 1 tablespoon at a time if needed, until the dough is moist and mostly holds together.

Lightly flour a work surface. Turn the dough onto the surface and knead 4-5 times. Divide the dough into two large balls. Knead briefly to shape, and divide each ball again. You will have four balls. Flatten each ball with your hands to about ½ inch thick. Use a table knife or scraper to cut into four wedges. Repeat with remaining three balls.

Place scones on prepared baking sheets and bake 18-20 minutes, or until the tops look dry and the bottoms are lightly golden. Remove from oven and cool on the pans for 5-10 minutes. Transfer to a wire cooling rack.

To make the glaze: Combine all ingredients in a small bowl. When scones are cool, drizzle with glaze and sprinkle about ¼ teaspoon zest on top. Serve and enjoy!

Makes 16 scones.

Wrap well to freeze. Surprisingly, the glaze withstands freezing relatively well, so you can enjoy the sweet touch on top without needing to make a fresh batch of glaze.

RHUBARB ALMOND MUFFINS

A *favorite at Ripe, Laurel's downtown deli, these muffins are light and cakey, rising above the rim of the tin. That makes them wonderfully showy, paired with a fluffy omelet or the perfect cup of coffee.*

For the muffins:

2¼ cups all-purpose flour
⅔ cup granulated sugar
½ teaspoon salt
½ teaspoon baking soda
1 teaspoon baking powder
6 tablespoons unsalted butter
2 large eggs
1 teaspoon almond extract
1 cup buttermilk or ¾ cup plain yogurt plus ¼ cup milk
2 cups rhubarb, diced

For the topping:

sprinkling sugar or turbinado sugar (coarse raw sugar)
sliced almonds

Heat the oven to 350 degrees. Spray a 12-well muffin tin with nonstick spray or use paper or silicon liners.

In a large mixing bowl, whisk together the flour, sugar, salt, baking soda, and baking powder.

In a small bowl, melt the butter. Whisk in the eggs, almond extract, and buttermilk or yogurt-and-milk mixture, then add to the dry ingredients and mix until combined and no dry streaks remain. Add the diced rhubarb and combine.

Scoop the dough into the muffin tin, filling about ¾ full. Sprinkle tops with sugar and sliced almonds.

Bake 22–25 minutes, or until springy to the touch and a toothpick inserted in the center comes out clean. Cool slightly before removing from the pan. Serve warm.

Makes 12 muffins.

Spice Up Your Life with Pepper and the Flick Chicks

KIR ROYALE

Legend says a French priest and Resistance fighter, Félix Kir, invented this cocktail when the Nazis invaded Burgundy in 1940, using a local dry white wine and adding black currant liqueur to mimic the color of classic French reds. The champagne version came later and is perfect for a celebration. Like getting together with friends on a Tuesday evening.

> For each drink:
> 5 ounces chilled champagne
> 1 ounce crème de cassis (black currant liqueur)
> lemon twist or blackberries, for garnish

Pour the wine into a champagne flute, add the liqueur, garnish, and enjoy!

KRISTEN'S FOUR-INGREDIENT ASPARAGUS TART

If you're cooking for two, cut the recipe in half by using one sheet of puff pastry. Make sure to use young, tender spears. If you're using fontina, toss it in the freezer for 30 to 60 minutes before cooking to firm it up for easier grating.

2 sheets (one package) puff pastry, thawed on a work surface
1-2 tablespoons Dijon-style mustard
8 ounces freshly grated fontina or Gruyère
1 pound asparagus, rinsed, woody ends snapped off

Heat oven to 425 degrees.

Use your rolling pin to flatten and smooth the puff pastry. With a table knife or paring knife, lightly score a line about ¾ inch inside the outside edge, as if drawing a frame. Transfer each pastry to a silicon- or parchment-lined baking sheet.

Spread mustard evenly on the pastry, inside the score line. Sprinkle the cheese on top of the mustard. Line up the asparagus spears like pickets in a fence, alternating heads and tails. Bake 25 minutes, until golden brown and puffy. (Don't freak out if it gets a little too puffy; it will calm down as it cools.)

Cut each baked sheet into quarters or sixths. Serve with a green salad and a glass of a sprightly white wine.

MOROCCAN CHOCOLATE MOUSSE

The classic chocolate mousse, with a Moroccan flair. Agave nectar, or syrup, adds just the right touch of sweetness. The combination of cumin and cinnamon—use your favorite variety of cinnamon or a blend—illustrates Pepper's observation that cumin can balance other spices, adding a delicate flavor without heat.

4 ounces bittersweet chocolate, coarsely chopped
3 large eggs, separated, at room temperature
1½ teaspoons agave nectar
¼ teaspoon ground cumin
¼ teaspoon ground cinnamon
⅛ teaspoon salt
1½ teaspoons granulated sugar
whipped cream or crème fraîche, for serving (optional)
berries or mint leaves, for serving (optional)

Melt the chocolate using a microwave-safe bowl, double boiler, or saucepan. Remove from heat and add the egg yolks, one at a time. Stir in the agave nectar, cumin, and cinnamon.

Beat the egg whites with the salt until they start to form peaks. Continue to beat, gradually adding the sugar, until the whites are shiny and form stiff peaks, about 5-7 minutes.

Spoon about a quarter of the egg whites into the chocolate and stir in gently. (This lightens the chocolate and makes folding in the rest easier.) Spoon the rest of the egg whites into the chocolate and fold with a rubber spatula, being careful not to overwork or deflate the mixture. A few streaks are fine.

Spoon into a serving bowl or six individual bowls, cups, or ramekins. Garnish and serve, or chill to serve later.

Serves 6.

Out on the Town

THE CUMIN NATURE BURGER

You don't need to be a spice spy or to stick your nose into murder to enjoy a tasty burger! Some people prefer an all-beef burger; at home, Pepper likes to lighten hers up by adding breadcrumbs and Parmesan. Your choice! Jalapeños are the mildest of the hot peppers, though the heat level can vary. Dice yours finely and test it, then adjust the other seasonings to your palate. If you're among the 15 percent who can't eat cilantro, leave it out or substitute parsley. And yes, that's a lot of cumin—remember, flavor, not heat!

For the burgers:

4 strips peppered bacon (optional)
1 pound ground sirloin or lean ground beef
¼ cup panko-style breadcrumbs (optional)
¼ cup grated Parmesan (optional)
2 jalapeños, seeded and diced
2 tablespoons freshly ground cumin seeds, raw or toasted, or a mix
½ teaspoon kosher salt

For the guacamole:

2 ripe avocados
⅓ to ½ cup mayonnaise
1 tablespoon lime juice
1-2 tablespoons fresh cilantro leaves, chopped
½ teaspoon kosher salt

Arugula, rinsed
Cilantro leaves (optional garnish)
Buns (optional; pretzel and brioche buns are both great!)

For the burgers: Heat oven to 400 degrees. Line a rimmed baking sheet with parchment paper. Lay the bacon strips on the sheet and bake 20 to 25 minutes, turning the strips halfway through. Drain on paper towels and allow to crisp up. (Cooking time will depend on the thickness of your bacon and preferred doneness; you'll want these strips fairly crispy.)

In a large bowl, mix beef, breadcrumbs, Parmesan, jalapeños, cumin, and salt. Shape into four patties. Grill or bake the burgers, as you prefer.

For the guacamole: In a medium bowl, mash the avocado with a fork. Stir in the mayonnaise, lime juice, cilantro, and salt. Adjust seasonings to taste.

Toast the buns if you'd like.

To serve, lay a bed of arugula on each plate. Top with a burger, one strip of bacon broken in half, and a dollop of guacamole. If you're using a bun, put a little butter or mayonnaise on each half, add a few arugula leaves to the bottom half, then top.

Garnish the plate with cilantro leaves, if you'd like.

Serves 4.

READERS, it's a treat to hear from you. Drop me a line at Leslie@ LeslieBudewitz.com, connect with me on Facebook at LeslieBudewitzAuthor, or join my seasonal mailing list for book news, free short stories, and more. (Sign up on my website, www.LeslieBudewitz.com.) Reader reviews and recommendations are a big boost to authors; if you've enjoyed my books, please tell your friends, in person and online. A book is but marks on paper until you read these pages and make the story yours.

Thank you.

Acknowledgments

IN THE LATE 1980S, I LIVED IN SEATTLE'S WALLINGFORD neighborhood, next door to Fremont. Back then, Fremont was quirky and homespun; now it's trendy but, happily, still quirky.

The Fremont Sunday Market and all the public art I've described are real, as are the Vintage Mall and the bakery, though it's been a while since I've visited, so my memories might be dusty. Speziato, the Belltown Bistro, and other businesses are figments of my imagination and stomach.

As always, I ask you to forgive me if the city on the page does not match the city of your memory or experience. Cities change, and I have occasionally renamed or relocated a business to better suit the story.

You've heard me rave about World Spice, but you haven't heard me tell you about their Cinnamon Toast blend. Try it. You'll be glad you did.

My Facebook reader community contributed to this book in a delightful range of ways. Thanks to readers Val Rogalla for the title and Kathy Rothwell for Ruth's personalized license plate. Readers talked to me about many things that worked their way into this story: Pet peeves in mysteries. The books their children took with them when they left home. Pepper's dream car. Salon experiences and jokes about foil wraps improving radio reception. What TV series Pepper might binge-watch. And Speziato, named by reader Mary Ann Giasson a few books back, returns on these pages for a special night.

Thanks as always to my longtime writer pal, thriller author Debbie Burke, for another astute read. Thanks to my editors Dan Mayer and Rene Sears, Ashley Calvano, publicist Wiley Saichek, and everyone at Seventh St. Books who helps make these books better and get them into your hands.

My husband, Don Beans, listens to me fret and helps me test every recipe. I couldn't live this crazy life without his steady presence.

And thanks to you, readers, for buying the books, for reading and listening and checking them out of libraries, for passing them on to your friends. For sending me exactly the right notes at exactly the right time. For taking my imaginary friends into your hearts and making them real. Stories truly are the spice of life.

About The Author

LESLIE BUDEWITZ IS PASSIONATE ABOUT FOOD, GREAT mysteries, and the Northwest, the setting for her nationally best-selling Spice Shop Mysteries and Food Lovers' Village Mysteries. As Alicia Beckman, she writes moody suspense set in the Northwest.

Leslie is a three-time Agatha Award winner: 2011 Best Nonfiction for *Books, Crooks & Counselors: How to Write Accurately About Criminal Law and Courtroom Procedure* (Linden/Quill Driver Books); 2013 Best First Novel for *Death al Dente* (Berkley Prime Crime), first in the Food Lovers' Village Mysteries; and 2018 Best Short Story for "All God's Sparrows" (*Alfred Hitchcock's Mystery Magazine*). Her books and stories have also won or been nominated for Derringer, Anthony, Macavity, and Spur awards. A lawyer by trade, she has served as president of Sisters in Crime and on the board of Mystery Writers of America.

Leslie loves to cook, eat, hike, travel, garden, and paint—not necessarily in that order. She lives in northwest Montana with her husband, Don Beans, a musician and doctor of natural medicine, and their gray tuxedo cat, whose hobbies include napping and eyeing the snowshoe hares who live in the meadow behind the family home.

Visit her online at www.LeslieBudewitz.com, where you'll find maps, recipes, discussion questions, links to her short stories, and more.